Caribbean Gold
Book II
The Treasure of Time

Michael Reisig

A Clear Creek Press Publication

This book is a work of fiction. Names, characters, locales and incidents are either the product of the author's imagination or are used fictitiously, and any resemblance to actual persons, living or dead, is entirely coincidental.

Clear Creek Press
P.O Box 1081
Mena, AR 71953
(501) 394-4992

Cover design by Powell Advertising and Design.
Editing by Dorrie O'Brien and Write Way Publishing, Aurora, CO.
Formatting by Cris Wanzer of Manuscripts To Go
ISBN 978-0-9863801-0-5

A NOTE TO MY READERS:
Over fifteen years ago I wrote a novel called "Brothers of the Sword/Children of Time." At the request of numerous friends I recently decided to revise it and turn it into a more modern "two-book" read. "Caribbean Gold – The Treasure of Time" is the second book of this new read, which was originally titled "Children Of Time."
I hope you enjoy.

— **Michael Reisig**

Other titles by Michael Reisig

Caribbean Gold Book I –
The Treasure of Tortuga

The Road To Key West

Back On The Road To Key West

Along The Road To Key West

Somewhere On The Road To Key West

As well as …

The New Madrid Run

The Hawks of Kamalon

The Old Man's Letters

To my lady, Bonnie Lee, who has always been my beacon in the misty seas of life.

Have you never walked into a room, or stood in a crowd, and gazed across that sea of people to a face that in a single heartbeat captured a piece of distant memory, buried like a treasure deep inside you?

Foggy swirls of remembrance curled around your brain, tugging in disconcerting fashion. Your rational mind shouted that you'd never seen that face before, but that small perceptive voice within you cried, "Hello again, my friend."

Chapter One

Key West, Florida
Summer, 1980

As the simmering yellow sun touched the horizon and slowly transformed itself into a diminishing blood-red orb, Travis Christian finished tying down the starboard wing of his Cessna 310 on the warm tarmac of Key West Airport.

It had been a long day. He'd delivered three passengers to Miami, then flown on to West Palm for two attorneys. The lawyers made him wait nearly two hours, finally showing up with what could only be two high-priced hookers on their arms. They had the audacity to tell him to "put the pedal to the metal," as their ladies were in a hurry to get to Key West. Travis figured mostly, their ladies were in a hurry to get their clothes off, so they could start earning some of the money the attorneys had promised them. But hey, what did he care? He'd fly the devil himself with a squirming bag of freshly stolen souls, as long as he paid in cash and didn't try to make conversation.

In any case, the attorneys and their women were long since gone, headed for The Pier House and a weekend of expensive debauchery. He smiled wryly, thinking he'd take a tanned island girl over an uptown hooker any day.

Travis was drawn from his thoughts as someone called his name. He stepped away from the wing of the plane and looked across the tarmac. Cody stood by the chain link fence that separated the ramp from the commercial area of the airport, yelling and waving at him.

William J. Cody, Jr., now there was a character. He was one of those rare, bigger-than-life people romance novelists were always writing about—shoulder length blonde hair and a Custer-type mustache, iridescent blue eyes, a roguish but disarming smile, and enough charisma to seduce a temple virgin during a commercial break. The man was barely five feet, six inches tall, but after you spent an hour with William J. Cody, Jr.—Cody to his friends—you never thought of him as being less than six feet ever again. He owned and flew for a small island crafts import business, and was simply the best pilot Travis had seen anywhere. If it made noise and lifted off the ground, Cody could fly it. Inside a cockpit, Cody Joe was like a master musician, a consummate artist—he didn't think about it and do it, he just thought it and it happened.

Travis and Cody had met at Sloppy Joe's, a Key West bar, almost two years ago. Travis had been playing pool and was having a fairly good night. He had pretty much taken all the money the players in the bar wanted to lose, when Cody stepped up and challenged him to a series of nineball. They played for two hours, trading games back and forth while drawing a crowd of onlookers as the stakes got higher and the contest became more exciting.

As they played, Travis studied his fellow competitor. There was something familiar about him, something completely comfortable. There'd been an instant rapport between them, like old friends seeing each other for the first time in a while, instead of opponents playing for prestige and money. They laughed, bought each other drinks and traded stories, while shooting some of the best pool that old table had seen for a long time.

When finally they quit, Travis was probably ahead by a few dollars. But at that point it mattered little, because one of those rare, inexplicable friendships that a man finds only once or twice in his lifetime had germinated from the seed of coincidence, and somehow they both knew it.

Cody, perhaps a little more drunk than Travis, said he was headed for Schooners, a bar on the docks. When he prepared to leave, Travis turned to him. "You know, it's a long walk to the docks from here, and you're in no shape to drive. I thought maybe you might like some company?"

Cody smiled that cocky smile of his. "Absolutely, absolutely!" Together they stumbled out of the bar and into the night.

Travis looked over from the airplane and waved back at Cody. He gave the aircraft one last check then headed for his friend. Cody stood there shading his eyes, the last of the afternoon sun accentuating his lean, hard body and lifeguard tan.

Travis moved across the tarmac in long, easy strides. He was a big man—almost six feet, with hazel eyes and dark wavy hair. He wasn't overly handsome—his features were a little too angular and heavy, but there was an integrity about him—a quiet, assured air that drew people and made them feel safe around him. His almost daily workouts at the gym and his natural sense of confidence left most men feeling slightly envious and most women wanting a second look.

Besides their common penchant for flying machines, both Cody and Travis loved the ocean. Cody owned a nice little sailboat, and with ladies in hand, they often spent a weekend in the Marquesas or the Tortugas. It was at sea their distinct connection seemed to be the most pronounced. On the ocean they both seemed so attuned to each other that it was uncanny. There was an innate understanding between them that required no words, as if the wind and the sea had been a part of them forever.

They played tennis together in the crisp mornings and, rum drinks in hand, made the rounds in town at least one night a week. In the interim, their friendship matured into a bond that few brothers experience.

As the last of the sun set, Travis walked over and hopped the small fence that separated them.

"What's up?" he asked, as they shook hands.

"Nothing, really. I was done for the day, so I thought I'd see if I could talk you into a drink at The Parrot before you run off into the night with some tourist."

"Sounds great to me," said Travis, "Lead the way."

No one could say that either of them lived a boring life, or an unpleasant one for that matter—with the girls, the flying, and the sailing. But that night, as they sat in a small bar called the Green Parrot, the circles of fate, circumstance, and timing closed around them and set in motion an adventure of such scope and excitement as to dwarf even the most interesting moments of their already adventurous lives.

It happened like this ...

Chapter Two

He sat on a stool at the bar in the back of a small, dimly lit saloon, one elbow resting on the rail, his back to the bartender. He was a little too drunk for his own good, talking too loud, telling a story about danger, adventure, and buried treasure. It was a slow Monday night and his audience consisted of maybe half a dozen regulars— fishing guides, shrimpers, commercial divers—and five or six of the ever-present tourists, vicariously experiencing the real Key West, Green Parrot style. With the exception of a periodical break on the pool table in the corner it was a typical quiet summer night. The French doors that led to the street had been thrown open, letting in the cool air.

He was a man of medium height, with a slight build, although "wiry" would have probably described him best. He wore his long, Indian-black hair in a tight ponytail down his back. His skin was tanned like brown leather and he wore a pair of faded jeans, a T-shirt, and a denim jacket. At his throat was a solid gold chain that had the look of legitimate antiquity about it. A two-inch faded scar blemished his right cheek, hardening slightly the mischievous look of his lean face.

His gray eyes sparkled with excitement as he related a brief history of an island on the northwest coast of Haiti, then went on to recount his own story. Travis and Cody sat at a table across from him and, while he talked, their conversation slowed, then ceased as they were drawn into the tale.

He was accustomed to telling a story. He spoke articulately, in a passionate narrative about the power and the glory of the sea, and the men who sailed on her waters. Gradually his tale evolved from past to present, and it was there that the attention of his audience became riveted on the man with the crooked smile and the flashing gray eyes.

"I researched for months, studying everything I could find on the razing of Havana by the pirates of Tortuga—called the Isle of Tortue today. The amount of gold and silver taken on that raid was far greater than ever imagined and much more than what was recorded lost by the Spanish.

"I found, while researching documents in England and France, a small segment of unpublished writings by the famous Esquimelin, a Dutch buccaneer with a touch of literary talent who sailed with Morgan. The man is credited with publishing the most factual documentation on the life of the buccaneers. His original articles were published in England in sixteen seventy-eight. What I found, however, never went to print. It was a description of the treasures taken from the cathedral in Havana and it told about a group of men called the Brothers of the Sword, who walked away with the lion's share of the treasure and buried it on Tortuga. Esquimelin's writing also goes on to tell about the Spanish retaliation, and the destruction of Tortuga's pirate stronghold. The intriguing part of this story is that it appears to have been told to Esquimelin by the only surviving member of this Brotherhood. The survivor told Esquimelin that he only took a portion of his share from the treasure trove, since he was bonded by his word never to touch his fellow pirates' loot. Bored with life and saddened by the death of his companions, this survivor decided to offer Esquimelin a number of hints, almost a riddle of sorts, as to the location of the treasure. It's my guess that because his conscience and his honor wouldn't allow him to touch the horde, he gave Esquimelin the opportunity to find it if he was smart enough—if he could decipher the cryptic, almost poetic group of passages he wrote. I'm certain Esquimelin failed to find the main treasure. He did find what he felt to be significant proof of its existence, however. He laments in the writings his inability to uncover the main treasure, and it's a documented fact that he died a poor man. He never published this segment of his writings, because he didn't want competition while searching for the treasure. It was only by the purest coincidence that I found a brittle parchment with his final words, and those details I prefer to keep to myself. I still have it, and with it, the riddle of the treasure of Tortuga."

The storyteller paused for a moment and nodded to the bartender, pushing over his empty glass. While it was being refilled, he pulled a small, dark cigarillo from his vest pocket and lit it, exhaling a stratum of bluish smoke.

"The lone survivor of the Spaniards' revenge was an Englishman named Will Devon. He must have been an interesting man—a man not without wit and a sense of prose. Such a fascinating tale he wove, and the poetry he left Esquimelin in the form of clues is, in itself, a statement of his intellect.

"He chose to make the search challenging, so he created a treasure hunt of sorts. He buried three bags of coins in the vicinity of the treasure. The first bag held twenty-five coins, the second fifty, and the third, one hundred. As the number of coins increased in each bag the closer you got to the treasure. When you found the last bag, you were within one hundred feet of the booty. In each bag, one of the coins had been beaten flat and etched with the clue to the next bag. The final bag held the greatest, most significant clue to the location of the treasure trove.

"Esquimelin found the first bag, and with it, the etched coin with the next clue. He said so in his final writing, while cursing the gods for his poor luck and Will Devon for his difficult clues. He did, however, leave the clue that was etched on the beaten coin, and the location where the first bag was found.

"I had these things when I reached Tortuga less than two months ago." As eyes widened in the audience around the man, he paused for dramatic effect and smiled, "Yes, eight weeks ago my partner and I sailed into Tortuga's little bay during the full moon.

"We searched the island for a month. The only people we met were the residents of the two small fishing villages. They didn't pay much attention to us. I'm sure they thought we were crazy, wandering up and down the hills, waving metal detectors over the ground wherever we went, doing our best to decipher Esquimelin's clues in relation to the remaining landmarks. Sometimes we slept on the sailboat, sometimes on shore, depending on how far into the island we were. After our initial contact with the villagers, they seemed indifferent to us, but removed and aloof became a more apt description as time passed. Only a few of them could speak any English, and they were reluctant to answer questions, pretending not to understand. We sensed that something wasn't right with them, but we were busy at the task of treasure hunting, so we gave up on conversation.

"It was frustrating at best. Three hundred years had gone by since Will had buried his coins and written his clues, and a lot had changed in that time. But we stuck to it, and in the end we were rewarded.

"Three weeks into the hunt, while camping deep in the island, we heard voices ... a distant wailing. We could also hear an underlying, hypnotic rhythm of drums accompanying the voices, pulsating in the dark night air. There were screams of more than passion intermingled with those voices. The chorus that carried through the trees was mesmerizing, but underneath there was a cry of terror, shrieks of pain. We moved closer to the fire.

"When morning came, the sun diffused the surrealism of the previous night, and we acted as if nothing had happened. Neither of us mentioned the screams.

"On we went, day after day. We searched the jungle and the surrounding hills. Not an hour passed that I didn't pull the notes from my pouch and read, one more time, the cryptic clue from Will Devon:

'She lies on her back and cries for her lover, gone to an honorable death.

'There 'tween her mounds, like a trinket on a chain, buried in the cleft of her flesh, lie the coins and the clue of a brother that was true, when his conscience was put to the test.

'Seek the stone, like a mole, 'tween the bosom of the lady in mourning.'"

A small group of tourists entered the front part of the bar noisily—a little drunk, interrupting the narration. The man relaxed for a moment, chewing the end of his cigarillo as he held it between his fingers while the newcomers found seats on the far side and settled down.

"Finally, when I was all but ready to give up, it came to me—in a dream.

"We'd scoured the hills that day, and by sunset I was so exhausted I could barely eat supper. After eating we talked for a while, then hit the sack. My head had no more hit the pillow than I fell asleep and I had the strangest dream. I found myself rushing back through time. Winds of change swirled and eddied around me as I plunged through a vortex of ages and eras. I felt my identity slipping, changing. Then, suddenly, I found myself in the village of Tortuga as it must have been three hundred years ago. I swear to you this dream was so real I could hear the children and the dogs and smell the boucan cooking. I was in another body, similar to mine, yet different, and I could only see from one eye.

"There was a path that led from the back of the village, through the jungle, and to the hills on the back side. As I walked that path I was overcome with fear. I could remember running like hell down that trail. I could hear men shouting as they chased me. It was the most vivid, terrifying dream I've ever had. The path led out of the jungle, and in the distance I could see two hills, like the breasts of a woman on her back. As we approached the hills, an incredible sadness overwhelmed me. Suddenly I knew with absolute certainty that between those mounds lay the bag of coins my other personality sought.

"I woke up and found myself back in the jungle, soaked with sweat and shaking like a scolded dog. Needless to say, I didn't sleep much the rest of that night, but I *knew* where the coins were.

"After a quick breakfast, we packed up and headed back to the ruins of the original village, which weren't far from where we'd anchored the sailboat. There was no longer a true path that led from the back of the village; the jungle had long since claimed it. There was, however, an animal trail headed in the right direction, so we headed out on that. After two hours of hacking through vines and undergrowth, just when I was beginning to doubt the dream, the treasure, and my reasons for being in a godforsaken jungle, we broke into a clearing. Perhaps two hundred yards ahead, lay the hills of my dream, and once more I was struck by despair and fear.

"I stopped in my tracks, my knees weak. My friend, Paul, looked over at me and, seeing the look on my face, asked if I was okay. There was no way to explain to him what I was feeling. How could I define something I didn't understand myself? I was, however, sure of one thing—the second bag of coins lay in the cleft of those hills.

"My partner touched my shoulder and asked again if I was all right. I nodded, gulping in deep breaths and collecting myself. Then I pointed to the hills. 'There,' I croaked. 'There.'

"We walked slowly to the base of the mounds, then up the incline to the pass. As we reached the center of the pass, I sensed an intense desperation, a sensation of violence strangely fused with conscience and honor. I stood there and the words etched on the first coin came to mind, 'Seek the stone like a mole' ... Not ten feet from me lay a round stone, maybe two feet across and a foot high. I walked over like a man in a trance, knelt and began to dig around it. I'm sure Paul thought I'd finally lost it, but he knelt and helped me all the same. When we could get our fingers under the stone we gradually lifted it, turning it over on its rounded back. There under the rock was ... nothing. Just dirt. My buddy sighed in exasperation and started to say something, but I stopped him, holding up my hand. I began to dig. I clawed at the soil with my bare hands, oblivious to the pain of bruised fingertips and bent nails. Six inches down I struck a deteriorated leather bag, which disintegrated in my fingers. But beneath the crumbling leather I felt the first of the gold coins. My heart was hammering as I withdrew my hand, clutching a handful of coins, and turned to Paul triumphantly, opening my fingers.

"'My God,' he whispered, 'you were right! It's impossible, but you were right!'

"We dug the coins out carefully and laid them on a cloth we'd put on the ground. The wonder of gold is that it never tarnishes. Three hundred years they'd been there, yet they glinted with the touch of the sun as brightly as they had the day the Spanish coin-smith struck them centuries before. Finally, near the bottom of the ragged bag, lay the coin I was looking for. It was twice the size of the rest, beaten flat and thin, and on its shiny surface were the words of the second clue.

'Stand on the lip of God's green table, here on the isle of the sword. Find the moon as she crawls from the sea amid the season of the storm.

When the glow of God's great lantern has finally been cast, it touches a tree that stands like a frigate's mast, there in the clearing below.

Fifty steps west in strides that are bold, lie the coins and the clue to the brotherhood's gold.'

"My hands shook as I held the coin and read Will Devon's clues. It was as if I was recalling the writing, not reading it for the first time. I stood numbed by this strange intuition, and again, my friend's hand on my shoulder brought me back to the present.

"I cleared my throat, then recited the inscription out loud, barely looking at the coin. This didn't escape my friend, who was beginning to eye me with the same kind of confused awe natives accord a witch doctor.

"When the coins had been stowed, I stood and walked to the rear of the pass and looked out. I was sure I'd find a tidal creek at the base of that hill. I was surprised to see that a small airstrip had been bulldozed into the land behind the hill, it being one of the few areas in Tortuga flat enough to put in a strip. I learned later that it was put in by a millionaire land developer from Texas, years ago. He wanted to make the island into a Caribbean playground for the rich and famous. The development never came to pass but the strip is still there.

"Looking across the island from the pass, I saw the tidal creek had been diverted, either by a hurricane or by man. It now ran through the far tip of the island, perhaps a half a mile away.

"It was evening now, and we moved off the pass to the clearing below to set up camp for the night. I was exhausted,both mentally and physically, but I was sure for the first time that we were going to find the treasure of the Brotherhood. We had a light supper, studied the coins by the firelight, discussing our plans, then decided to call it a night. We'd only been in our bedrolls for a few minutes when we heard the drums again—closer ... much closer."

The man paused for a moment and looked around the bar. "I can't really explain what happened that night. The closest I can come is to describe it as an experience in the fascination of terror. I got a first-hand look at the midnight realms of madness, of frenzied bloodlust and the narcotic passions of pain. If that seems a bit much, listen on. When I'm done, you'll find the description weak." A slightly bemused smile touched his lips. He took a sip of his drink and continued.

"I rolled over and looked at Paul. He listened for a moment longer. I didn't know why, but the compelling voices and the nearly hypnotic rhythm of the drums seemed to be beckoning us—a seductive invitation that offered to satisfy our curiosity. We both sensed it. 'Okay,' he said, 'let's check it out.'

"The drums were close, but the jungle at night is no walk in the park. It took us a half an hour to pinpoint the location. As we crept slowly forward, we began to glimpse the light of the huge fire in the tops of the trees ahead. It is hard to explain exactly, but somehow that night, fear changed into need ... I had to see, we had to see, what lay behind the haunting voices and the horrible screams.

"Closer and closer we crept toward the firelight. Finally, with my heart thumping, I knelt and pulled back the broad leaves in front of me.

"In the clearing before us was a scene of torch-lit lunacy—a scene as close to hell as you're going to find this side of death.

"The huge bonfire painted a swaying circle of glistening bodies in fiery colors of orange and yellow. The flames from the fire licked at the black sky through the hole in the dark green canopy above. Blazing timbers in the fire crackled and popped, throwing showers of sparks on the spellbound souls surrounding it, but they were oblivious to all but the spectacle in the center of the circle.

"Beside the fire stood a giant of a man. His skin shone like burnished mahogany and his powerfully muscled body gleamed from the heat of the flames as he stood there, legs apart, and raised his bloodied knife to the moon above, chanting incantations. Beside him was a wooden altar, and bound to the altar lay a woman—a girl, really. Streams of blood ran from her body where the sharp knife had already touched her.

"I'm not a newcomer to the baser side of life. I've had my share of experiences I wouldn't tell my mother about. But that night, I was seduced by terror and pain. I couldn't pull my eyes away from that gleaming blade as it cut that girl again and again. Raw excitement swelled in my breast. The passion of horror shortened my breath and slicked my palms. The high, chanting voices crawled inside my brain, plucking at pieces of my sanity. I poured with sweat from the heat of the night and the fire of wicked emotion burning inside me. Through it all, my eyes remained riveted on the center of the circle.

"Each time the knife descended, the girl's shrieks rose above the eerie chorus, the circle undulating inward with each slash of the blade, then writhing outward again, like a snake devouring itself. Throughout this whole ordeal, the most amazing thing of all was the tortured girl's eyes. She screamed when the knife touched her, but she watched the blade descend with desire. Yes ... desire, eager for the pain, like a new bride on a wedding bed. There was no fear in her eyes, none at all ... There was need.

"The ceremony continued and, gradually, like a storm wind coming off the sea, the voices rose, the chanting increased in intensity as it reached a crescendo. The giant priest, like an actor sensing the finale, raised his bloodstained knife to the heavens again and cried out. I had no idea of the meaning or the language but the words sounded ancient and evil. The shimmering circle of bodies cried back at him, repeating the phrase. Again he shouted, and once more they repeated his words, their intensity still rising.

"Suddenly the drums and the voices stopped, as if they had never been, and the knife fell one more time."

The storyteller took a sip of his drink, his bright eyes darting around the audience to insure attention. It wasn't necessary. No one was going anywhere. He set his drink down and returned to the tale.

"The noise of the jungle died with the girl, and for a moment the only sound was dripping blood as it pooled on the ground at the priest's feet.

"The sacrifice completed, the priest moved toward the members of the circle, carrying a small half-gourd of blood collected from the girl's severed throat. The congregation of this hellish communion stood stock-still while he anointed each one of them on the forehead and the lips with the warm blood, muttering syllables from a strange language. As the ritual neared conclusion, my friend, who was slowly returning to his senses, shifted his position slightly. In the process, his foot tipped a rock that rolled down the slight incline of the clearing and stopped at the feet of the worshipers. They looked up as one. A wild-eyed woman in the center raised her hand slowly, gesturing at us, and howled ... We drew back, but it was too late. The giant priest in the center shouted harshly and pointed, and en masse, the screaming throng broke, scrambling across the ravine at us.

"Fear slammed adrenaline into our veins and we were up and running before we thought about it, shaking the narcotic sensations of the ceremony as we ran. We tore through the brush like two madmen. The wide leaves of the jungle plants slapped us, and the vines in the trees and on the ground reached for us, clutching and clinging like desperate lovers. We stumbled and fell a dozen times, but each time we clawed our way to our feet and ran on.

"Our pursuers, having clambered up the ravine surrounding the clearing, were no more than fifty yards behind us. Their frenzied shrieks terrified us as we bolted with panicked abandon.

"Racing through the dark jungle, we struck a trail. When we reached the trail, I could just see light from the moon as it worked its way off the water and into the treetops, and I knew the direction of the sea and the boat. Grabbing my rapidly tiring friend, I shoved him ahead of me and on we rushed.

"By the grace of God, we lost our pursuers for a few minutes when they turned the wrong direction on the trail. After running maybe another half a mile, we paused for a moment to catch our breath. I massaged my cramped legs as we sucked in oxygen, just beginning to think we'd lost them, when faintly in the distance, up the path, we heard their cries. I looked at Paul. I could see the desperation in his eyes. He was a sailor, not a marathon runner. He was exhausted, and terrified.

"'Come on,' I said, reaching for him and pulling him up, 'we can't have more than another half mile to the beach.' He took some comfort in that, and struggling to our feet, we stumbled on again, the cries of our pursuers growing closer.

"The moonlight beamed through the canopy above, sending streamers of smoky light to the jungle floor. We had awakened the creatures of the jungle and they chattered and shrieked, indignant and angry. We staggered down the trail, exhausted now to the point of collapse. All that kept us on our feet were the sharp jabs of fear as we heard the cries from those hellish bastards behind us. The gap between them and us had closed to about seventy-five yards.

"Taking the lead, I followed the trail the best I could. Each time it veered off, I took the path toward the moon, and hopefully the water. Just when I had begun to doubt our position, I broke free from the jungle and stumbled, sprawling onto the moonlit sand of the beach. The wind was up and I could see the waves pounding the shore. Our sailboat bobbed just a hundred yards down the beach and another hundred offshore. It was more luck than we could have possibly hoped for, breaking out of the jungle near the boat."

The narrator crushed out his cigarillo, took a swig of his drink, and continued. "We were close, but they were closing the gap. Once again, the crazed shouts drove us to our feet, and we stumbled toward the sea.

"I somehow knew that those creatures behind us had a fear of the water. I don't know how, but I knew. I was sure if we could make it into those waves and the deep water beyond, we'd be safe. We'd made half the distance to the sea when the maniacs behind us broke out onto the beach. Sighting their prey, they screamed and scrambled after us.

"There was a hurricane inside my head. My legs began to disobey commands from my oxygen-starved brain. My lungs levered like a blacksmith's bellows, but I just couldn't seem to get enough of that sweet salt air inside them. The water was so close now, only steps away ...

"When Paul and I finally reached the surf, there were no more than two dozen yards between them and us. The bite of the cool water revived me, giving me the final ounce of strength I needed to force my way through the waves and into the sea. The single-minded thought of survival had gripped me so completely that I didn't look back again until I had cleared the breakwater. Fear had driven my friend that far, but as we entered the water and the waves rose and thrust against us, Paul's weary body refused to obey anymore. He couldn't force his way past the shore surge. He staggered out, only to be knocked back by the surf. The creatures that had chased us so relentlessly were at the water's edge now, wading in, reaching for him.

"I watched with horror as he staggered out into the waves again like a drunken man, only to be bowled over and washed back into the hands of the devils in the shallows. He wailed in terror as they dragged him from the water, screaming and kicking as they pulled him up onto the beach. Three of them held him as one drew something from his belt, and I saw the moonlight glint off the knife blade as it rose and fell, cutting his shrieks like a needle being ripped from a record. I watched helplessly as they slashed and stabbed him again and again. Then they turned and looked at me. There was nothing I could do. I spun quickly in the water and swam for the boat.

"Halfway to the sailboat, I began to feel the strangest of sensations—a tugging at my consciousness. I turned back and peered across the water. There, at the sea's edge, they stood, maybe twenty or thirty of them. In the light of the moon they saw me turn, treading water. Quietly at first, like the wind carrying a sound from far off, they began to howl. Never in my life have I heard such a chilling sound, and I've never seen anything to compare with the nightmarish scene of those creatures standing on that moon-bathed beach, reaching out to me and howling. I treaded water for a moment and listened to that eerie wailing. Suddenly, I began to feel the threads of my sanity being undone again. I was drawn once more to the beach, and there in the center of his disciples stood the huge priest with those horribly intense eyes. He was reaching out to me and howling in sweet supplication. All of a sudden, going back to the beach didn't seem like such an awful thought. Part of me could feel my rational mind screaming in terror, but I didn't care. My sanity was being covered with thick, warm honey and it felt good. I was almost looking forward to the touch of their hands ...

"I had actually turned and began a few tentative strokes in the direction of the beach, the logical, sensible part of me crying out in panic that I *should not* go back, when a freak wave struck me from behind and buried me in the cool salt sea, shocking my senses and silencing the voices on the beach. I burst to the surface choking and gasping. I had been jolted back to reality and the voices on the shore held only terror for me. I turned and swam toward the sailboat as the howling on the beach rose from soft entreaty to desperate rage."

The man with the sparkling eyes looked at the glass he held and spoke with a sad smile. "I've had too many of these again, but the booze is all that lets me turn off my mind when I close my eyes at night." Everyone waited in respectful silence as he came from his musings.

"I stayed with the deep water and sailed around to the western end of the island that night. I dropped anchor about a quarter-mile offshore and tried to sleep. I was as tired as I'd ever been, but sleep came slowly, and it brought nightmares as baggage. The gray dawn found me sitting in the cockpit, willing the sun out of the horizon. When I could see, I upped anchor and plotted a course for Key West. Five days of sailing and maybe a dozen hours of sleep found me back in the harbor here."

Again the man paused and looked at the faces around him. He had saved the best for last. "There's probably none of you here that doubt I tell a hell of a good story. But you might be asking yourselves, *is he telling the truth?*" He continued speaking, reaching down into a leather pouch at his waist. "After we found the coins in the pass, we split them up that night after supper by the fire. Gold does funny things to a man—you want your share. I kept my twenty-five, including the beaten coin, in a pouch I wore at my side. I still had it that night when I reached the sailboat." He drew his hand up and laid a handful of glittering gold coins on the tabletop. "And this, ladies and gentlemen, is the proof in the pudding. True pirate's treasure, but only a small piece of what lies buried in the hills of Tortuga."

There were audible gasps from his audience, and three seedy-looking characters who had been lounging at a table near the back of the bar suddenly sat up and took notice. One of them muttered to his companions, "Jesus! He was tellin' the truth! Look at that damned gold!" His friend next to him stopped him with a touch to his arm and a look. The man halted in mid-sentence, his hard eyes flashing with understanding.

Most of the people were too intent on the coins to hear the comment or see the silent exchange that took place with the men in the back. It didn't escape Travis and Cody, however. Cody leaned over casually and whispered, "That could be trouble." His friend nodded almost imperceptibly as he sipped his drink.

When the man with the coins had finished answering a few questions from the people around him, he rose to leave. He was still steady on his feet but his movements carried a stiffness and deliberateness that marks a man who's had one too many. He was offered a ride home by a couple of the patrons but he refused, saying it was only a few blocks to the house he was renting, and that the night air would do him good. He said goodnight to all and walked out into the warm summer evening. Cody had just turned to Travis, remarking on the incredible tale they had heard, when the three men in the corner rose, paid their bill and left the bar.

Travis turned to Cody and their eyes met. They didn't say a word for a moment, then Travis spoke: "Yeah, I know. All right, let's go."

When they got outside, there was no one to be seen, but Travis had watched the men turn to the left as they exited the bar, so that was the direction they headed. There was an alley about a hundred yards down the street.

Actually, it was a small street from old Key West that had never been widened. There were a few houses along it, several big trees, and a lot of shadows. As they walked quietly along the main road, they heard voices down the side street. They moved forward cautiously, but as they entered the alley, the voices stopped. The street took a slight bend and, as they came around it, they saw the storyteller. He lay inert against the base of a large banyan tree.

Travis knelt by the man and checked his pulse. He was still alive. Carefully they brought him around. When his eyes cleared, he looked up at them and started.

"It's okay," Travis said, "we're on your side. Are you all right?"

The man sat up and winced as he moved, bringing his hand to the back of his head. Then, suddenly, with a spark of alarm, his hand shot to his pocket where his bag of coins had been. He sighed. "Gone," he said. "They took my coins."

"Did you get a look at them?" Cody asked, knowing full well who they were.

"Yeah, but not a good look," the man relied a little shakily, as he stood up. "They approached me in the shadows—big men—two of them. They wanted to know what time it was. Then they wanted directions to the Pier House. About the time I was starting to feel like a tourist information center, someone comes up behind me and whacks me on the head."

"They take anything else?" Travis asked.

The man checked quickly. "Nope, just the coins. Looks like they knew what they were after."

"Listen," said Travis. "We're sure we know who did this. We were there at the bar when you told your story." The victim nodded, remembering them. "The three big guys in the back left right after you did."

"Yeah," said the fellow, rubbing his head. "I think that's them. Jesus! I don't know what I was thinking. I should never have told the whole tale there. The frigging rum did it to me again. I just got a little lit and the story came rolling out."

"You could have told the story," said Cody, "without flashing the coins. Sorry, but that was stupid of you."

"Lord, you're right there."

"You know," said Travis, "this whole thing just pisses me off. If the story you told was true, you earned those damned coins."

"Oh, it's true. Every friggin' word."

Travis sighed angrily, pausing for a moment. "Listen," he said. "I know how guys like those think. They let their ego and their arrogance get way ahead of their intelligence. I'll bet you dollars to donuts those three are in a bar not a mile from here, having a drink and celebrating." Travis glanced over at Cody. "What do you think?"

"Come on," said Cody. "Let's go find them."

Before they moved off, they introduced themselves. Their new acquaintance was Sirus William McCree, Billy McCree for short. As they walked, they talked, and the rhythm of their conversation was so smooth and natural, a stranger would have thought they'd known each other forever.

Travis considered this new man at his side as they walked the streets of Key West. Being a man who understood justice or injustice, and the territory in between, it would not have been unusual for him to feel a good deal of empathy for this fellow. But he couldn't understand for the life of him why he felt this overwhelming desire to right the injury this man had suffered. Where he might have felt sympathy for another in this situation, here he felt anger and indignation. His mind kept flashing back to the coins ... It wasn't as though he wanted to keep them. He just wanted them back.

It took two hours and eight bars, but as they walked into the second-floor bar of the Bull and Whistle on Duval Street, they saw the three men playing pool. Actually, two were standing shooting pool, the other sat at a table nearby. When they walked in, the trio glanced over, surprised, but not particularly concerned. One stood framed by the big picture window that looked down on the street below. He was five foot eight or ten with a thin but sinewy build and stringy, sandy blond hair. Another, shorter and heavier, with dull, watery-blue eyes and the same dishwater blond hair, grinned and chalked his cue stick as he leaned against the wall near the table. The third remained seated on the far side of the pool table. He was bigger than the others, and harder-looking. His shoulder-length hair was light brown. The muscles of his arms strained the fabric of his faded Hawaiian Tropic T-shirt. The lines on his face and the look in his glacial blue eyes said he wasn't much amused by life—that he expected little quarter and gave none.

Travis never hesitated. He walked over to the biggest of the three, the man seated at the table, and, looking down at him, said, "You have something that belongs to my friend. I want it back, now." As Travis spoke, Cody edged himself between the two men standing by the pool table, leaning casually against the rail. The man by the window was maybe ten feet from him, the other, another ten behind him. Billy McCree stood off to the side of Travis, toward the front of the pool table.

The man sitting at the table feigned surprise. "And

what could I possibly have that would belong to you or your friend?" He was smiling, but the smile never made it to his eyes. The other patrons in the bar melted away, having recognized the violence in these men and the oncoming confrontation. The bartender wasn't even going to get into this one. These boys were out of his league. He was already dialing the police.

"Ten seconds," said Travis.

"What?" said the big man, no longer smiling.

"You've got ten seconds to give the coins back," Travis said, leaning both hands on the table and looking him in the eyes. "Then you and I are going to dance, and you're not going to like the tune."

There was just a glimmer of uncertainty in the man's eyes as he faced the powerful-looking stranger leaning over him, but unfortunately, it passed. "Screw you!" he spat as he snatched up a beer bottle from the table and swung it at his opponent's head. Travis reached out like a striking snake, never taking his eyes from the man, and caught the fellow's hand in midair. The shock on the man's face from being stopped so easily was followed by a flash of fear, as Travis hammered a hard, straight right to the man's nose, smashing cartilage, bursting blood vessels and limiting his appeal to the ladies for some time to come. As the fellow cried out and put his free hand to his face, Travis reached over and snatched the beer bottle out of his other hand. Taking it by the neck, he smashed it on the edge of the table. Grabbing the stunned man by the hair, he ripped his head back and put the jagged edge of the broken bottle against his throat.

As the action started with Travis and the guy at the table, the man by the window started to move in, bringing his cue stick around like a club. Before he'd taken two steps, Cody was standing in front of him.

Cody smiled, and held up his hand, wiggling his index finger as if to say, "No, no, no." The guy with the cue stick was an easy hundred and seventy pounds. When he saw the small man with the long yellow hair step in front of him, he stopped and smiled nastily. He had no idea that the little blond guy had spent a good portion of his adult life in a karate dojo. Without warning, he swung the cue at Cody's head as hard as he could. Ducking the cue stick as it passed over his head, Cody Joe stepped in on the man. With the tips of his fingers, he jabbed his opponent sharply in the underside of his extended arm. The man screamed like he'd been touched with a branding iron and his arm fell to his side, his lateral nerve temporarily damaged. Not learning from his first mistake, the fellow turned with the cue stick in his good hand and swung again at Cody's head. Like the saying goes, "Those who don't learn the first time, are destined to repeat ..." Cody simply ducked the cue again, spun and side-kicked the guy clear through the picture window. He sailed out in a shower of broken glass and tumbled fifteen feet onto the top of a new Cadillac convertible parked below, caving the canvas into the backseat.

When Cody jabbed the man's arm and he screamed, the guy against the wall decided to get involved and moved toward Cody's back, raising his cue. Billy was at the far end of the table, and couldn't reach the man in time to stop him. Suddenly he looked down and saw the cue ball by the corner pocket. Grabbing it up, he wound up and hurled it like a baseball pitcher.

The man with the stick had just begun the downward stroke at Cody's unprotected back when the cue ball struck him solidly on the back of his head and ricocheted out the broken window. The fellow dropped like he'd been pole-axed, his cue stick clattering to the floor. Cody looked over at Billy and smiled in appreciation of his fastball.

Meanwhile, Travis jerked the seated man's head back a little farther and drew just a touch of blood with the jagged glass. Riveting the terrified man's eyes with his own, he whispered, "Seven. Six. Five—"

"Here! Here!" the thief cried. "In my pocket! Take them! Just take 'em."

The fellow reached down slowly with shaking hands and produced the bag of coins. Travis grabbed them, then pushed the man's chair over, sending him sprawling onto the floor. Travis looked over at Cody, who grinned broadly, then over to Billy who smiled and gave him a thumbs up.

"Let's go, boys," he said with a smile. "Our work in this 'ere town's done." Cody and Billy laughed at him as together they walked down the stairs and out of the bar, into the early morning of Key West. A dozen policemen charged into the bar behind them. They just grinned and kept walking. About a block away from the bar, Cody looked over at Billy. "You know, Bill, with that arm of yours, you ever get bored with treasure hunting and tall-tale telling, you might consider major league baseball."

Chapter Three

After retrieving Billy's coins, they found a quiet little bar at the end of Duval Street and had a couple of drinks to celebrate the success of the "mission."

As drinks were downed and stories told, Billy realized that although Travis and Cody were as different in looks as night and day, they had most everything else in common. They were in their early thirties, had a passion for flying, and both had experienced Vietnam up close. Billy learned that Cody had flown spotter planes and forward observation aircraft in 'Nam—Cessna 337s armed with rocket pods, as well as bigger cargo planes like C-47s and C-54s. He also flew the drops for the boys when they went into the places they weren't supposed to go.

"This son-of-a-bitch was either the luckiest, or the best damned pilot Vietnam ever saw—maybe both," said Travis as he waved his drink at Cody. "He got shot out of the sky or crashed-landed airplanes seven times in the two years he spent in 'Nam. Two times he fought his way out of the jungle after losing his plane in VC territory. Don't let him give you that, 'ah shucks, it was nothing' crap. He has a boxful of medals that would make a pawnshop envious, including two purple hearts. I didn't know him then but I had heard of him. Lots of grunts owe their lives to this guy and his little rocket-spouting Cessna. He gave the ground troops immediate support when they just couldn't wait for the big boys in the jets."

Cody smiled. "As usual, he exaggerates when he gets drunk. If you're fortunate, you start with a bag full of luck and an empty bag of experience. The trick is to fill the bag of experience before you empty the bag of luck." He looked over at Billy. "While we're talking about timing and courage, let me introduce you to Captain Travis Christian of the Vietnam era. Our mild mannered buddy here was a helicopter pilot, and during his two tours, his flying abilities were almost legendary. He had a reputation for sensing danger before it happened and getting his people in and out alive. During combat missions, the friggin' platoons drew lots—drew *lots*—to see who'd get to fly with him. This boy could put a Huey into places that left the pilots above him slack-jawed and the soldiers on the ground cheering. The grunts in the forward bases called him 'The Magician.' I'd heard of him, too."

They discovered another remarkable coincidence about the three of them—they were all pilots. Billy had a fixed-wing commercial license and had worked for a small cargo company out of Miami for several years. He was a little younger than the other two and had missed the Vietnam experience.

As the first tendrils of light from the new sun started to paint the horizon in colors of blue and rose, Travis pushed back his seat and stood, wobbling just a little. "Well, I think I've had all the alcohol and tribute I can handle for one night. I'm going to call it a morning, go home and get some sleep." He looked at Cody and Billy. "Gentlemen, it's been a pleasure—an interesting evening. I think we ought to get together and do it again sometime."

Cody rose as well, balancing with an arm on his high-backed chair. "You know, I was thinking about a day sail to the Marquesas on Saturday. You two want to come along?"

Travis thought for a moment then shrugged. "Sounds good to me. I'm off Saturday. What about you, Billy?"

Billy eased back in his chair and smiled. "You're on."

"You two just bring your snorkeling gear," said Cody. "I'll have everything else we need on the boat."

The trio sailed out of the Key West harbor and into the Caribbean aboard Cody's 44-foot Pearson at dawn on the following Saturday. Jimmy Buffett's *Son of a Son of a Sailor* rolled out of the cabin speakers and the rigging sang a contented, taut harmony as the sleek little sailboat sliced through the waves. The sky was clear and soft and there was a fair breeze from the southeast that rippled the rolling sea and filled the sails. It was like coming home.

Cody was at the tiller. Billy and Travis sat on each side of the cockpit. Billy lit one of his little cigars and looked over at Cody. "From what I hear, you're quite the colorful character—fairly well-known on the island. How about a two-minute dissertation on the life and times of Cody Joe, so I won't have to wait until they make the movie."

Cody chuckled. "Not that much to tell, really— anything you heard was grossly exaggerated, I'm sure. Drinking and talking about people are the two favorite pastimes in Key West. If you don't have an interesting story, no one will buy you a drink. You, of all people understand that." Billy smiled and motioned him to continue.

"I run a little business based out of Miami and Key West that imports arts and crafts from the Caribbean and South America—nothing too fancy, but it pays the bills."

"How'd you get into flying?" Billy asked.

Cody took a swig of beer. "My mother had a brother, my Uncle Ray. He was a rock and roll musician of some success and had his own small plane. He got me interested in flying when I was seventeen, and helped me get my private license." Cody smiled. "One day Jim asked me if I wanted to go flying with him. I said sure, why not. He took me up—did a handful of tight turns, loops and stalls and basically scared the crap out of me. I couldn't wait to get my feet back on the ground. The funny part was, a couple of days later I couldn't wait to do it again. I realized something about myself then—I liked being on the edge—which probably saved me from becoming a lawyer or a banker. Went into the service during Vietnam, and flew for the Army. I survived that somehow, came home, got discharged, and afterward sort of spiraled down across the country until I ran out of land and ended up in Key West. Now I fly airplanes for Caribbean Cupboard."

"Somehow I think that's the Reader's Digest version," Billy said wryly.

Travis listened, suppressing a small smile.

It was almost six months after their first meeting in Sloppy Joe's that Travis actually learned what Cody did for a living. Cody had maintained, as he did presently, that he was a corporate pilot for a small company. Eventually, when he came to trust Travis, he divulged a little more information about his profession. First, Cody Joe didn't work for the company, he owned it, and secondly, the "business" of the company was smuggling.

For Travis, it certainly explained the lovely sailboat, nice little sports car, and never-ending wad of money Cody was always pulling from his jeans pocket.

Cody was a smuggler. He told Travis that, no matter where you went, there was always someone who wanted something delivered without the curious eyes of customs. He smuggled pre-Columbian gold and emeralds out of Columbia, fine paintings into Venezuela and Mexico, rare birds out of Ecuador, and money into the banks of Caribbean Islands. He had even smuggled diamonds out of Africa. You could argue ethics with him, but not integrity. The man had a sterling reputation in a dubious business. He always delivered.

But Cody wouldn't smuggle drugs of any sort. It was a hard and fast rule with him and he never broke it, no matter how much money was offered. In a time when those around were becoming overnight millionaires, it was a statement of his character.

The company that Cody finally admitted to owning did just as he said—imported items like carvings, baskets, and paintings from the Caribbean and South America. It was the perfect cover, explaining his numerous trips out of the country while allowing him to funnel a good amount of money through it as well.

Up to this point, Travis had resisted Cody's offer of midnight flight employment, but it was difficult. He worked about thirty hours a week flying a cramped 310 with impatient, arrogant passengers and made about four hundred dollars for it. Cody, on the other hand, flew for "business" maybe once a month and had more money than Midas.

Billy turned to Travis. "Okay, what about you?"

"I'm afraid I'm a lot less interesting," said Travis as he tightened the mainsail. "I was born in California—Napa Valley. Got interested in flying early—I was fifteen when I got a job cleaning out a hanger at the small airfield near home. The owner of the FBO there took a liking to me and started teaching me to fly. I had a fixed-wing license at sixteen, and could find my way around in the cockpit of a chopper by eighteen. Then 'Nam came along. Got my commercial license on the G.I. Bill afterwards, and wandered around trying to find someone who would hire me. Took a trip to the Keys with some friends, just to see what it was like, and never left. Got a job with a charter company here in 'seventy-eight, and I've been doing that since."

Billy nodded. "Well, for your own edification, I'm a South Florida boy—born and raised in Miami. As a young man, I read all the books by the great adventure authors—Hemingway, Michener, Robbins, and decided I wanted to be one—an adventurer, that is, not an author. After squeezing my way through high school, I got a job on a shrimp boat for about six months. The ocean and far away places got into my blood and I've never been very good at staying in one place since." He glanced at Cody. "Spent my share of time on the edge of life, but it makes my shorts ride up after a while and I have to back off and take a break. Taking a chance or two, I managed to make enough money to pay for a commercial pilot's license along the way, and I've stayed one step ahead of the landlord and the jailer most of the time, which is more than I can say for quite a few men I've known."

Cody smiled. "Sounds like a familiar song."

When they reached the shallow waters of the Marquesas, they anchored and did some snorkeling. Travis took a spear gun in with him and shot a hog snapper, which they filleted and grilled on the hibachi. Cody warmed up some vegetables and lunch was served topside.

As they ate, the conversation came around to Tortuga. Travis looked up from his plate to Billy, who was munching on a piece of fish. "Do you plan on going back, or was the last time enough for you?"

Billy swallowed and stared at the seabirds diving on shallow baitfish off the bow. "If you'd asked me that question the day I made it back to Key West, I would have probably said 'No, I'm not going back.' But time does heal most wounds." He sighed. "There's not a night goes by that I don't lie on my back, stare at the ceiling and dream what it would be like to find the hole where they stuffed all that booty! At just a rough guess, there's got to be eight or ten million in gold and jewels buried somewhere on the island. But it's not just the money. I feel as if I have to go back, like I left a situation unresolved—as if there's a piece of me there, or maybe a piece of my destiny." He shook his head, smiling strangely. "It's hard to explain, gentlemen. I think you had to be there." He looked at Travis and Cody again. "Even if I was ready to go, and I believe I'm getting close, there's still the matter of mounting an expedition, transportation, supplies and equipment. The sailboat I came back on belonged to my friend. It's been given to his relatives. I have my coins but it will still take time to turn them into cash. I can't just walk into a bank and say, 'I'd like some money for these coins I took from a treasure in Haiti.' There would be way too many questions to answer."

Cody looked up at Billy, his eyes suddenly intense. "How much cash do you think you'd need to put this thing together? To go back?"

"Maybe ten to fifteen thousand, plus a sailboat or a plane to get over and back in."

Cody smiled and glanced over at Travis. As soon as their eyes met, Travis knew what was coming. Cody turned back to Billy. "What if I told you I had the resources to put fifteen thousand dollars in your hand tomorrow morning, and have this sailboat and a twin-engine Beechcraft at your service by tomorrow night, plus connections to get us in and out of Port au Prince with minimal red tape?"

Billy looked up in disbelief. "Are you serious?"

"As a heart attack."

Billy paused for a moment, then glanced from Cody to Travis, who were smiling. "You are serious, aren't you?"

Cody nodded.

"Then I guess I'd have to say, when do we leave, partners?"

If the trip out had been fun, the trip back was euphoric. They were going treasure hunting! This was not a "maybe it's there" treasure—not a myth. This treasure lay buried in the hills of Tortue and they were going to find it! They had the friggin' directions on a beaten coin!

Billy got fairly ripped as they headed back for Key West. Standing on the bow, holding the rigging with one hand and extending the other as if with sword, he shouted into the wind, "Onward, me buckos! Onward to adventure, off to the lure of the yella gold and the sparkle of Spanish jewels! Avast me hatches! Batten the halyards! Shiver me timbers!"

Travis looked over at Cody from the steering cockpit. "You sure you know what you're doing—risking that kind of money and your equipment on this?"

Cody smiled. "I've been risking my money and things on what my gut tells me for a long time. My gut tells me this is for real, that we just might find that goddamned treasure."

"What about these crazy natives with their voodoo ceremonies and their sacrifices?"

"Travis, neither of us are newcomers to danger. Besides, a little war is good for a man. It makes the times of peace a touch sweeter. It gives you a story or two to tell. Let's face it; we walk on the edge because we like it there. You can't fool me, amigo, you're just as excited about this as I am, natives or no natives. Or maybe because of the natives."

Travis grinned and shook his head, knowing his friend was right. God! They were going treasure hunting on the isle of Tortuga!

The next three weeks were a flurry of activity, as equipment from camping gear to metal detectors was purchased and stored. Non-perishable foodstuffs were bought and stowed on board the boat, extra parts from spark plugs to spare airplane tires were boxed and loaded—and weapons were picked out. They all knew it was highly illegal to bring weapons into Haiti, but there was no chance they were going into this situation without them. Cody knew that once past customs in Port au Prince, they would probably be safe. The isle of Tortue, as it was now called, had little more than a couple of fishing villages on it. There were no government troops to speak of there. When Travis asked about getting everything through customs, Cody smiled and showed them the secret compartments that had been built into the inner hull.

Travis whistled. "God, Cody, even when you know where they are, you don't know where they are. That's some fine carpentry."

"Yeah," said Cody noncommittally, "cost me the price of a small Mercedes to have it done, but it's already paid for itself."

"I bet it has," whispered Travis, still admiring the work.

None of them were strangers to weapons and each had a favorite. Cody's gun was a Thompson submachine gun, a weighty little snub-nosed thing that threw heavy, .45 caliber slugs. Travis chose an M16. Billy's preference was a riot shotgun. "Don't have to aim," he said, "just point and pull the trigger." The guns were no problem. What Cody didn't have "in stock," he simply placed a discreet call for, and they arrived that afternoon. Cody had a couple more surprises for them along that line. The first was a smallish wooden box that had "U.S. Army" stamped on it. When Cody opened the lid, there lay a dozen fragmentation grenades.

"I'm not even going to ask," said Travis.

Cody smiled. "A little box of discouragers. You throw one of these at someone and it discourages almost any plans they had." Then he pulled out another box, about the same size, with the same markings on the outside. Inside were neat little packages of C-4 plastic explosive, probably ten pounds, plus detonators.

Travis whistled again.

"A parting gift from Uncle Sam, for my services in 'Nam."

"I'll bet," said Travis. "Jesus, Cody, what are you planning on doing, redefining the geography of the island?"

"Perhaps. If we figure out where the treasure is, and if it's buried deeper than we care to dig, like say in the side of a mountain, we can use a little of this to get to it. You never know. Anyway, let's get this stuff and the weapons tucked away in my little compartments and get on to other projects."

After storing the armory, Billy and Travis took charge of procuring the remainder of what they would need for the trip, while Cody began laying the groundwork for entering Haiti.

Cody told them that Haiti was not necessarily a fun place. In fact, on the list of "Not So Fun Places" in the Caribbean, it ran a close second to communist Cuba. It was run by a paranoid dictator named Jean-Claude Duvalier, who had become President for Life after his cruel-fisted father, Papa Doc, died.

"If they have any idea of our intent," explained Cody,

"they'll either kick us out of the country immediately or try to make a deal with us that they'll never keep when we find the treasure. The only way to do this is to have a good cover, an excuse for being on Tortue. Then, when we find the treasure, we load it up and we're out of there in a blink. That's where the plane comes in.

"We'll sail the boat over first and clear customs in Port au Prince. Billy and I are going to be journalists, writing a novel on the history of Tortue—a wonderful tale about buccaneers, sailing, etcetera." He looked over at Travis. "You are going to be our pilot/boat captain. The editor of the *Key West Citizen* is a good friend of mine. He owes me a serious favor. He got himself in trouble once and didn't know who to turn to. It's a long story, but let's just say he owes me big time. I'm going to have him write me a letter of introduction, stating that we're freelance reporters of high caliber, writing a great book that will surely shed a favorable light on Haiti. All this will give us license to wander around on Tortue.

"Now, as I was saying, we'll sail the boat over and get situated on Tortue, then I'll catch a flight to the States and bring the Beech back over. I'll give them some cock-and-bull story about needing a plane to reach some of the other islands in the Caribbean that are part of our research. Once they've called the editor and verified our story, I don't think they'll care much about us one way or another."

Winston Magruder, special agent for the Internal Revenue Service, was a happy man. He was closing in on his prey. He thought of all his assignments as "prey." He didn't care if it was a grandmother in Des Moines or a smuggler in the Keys. To him it was, "In for a penny, in for a pound," and he was going to get them.

There are some people in this world who simply take their job too seriously. Magruder was one of them, or maybe he just really liked his work.

Magruder stood in front of the bathroom mirror in his motel room and combed his short brown hair, studying himself. All right, so he wasn't Robert Redford, he had plain brown eyes, a pale complexion, and he was a little overweight. But he was a special agent now, by God; after all these years of pushing papers and knocking on the doors of people who had screwed up their tax returns, they had finally promoted him. This was only his third assignment in the field, but it was a big one. He was a little surprised that the boss had given him a shot at it, but he was pleased as punch at the chance to really perform.

Life had not been all that kind to Mr. Magruder up to this point, or perhaps it was fairer to say that people had not been all that kind. His father left his mother when Winston was ten years old. He simply went out for a pack of cigarettes and never returned. Winston, dominated and protected by his mother, was a late bloomer. He was not necessarily introverted, but suspicious of most everyone and their intentions. Finally, at the age of twenty-seven, he met a quiet, sincere woman to whom he, with a touch of reservation, gave his heart to and wed. They had only been married six months when Winston caught her in his bed with his best friend—or maybe he wasn't his friend at all.

Three months ago he'd been assigned to this slippery smuggler in the Keys. The guy was smart, no question. Up to this point he'd eluded the law completely. The fellow was so clean he didn't even have a traffic ticket. The authorities suspected that he was funneling money through one of his businesses, but they couldn't prove that either, so they called in the IRS. Magruder had been on the case all this time with little or no luck. He had to admit this William J. Cody was a pretty slick character, but Magruder was as tenacious as a pit bull, and finally his dedication paid off. The word from his snitches was that this Cody guy had teamed up with another gentlemen of questionable reputation, and together they were planning on stealing some gold from a foreign country then sneaking it back into the U.S. This was wonderful! If they found all the gold they were looking for, he'd trail them back to the States. When they hit the border, he and customs would be all over them like a cheap suit! He'd have 'em on antiquities violations for the United States and Haiti, and revenue violations. Jesus! This was the kind of case careers were made from!

He'd learned they were leaving at the end of the week. He contacted his superiors and filled them in. With their authorization, he bought his tickets for Port au Prince and packed his bag. God, this was great; he felt like Batman, James Bond, and the Lone Ranger all rolled into one. He was gonna get this thief and his friends and bring 'em back in chains!

Cody finished the final inspection on the boat while Billy picked up the last of the metal-detecting equipment from the UPS and checked its function. They had ordered several hand-held detectors from Garrett Electronics in Texas, including an underwater model.

Now that they had the supplies, equipment, and the wherewithal, they were ready to go.

Chapter Four

As the first rays of the rising sun touched the top of the mast, they unfurled their sails and headed into the Caribbean.

Cody set a south-southeast course that would take them down toward Cuba, then along that coast toward the Windward Passage, being careful to stay well outside Cuba's twelve-mile territorial limit. Cody had friends who were still "guests" of the Cuban government, caught in those waters while trying to shave some time off their trip home. Captured with weapons or drugs, or both, they were destined to grow old eating rice and beans, and playing baseball in the prison yard twice a week.

The first day of sailing was perfect. The wind was a healthy fifteen knots and running abeam of them. The sleek Pearson fairly skipped over the water. Schools of bottle-nosed porpoise ran next to them, submarining in and out of the waves. Gossamer-winged flying fish sailed across the bow and sunlight danced off the aquamarine sea. As night began to fall they neared the Cuban territorial limit, so they adjusted to a more easterly course. They split the time at the wheel into three eight-hour shifts. Travis took care of the navigation, operating the Loran and plotting their courses.

During the first day of sailing, the three of them sat in the cockpit and traded stories about Haiti. Cody told them about his experiences there, both business and pleasure, giving them a picture of everything from customs to hotels. Billy told them about what they could expect on Tortue. He provided insight into the religious practices and political unrest there, relating it to the death of his friend.

"Since my return to the States, I've done a considerable amount of research on Haiti. I was particularly interested in the voodoo ceremonies. I wanted a better understanding of what I witnessed—what had taken place with me that night. This research, strangely enough, led to the political arena.

"In my studies, I discovered that voodoo is still the most popular of the theological principles practiced by the traditional Haitian society. It is the grass-roots belief of the people—the base of their African heritage, and they've refused to let it go.

"Voodoo, and voodoo rites, represent some of the most controversial phenomenon in paranormal, occult, and theological circles. There are those who believe that voodoo is the purest, most successful philosophy practiced today in the field of metaphysics. Its origins go back to the bowels of ancient Africa when a more basic understanding of metaphysical elements was commonplace. Many religious philosophies tell you simply to have faith and hope for a miracle, that retribution, good or bad, is on the other side. Voodoo isn't so hip on heaven or hell, or waiting for results. It offers formulas for results right here and now. It is a way of life to the Haitians as much as it's a religious philosophy, and although it promotes birth and growth of the soul, it's also very much a philosophy of violence and revenge.

"There are good and bad priests, just as there are good and bad societies of all kinds. A priest who practices sorcery or black magic is called a *bokor*. It was a *bokor*, I believe, I ran into that night on Tortue."

Billy took a sip of his beer as Cody pulled the luff from the jibsail, then continued. "Since the death of Papa

Doc Duvalier, Jean-Claude, his son, has become president for life in Haiti, like his father was. During his reign, he has done little or nothing for the island. The country is in desperate shape economically, socially, and politically. It is being run by a handful of folks who pander to the rich and powerful both there and abroad. They are continually bleeding the island of its limited resources and sending the wealth abroad while virtually ignoring the people. The leaders of that country remind me of a man standing in a pool of gasoline while smoking a cigarette. Sooner or later an ember is going to fall.

"The ember may have already taken the form of a new religious leader. It seems there's a powerful voodoo priest, or *houngan*, making political waves in Haiti. There are many, however, who think of him more as a *bokor*. He calls himself Nyakang, "Night God" in ancient African. He claims to be the reincarnation of one Boukman Dutty, the man most credited with uniting the African slaves of Haiti in their revolt against the French and English in the late seventeen hundreds. It's claimed that Dutty used voodoo as the catalyst to bring the African slaves together. He traveled from place to place practicing ancient rites, performing ceremonies around huge bonfires in the forests and the jungles near the white plantations, exciting and frightening the superstitious slaves while reminding them of their African heritage. With Dutty's charismatic leadership, the slaves of Haiti rose up and threw off the brutal European dominance, destroying every single plantation and killing every European who remained in the country, even all of the emerging middle-class blacks with French and English blood. In the end, the country was cleansed of external influence, but it was also completely devastated—void of a living soul who knew anything about economics, industry, or modern agriculture. Since then, Haiti has had a succession of inept leaders and has continued in an economic downswing, reliant mostly in recent years on foreign aid.

"Anyway, I know a freelance reporter who's over there now, and the story he's getting is that this new *houngan* or *bokor* is doing the same thing that Dutty did two hundred years ago. He's taking his act on the road. Word goes out on the coconut telegraph that he's going to be at a certain place one night, and the natives from the local villages show up. He appears out of nowhere and preaches to them for an hour or so about becoming traditional Haitians again, rising up and destroying every vestige of European influence in the country, just as they did in seventeen hundred and ninety-one. He talks about returning to the land, of huge farms where everybody shares in the work and everyone gets a piece of the pie— a Caribbean utopia. Basically, it's the same rhetoric the communists have been preaching for years, but this has a bit more of a cultural twist to it. The middle and lower classes in Haiti have suffered such a bad deal for so long, they're open to anything that will put an extra plate of food on the table, and they're listening. He's just beginning to draw enough of a following that the authorities have started to look for him.

"His hook is, of course, voodoo," he continued. "Even those who don't like him seem to have great respect, even fear, for his powers. There was a tale told by the slaves to their children and repeated through the years of the *Neg Guinee*, the child of Africa, who would come someday to slay the oppressors and free the slaves of Haiti. Dutty is credited with being the first *Neg Guinee*. This Nyakang claims he's the second, and he practices the same ancient rituals that Dutty did, including sacrifice.

However, the rituals Nyakang performs are said to include human sacrifice. They are so physically overwhelming, the intensity of the sacrifice so terrifying yet psychologically seductive, that the people walk away believing he is the *Neg Guinee*, come to cleanse the land for them. He has but one demand of them—when he snaps his fingers, they are to rise up and serve him in the eradication of all European and Western influence. It's a pretty spooky situation and it has more than a few people sitting uneasy. You might wonder how this could happen in a country with considerable American influence. But keep in mind that you are dealing with a land that has a literacy rate of less than forty percent and poverty of epidemic proportions—a country where voodoo is very much a way of life and there is still a strong tie to African roots."

Billy paused for a moment, looking out over the sun-sparkled sea, then turned abruptly to his companions. "I'm fairly certain that it was this man my friend and I stumbled upon that night in Tortue." Suddenly his gray eyes went hard as marble. "I'm not gonna go looking for it, and it's not your business, but if I get a shot at that bastard, I'm gonna take it."

Travis and Cody nodded. They understood.

The first two days of sailing were as pleasant and peaceful as a sailor could ask for. Evening of the third day found Billy at the helm as the gorgeous orange sun set the sky on fire over the mountains of Cuba and the shadows of night crept across the graying waters. After a supper of Dinty Moore Beef Stew and a garden salad, Cody took the tiller. He had the night watch.

By eleven o'clock, Billy was fast asleep, lost to a five-beer slumber. Travis lay in his bunk, trapped in that surreal landscape between consciousness and sleep, where dreams and reality mix, weaving a tapestry you oftentimes can't control. He was captured by vaguely familiar images and emotions that pierced his thoughts like poorly spliced segments of film on an old projector—and he found himself enveloped by cold, uncompromising fear. There was an overwhelming certainty that death lay only moments away, and the acceptance, the courage he had hoped for was suddenly slipping away—his hands shook and the bile of panic rose in his throat.

He forcibly pulled himself from the scene and came to with a start, wiping the perspiration from his face and drawing in a few deep breaths. He calmed himself, listening to the rhythmic slap of the waves against the hull and feeling the gentle roll of the boat. It wasn't a new occurrence. These short, terrifying segments had been coming to him periodically since he'd returned from Vietnam, although he couldn't seem to draw a connection there. It was a confusing and unnerving experience that had cost him many hours of sleep.

While Travis finally succumbed to an uneasy slumber, Cody sat alone in the cockpit with the bright stars and the quiet sea as companions. The adventurer in him was excited about this new "mission"—a chance to step out on the edge again. But there was a small part of him, well hidden by layers of bravado, and his passion for risk, that hummed uncomfortably. He wasn't accustomed to that.

About one o'clock in the morning, he stood, stretched, then stepped up on the stern of the boat and unzipped his fly. After emptying his bladder, he turned to step back down into the cockpit but lost his footing. Grasping for the rigging and missing it, he fell headlong into the boat, banging his head on the fiberglass rail of the cockpit and knocking himself out cold. It might not have been a major problem, but he had turned off the autopilot just a few minutes before, to "feel" the boat as he sailed for a while.

Travis awoke to the thump topside, but hearing nothing else, he figured it was just Cody moving around and went back to sleep.

Travis felt the first rays of the early morning sun streak through the porthole of the cabin, and began to stir. Rising at about dawn had been a custom of his for as long as he could remember, except in those instances when wine or women ordained otherwise. He got up, ran his fingers through his hair, then climbed the small stairwell to the deck. As he came out of the hatch, he saw Cody, lying askew in the bottom of the steering cockpit. Travis quickly moved to his side, lifting Cody's head to inspect the ugly bruise near his temple. Cody began to come around.

"Easy, buddy, easy," Travis whispered. "Looks like you banged yourself pretty good."

Cody's eyes focused on Travis and he winced as he tried to move. "Jesus," he muttered. "I feel like someone clobbered me with a hammer."

"What happened?" Travis asked as he helped his friend to his feet. Cody moved his head back and forth a moment, massaging his forehead gently. "Well, as stupid as it sounds, I think I tripped while taking a piss and knocked myself out. Must have been around one or two in the morning."

With those words Travis's attention was drawn outward toward the mountains of Cuba. They were close, way too close.

"Christ on crutches!" he shouted. "For the last couple of hours we've been drifting in Cuban waters! Get the sails out, everything we've got, we gotta get out of here before those sons-of-bitches find us!"

Billy came through the hatch, rubbing the sleep from his eyes. "What's going on? What's all the shouting about?"

"Billy! Help Cody with the sail. We've drifted into Cuban waters and we've got to get the hell out of here right now!" Travis headed down below. "I'm gonna take a Loran reading and find out just how much trouble we're in."

Cody, scanning the horizon, shouted down, "While you're there, break out the weapons. I'm not spending the next ten years of my life in a Cuban prison! If they spot us, I'm not going peacefully."

The Loran confirmed their worst fears; they had drifted nearly five miles inside the twelve-mile limit. They were sitting on the northeast end of Cuba, an area popular for patrols. It was a small miracle the boat hadn't been spotted already. They set a north-northeast course, the most expeditious path out of their predicament, scanned the horizon, and loaded their weapons.

A half an hour later, when they had just begun to gain a little confidence in surviving the situation, Cody whispered, "Speaking of sons-a-bitches," and pointed. Coming from the direction of the island and moving fast, was a forty-foot Cuban gunboat.

Captain Hector Roberto Ortiz was in a foul mood. The three members of his crew were keeping their distance as much as possible. The captain was not a man of overly good temperament to begin with, but that morning they thought he'd been acting as if he was bent on homicide. Actually, they were right. He had someone particular in mind, but his bad mood had bubbled over to the point where almost anyone would do.

Last night his wife had boldly informed him that she

had a lover. She had been seeing "Enrico" for almost a year and was leaving Hector for him. Rico was an artist—so gifted, such genius. *Madre de Dios! A painter!* He could still hear her as she extolled his talents, both standing up and lying down. The words seared his brain, torturing him.

When he saw the boat on the horizon, it gave focus to his fury. *Smugglers! Dope runners!* He'd rip their boat apart. He'd find the guns or the drugs, and if they offered the least bit of trouble, he'd give them and their boat a burial at sea. He'd done it before.

As they closed on the sailboat, he put Martinez on the deck-mounted heavy machine gun at the bow. Martinez didn't have a problem shooting people. Ortiz liked that in a man. He left Lopez at the wheel in the cabin. Lopez didn't have much in the way of *cajones*—it was the best place for him. While they moved up on the sailboat, the captain and his first mate Santera armed themselves with AK-47s and stepped out onto the deck.

Not knowing what to expect, Travis had pulled out Cody's Thompson, Billy's shotgun, and the M16. When he had started to close the lid of the compartment, he looked at the box of grenades lying there and decided to grab a couple—just in case.

Billy moved forward to the bow, and, standing where the top of the cabin would give him cover if he needed it, he slipped his shotgun under the mainsail that lay doused on the cabin roof. All the sails were down. There was no point in trying to outrun the Cuban Coast Guard in a sailboat. Cody looked up at the rapidly approaching boat, threw back the bolt on his Thompson, and muttered, "Buckle up, boys. It's about to hit the fan."

Cody and Travis stood in the cockpit, their guns

below them, out of sight, and watched as the gunboat pulled aside them, maybe thirty yards off.

Captain Ortiz saw the American registration on the boat. He could see the men standing on deck, so he shouted in English as his craft slowed and came along side. "Stand where you are, everyone on deck. You are in Cuban waters. Prepare to be boarded."

Cody shouted back, "We're an American vessel, headed for Haiti. We had some difficulty and got off course during the night. There's no problem—"

"I didn't ask for an explanation," shouted Ortiz. "Now shut up and do as I say. Prepare to be boarded!"

"Wait just a minute." Cody was getting angry. "We're American citizens, we have a right—"

"You're shit!" the Cuban spat back. "You're in Cuban waters and you have no rights. You're on your way to Havana whether you like it or not!"

"Who the hell do you think you are? We've done nothing wrong, so screw you and the horse you rode in on, buddy. We ain't going nowhere!" Cody shouted back.

On a good day, Ortiz had the tolerance level of a pit viper. It was safe to say that this was not one of his better days. This smuggler, standing there, shouting at him, with his long blonde hair and his blue eyes, suddenly reminded Ortiz of an artist. He turned to Martinez on the machine gun. "Kill them all," he said. Martinez looked over at the captain to make sure he'd heard right—this was unorthodox even for Ortiz. The captain swung around, locking him with furious eyes. "Kill them all, I said!"

Both Travis and Billy spoke fairly good Spanish, but they missed Ortiz's command the first time because he spoke quietly. The second time they got it loud and clear. They were diving for their weapons as Martinez squeezed the trigger. Even so, there was really only one thing that saved them: Martinez was a little careless. He had forgotten to draw back the bolt on the machine gun as they sidled up to the sailboat. When he pulled the trigger, nothing happened. In the time it took him to realize his mistake, then quickly throw the bolt, Billy and Travis had their weapons in hand, Cody following suit. Immediately upon hearing the command from the Cuban captain, Billy dropped to his knees and grabbed the stock of his weapon. He lifted the gun, finger on the trigger, and fired right through the canvas sail. He didn't know it then, but the second he saved by not pulling it clear of the sail saved his life. The buckshot from Billy's first round caught Martinez from his ribs to his neck, knocking him off his gun just as he pulled the trigger and sent a spray of bullets harmlessly into the air.

Ortiz stood there expecting to see Martinez cut these *gringos* to pieces when, instead, the *gringos* whipped out weapons and beat Martinez to the punch. He swung his AK-47 around and let off a burst in the direction of the sailboat as he dove for the cover of his gunnels. Santera, standing next to him, wasn't as quick to react and took three rounds from Cody's gun in the chest before he could get behind the cover of the rail. But after three .45 slugs in the chest, being protected by the rail was no longer an issue.

Ortiz rose up and let off a burst that tore up the fiberglass of the cabin in front of Billy, while shouting to Lopez in the wheelhouse to get them out of there.

Travis knew that if the Cubans got away, they were finished. They'd be in a Cuban prison by nightfall, and that was the best they could hope for. He grabbed a grenade and pulled the pin. "Cover me!" he yelled to Billy and Cody as he stood up.

Lopez, at the wheel, slammed the throttles to the panel and the big diesels started to whine as Travis reared back to throw. A hundred feet isn't a long toss, but the only chance of that grenade doing enough damage to stop the boat was to get it in the wheelhouse door—a three-by-five-foot opening.

As Cody and Billy blasted the gunboat, keeping Ortez down, Travis heaved the grenade—not so much in the fashion of a soldier, but more like a quarterback tossing a pass to a deep tight end. The deadly projectile sailed through the air. The boat was pulling away ... Travis held his breath as the grenade struck the very top of the gunnel. Two inches shorter and it would have glanced harmlessly off into the ocean. It hit the rail and bounced right though the wheelhouse doorway. Lopez heard something slam against the bulkhead inside the cabin and looked down as the grenade wobbled to a stop at his feet. He took one look, let go of the wheel and jumped out of the door on the other side, over the rail and into the ocean.

Ortiz rose to blast the sailboat once more, unaware of the grenade's arrival and Lopez's departure. Travis was caught standing there, like a quarterback who watches his pass received, then gets blindsided by a lineman. Ortiz smiled and aimed—and the grenade blew.

The captain was less than eight feet from the door of the wheelhouse. The explosion all but tore off the small cabin, sending shrapnel of metal, fiberglass, and wood for a hundred-foot radius. Ortiz was blown out of the boat, a dozen six-inch daggers of fiberglass buried in his back. As he struck the water and began to sink, he watched his final exhale forming bubbles that danced to the bright surface. Everything darkened and he died with a single thought ... *Madre de Dios. An artista!*

When the smoke cleared, the gunboat lay dead still in the debris-covered water. The wheelhouse was a charred and mangled wreck. Cody, Billy, and Travis slowly stood up. Billy shook his head. "Christ! What a throw, Travis. I think we have the makings of a hell of a baseball team here."

They saw Lopez floating quietly by the stern of the Cuban boat. Swinging around, they motored over to the gunboat and tied up to it. Travis jumped over onto the other deck and released the foam-filled life raft from the stern, pushing it into the water next to Lopez, holding the line to it. When the Cuban got into the raft, Travis looked down at him and drew the bolt back on the M16. Lopez crossed himself and closed his eyes.

"Do you speak English?" asked Travis

The Cuban opened his eyes. "*Si* ... yes, I speak some."

"You know we should kill you, don't you? You can identify us and our boat." Travis paused, letting the point sink in. "What's your name?"

"Juan Lopez," the Cuban said shakily.

"Tell me, Juan, are you married? Children?"

"*Si Jefe, dos ninos.*"

Travis took a deep breath. "Listen, Juan. You're going to make me a promise, and I'll tell you why you're going to keep it. You're going to promise not to mention a word about this little fight today. You're going to float in on your raft and tell the authorities you had an explosion in the engine room and your boat sank. The others drowned or were killed when the boat blew. You're going to do this for two reasons: one being that you're an honorable man and it is your repayment to me for letting you live. The other is that if we are caught, we are all going to tell the same story—that when the fighting started you were a coward and jumped into the sea, leaving your friends to deal with us. My guess is that even if your superiors are not positive we're telling the truth, they will find other work for you. Your reputation as a man will be destroyed. My guess is that you'll probably end up cleaning the bottom of these boats, rather than riding in them."

The Cuban gulped and nodded. Travis tossed the securing line to him. "Paddle away now. The winds will take you to shore in less than a day. You'll make it. Remember my words, Juan."

As Lopez drifted away, concocting the story he planned to tell, Cody took a small stick of plastic explosive and planted it in the stern by the outdrive, setting a ten-minute timer on it. Cody and Travis got back into the sailboat, unfurled the sails, and headed out of Cuban waters. From a safe distance they watched the stern of the gunboat buckle and blow. In moments there was nothing but an oil slick and a few bubbles to mark its passage.

Chapter Five

They cleared the coast of Cuba without further incident. A Cuban fishing boat discovered Juan Lopez later that day, and that night in Havana he told his story of an engine explosion to the authorities. Cody and his crew entered the harbor of Port au Prince the following evening.

Customs sent a boat out as they entered the harbor and three taciturn Haitian officials requested their papers and the purpose of their visit, while doing a fairly thorough search of the boat. They discovered nothing, passing right over Cody's secret compartments. The newcomers were directed to a marina, where they rented a slip for a few days. Travis figured they would need three or four days in Port au Prince. They had to contact the government and inform them of their plans to travel to Tortue for the purpose of researching a book. Cody had his letter of introduction from his editor friend in Key West, and he hoped that would ease the way. They were also going to need an interpreter and a guide, someone who knew their way around and spoke English fluently. Both Billy and Travis were good with languages, but Haitian was impossible. It was a combination of African, Spanish, French, and Creole that had been ground together into a patois that sounded like someone trying to talk with marbles in his mouth.

Cody felt that the boat would be safe enough at the marina, so they decided to stay at a downtown hotel for a few days. They would be more centrally located and could get a bit of a feel for Port au Prince. After securing the boat and paying an initial fee to the marina manager, then dashing him a bit more to keep a good eye on things, the trio caught a cab for town. The sun had already set, and the warm, humid darkness of the moonless Caribbean night settled over the island. That nighttime drive into town was an experience in itself, giving them their first look at the desperate masses that overwhelmed the country's limited resources and inept government. As they rode in the rattling taxicab dodging potholes on a road that wound along the coastline of the bay, the darkness surrounding them was illuminated by thousands of fires. Near the road they could see people huddled around small fires beside the wrecked, stripped carcasses of ancient cars, or peering out from under cardboard and corrugated tin lean-to's. The fires extended from the edge of the road up into the hills, creating a surrealistic atmosphere. People looked up as the taxi passed, the whites of their eyes reflected in the firelight like animals caught in the glare of a car's headlights. It was unexpectedly eerie and cast a spell of uneasiness on the excitement and anticipation.

A few minutes later they entered the city, traveling along dimly lit streets lined with hookers and hawkers shouting their wares. Gutters were covered in excrement and ash, and the stench of fish and diesel fumes pervaded the air. As the cab bounced along, they saw the contradiction that was typical of third-world countries—a sprawling carnival of harsh poverty amidst the incessant optimism of daily enterprise and the opulence of presidential palaces and government buildings. But beyond the monuments to man's ego and the plague of poverty, there was to be seen in much of the populace a sense of pride, a jauntiness—they moved through the streets in their colorful clothes, the women with baskets on their heads, hurrying home for the evening, the men on their way out for a rum drink and perhaps a game of dominoes or dice.

When they arrived at Le Bougainvillea, the hotel recommended by the marina manager, they paid the driver and disembarked.

As the three Americans left the marina and headed for the hotel, the marina manager watched, then went to the phone in his office. He placed a call to a small hotel/bar on a hillside overlooking the bay and asked for room 17.

"Hello, Mr. Magruder. I have the information on the people you were inquiring about. Yes, that's right. No, come at eight. I'll be busy until then, and bring the fifty dollars you promised me."

Magruder was ecstatic. The first part of his plan had worked! There were only two or three decent marinas in Port au Prince. He'd gone to the manager of each with a description of the boat and the men, and a promise of money. He would be on them from day one. He got up off the bed and tucked in his shirt. He had about two hours to kill. He would get something to eat at the hotel restaurant and be on his way. "*James Bond ain't got nothin' on me*," he thought with a smile, as he walked out the door.

Travis and his companions settled into their quarters—a large villa-like affair with two double beds in one room and a single in the next, as well as a balcony overlooking the courtyard below. After each of them grabbed a quick shower, they decided to have dinner in the city and explore a little. The manager of the hotel recommended a popular restaurant/nightclub within walking distance.

The restaurant, Chez Caribe, was fairly crowded for a

Thursday night. It was an upscale establishment specializing in French and Creole cuisine, with an attractive disco for the tourists and the younger, affluent crowd in Port au Prince. The maitre d' showed them to a table off to the side of the entrance with a good view of the restaurant and the dance floor. The entertainment wouldn't start until ten. Right now there was soft music playing through the speakers on the stage.

They had only been seated for perhaps five minutes, having just received their drinks, when Travis's attention was drawn to the entrance. An older but attractive man, well dressed, with the natural, confident air of the affluent came through the door. The maitre d' rushed to his side immediately, greeting him with obvious deference, shaking his hand and escorting him and the lady at his side to a table across the floor from the three Americans. The man was obviously a person of some importance, but it was the woman on his arm who halted Travis almost in mid-sentence. She was of medium height, with short, sun-streaked auburn hair, a dark tan and a lithe figure. She was pretty, and carried herself with pride, yet few men would have called her beautiful. She gave more an image of dedication and tenacity—of days spent in the sun without the amenities of a sandy beach and a bottle of suntan oil. No, she wasn't necessarily stunning, but her eyes—her eyes captured him. They carried the bright, pale blue of Caribbean shallows in them and flashed with a touch of green found on offshore reefs, where the water is deeper and more compelling. There was honesty, strength, and intellect in those eyes—and something else—the timeless warmth of an old friend's caress—guileless, unfeigned, and offered without pride or price.

As the two walked across the room, Travis wondered what she was doing with a guy twice her age. But when he watched the older man dash the maitre d' with a twenty, he figured he knew the answer.

When they reached their table and the maitre d' had seated them, the lady glanced around the room, appraising her company. Her gaze moved slowly across the restaurant until she reached Travis's table and their eyes touched. For a moment she lost her confident air as she looked at the tall, dark-haired man at the corner table. They simply stared at each other. The older man was talking to her but she wasn't paying attention. Billy was speaking to Cody and Travis, but Travis couldn't have told you what he was saying. All his senses had room for were those dazzling blue eyes.

He was pulled from his trance as Cody nudged him. "Hey, buddy, it's not polite to ogle. Let's not have the locals thinking we're after their women. At least not right away."

The woman pulled her eyes back to her companion and his conversation, but not without first offering the faintest of smiles.

It wasn't just that Travis found her attractive, it was something else, something he had never before sensed with a woman. He couldn't remember meeting her before. But it was like, well, he just wanted to go over to her and say, "Hello, it's good to see you again."

They struggled through dinner, trying to keep their eyes off each other, catching one another staring. The whole affair didn't go unobserved. Her companion, at one point, remarked sharply that perhaps she would be more comfortable at another table, and Cody finally asked Travis how he knew her.

Travis studied the woman, chatting with her friend, and smiled. "I don't know, Cody. That's the funny part, I don't know."

At ten o'clock, the band came on stage and began to play. The couples at the tables drifted onto the floor to sway and bounce to island versions of songs from Billy Joel to Cole Porter. She was out on the dance floor with her partner while the band played a snappy version of "Joy to the World," by Three Dog Night. As the song ended, the band went right into a silky rendition of Jim Croce's *Time in a Bottle*. Cody was in the middle of a story when Travis abruptly excused himself and walked over to the couple on the floor. He tapped the older man on the shoulder. "May I?" he asked. The fellow was slightly perturbed, but he was a gentleman. He looked to the woman, she nodded, and he returned to his table.

Travis took her in his arms as his mind raced for something witty to say. She looked up at him with sparkling, mischievous eyes, and with a soft French accent asked, "What took you so long?"

Travis chuckled. "I was letting my dinner settle a bit, in case I had to fight your boyfriend for you."

She giggled, throatily, sensuously, and Travis's knees wanted to buckle.

They introduced themselves as they danced, her eyes leaving his only when he gently pulled her closer. Her name was Michelle. Michelle Dubonnet. With the fragrance of her perfume engulfing him and her body molded against his, Travis, at that moment, would have given his share of the treasure for the music not to stop.

But eventually the song came to an end. They held each other a moment longer. When Travis reluctantly released her, she took his hand. "Come, Mr. Christian, let me introduce you to my boyfriend."

Travis hesitated. "I don't really want to cause you any trouble."

She looked at him mischievously. "Trust me, he is jealous of any man I'm with. You will be no exception."

When they reached the table, the older man stood. She went over and gave him a hug and a little peck on the cheek. "Papa, I would like you to meet Mr. Travis Christian from Florida, and thank you, Papa, for being polite and not having him thrown out when he cut in on you."

The man smiled, knowing he was being worked, but was mollified somewhat by the hug and kiss from his daughter. He extended his hand. "Welcome to Haiti, Monsieur Christian," he said with a heavy French accent. "Would you care to join us for a drink?"

Travis hesitated politely for a moment, then looked over at Michelle who smiled and nodded. "Well yes, thank you. I'd be pleased." They all sat down and ordered cocktails from the waiter who appeared and disappeared on cue.

While they waited for the drinks, the older man spoke. "My daughter is lovely, but sometimes her manners are lacking. My name is not Papa; it is Pierre Dubonnet. Tell me, Monsieur Christian—"

"Please, call me Travis."

"Very well," replied Pierre, "and you may call me Monsieur Dubonnet—until I decide if I like you." Then he winked at his daughter. "Anyway, Travis, what brings you and your friends to Haiti?"

Travis explained the book that Billy and Cody were writing, adding that he was the pilot and captain of the enterprise.

The Frenchman's eyes lit up at the mention of flying. "I, too, am a pilot. I flew fighters for the French until there were no more to fly, and later I flew for the British in World War Two."

Travis spoke of his genuine respect for the men of that era, mentioning, in the process, that he had flown in

Vietnam.

"Ahhh, Vietnam," repeated Pierre. "A French disaster repeated by Americans too arrogant to have studied their history beforehand."

Travis readily agreed.

For the next half an hour the conversation ranged from American aircraft to Haitian agriculture. The Dubonnet's owned one of the largest sugar interests in Haiti. Monsieur Dubonnet was a widower—his wife had been killed in a car accident five years before. He and his only child, Michelle, ran the business—a huge, sprawling plantation on the outskirts of Cap Haitian, near the northwest end of the island. They exported sugar and molasses.

They all got along famously, and at the end of the first half hour the Frenchman decided he liked this Travis Christian somewhat, but still insisted on being called Monsieur Dubonnet.

Finally Travis excused himself for a moment to check in on his friends and to use the restroom, promising to return and dance with Michelle again.

Cody looked up and smiled. "So?"

"It's her father, not her boyfriend, and they are both very nice people."

Billy glanced over to them and back at Travis. "She's very nice people. Very nice."

"Down, boy, I'm on my way to the restroom. Then I want to dance with Michelle once more. Can you guys hang on for a while longer?"

"No problem," replied Cody. "The music's good, the drinks are great, we're fine."

Travis grinned at them both. "Thanks, be back soon."

A few minutes later, Travis was stepping from the men's room at the far end of the restaurant when four

Haitians burst through the entrance and into the dining room, weapons in hand. The leader of the group leaped into the center of the room and let go a burst of fire into the ceiling from the automatic rifle he carried. Women screamed and people melted into their seats in terror. As his companions fanned out into the room, he shouted, "No one moves! Darkness falls on this land for the rich and the corrupt. The African sun dawns on Haiti. Hail Nyakang!"

The man in the center quickly surveyed the room. When his eyes reached the Dubonnet's table he stopped and his face went hard. He pointed and shouted something in Haitian, and two of his men moved toward the table while the third took a position on the other side of the room, maybe fifteen feet from Cody and Billy. As the exchange began, Cody looked over to the restroom and saw Travis. Travis motioned with his hand to stay calm and drew back into the shadows of the hallway for a moment.

Travis and Cody had on snakeskin cowboy boots, a favorite with both of them. Each had had their boots altered. On the inside of Travis's left boot was a calfskin holster that held a .45 caliber, two-round derringer with a three-inch barrel, for better accuracy. He'd been through enough tight spots in his life to appreciate the advantage. In Cody's left boot was a sheath that held a boot knife, perfectly balanced for throwing.

As the two Haitians on the dance floor moved toward the Dubonnet's table, Travis slid out of the shadows and quickly palmed the pistol to show Cody, avoiding the attention of the other two men.

The big Haitian with the automatic rifle stood in the center of the room shouting slogans about the coming purge in Haiti, while the fourth produced a canvas bag and began moving from table to table taking money and jewelry from the terrified patrons. He was ripping the necklace from a petrified, heavyset lady at the table next to Cody when, across the room, the two men reached Michelle's table. One of them held a revolver. The other had a long, wicked-looking machete. The man with the pistol looked down on Michelle and her father.

"Dubonnet," the man spat. "You bleed the sweet gold from the land and give nothing back to the people. Their sweat and blood purchase your pleasures, yet your sugar touches only foreign tongues. You are a thief and your daughter is a whore!"

The older man rose angrily from his seat, but the gunman grabbed him as he came up and slashed the barrel of his pistol across the Frenchman's temple. Pierre collapsed across the table, unconscious. Michelle screamed and lurched to her feet, trying to reach her father, but the man with the machete grabbed her.

The Haitian in the center of the room moved quickly up the three stairs to the slightly elevated section of the dining room where they were. He took a can of spray paint from the pouch at his side and hastily drew a strange voodoo pentagram on the wall above Michelle's table.

"Hail Nyakang," he shouted as he finished, looking around at the frightened people with fierce, fanatical eyes. "Night falls on all of you! Death to all who enslave Haiti!" he screamed as he brought his gun up to shoot Pierre.

Sixty feet is a long shot with a derringer, especially a .45 caliber derringer, because it kicks like a little mule. But Travis was good with a pistol. In fact, he was better than good.

Travis watched from the shadows as the scene moved toward a crescendo. When the Haitian with the rifle brought the weapon up at Pierre's head, Travis stepped out, aimed, and fired. The bullet struck the man's temple; his head snapped like he'd been sucker-punched, his knees gave, and he crumpled to the floor. Everyone in the room, including his two companions at the table, swung around and stared at Travis, framed in the restroom hallway. The Haitian with the pistol at the table, and the one on the floor taking the jewelry started to bring their guns to bear on Travis. The American never hesitated. He targeted the one next to Michelle and shot him through the chest. The thief lurched back against the wall, his gun slipping from his hands as he slid slowly down to a sitting position and quietly died.

The man on the lower level took a second to drop his bag of goods. Cocking his big revolver, he brought it up with both hands at Travis, who was out of ammunition. Cody rose from his chair and shouted. Already unnerved by the death of his two companions, the startled man turned. As the Haitian came around, Cody snapped his arm out from his chest, flicking the boot knife. The movement was so swift that his assailant had just enough time to blink before the sharp steel buried itself in his chest. The bandit gasped in shock, the gun in his hand discharging into the floor as he dropped to his knees. He stayed like that for a moment, then, just when it appeared he was going down onto the carpet, the man seemed to get a second wind. Blood ran from the corner of his mouth as he sucked air into his ruined chest. The revolver had fallen to his side, almost forgotten. With exaggerated slowness, he began to bring it up again. The people around Cody and Billy gasped, frozen with fear. As the gun rose, Billy saw the empty wine bottle in the ice bucket next to him. In one swift motion, he snatched it out of the container and hurled it at the kneeling gunman.

For all Billy's potential as a major league pitcher, this throw was high and wide; the bottle sailed over the Haitian, missing his head by six inches. Blood covered the man's chin and dropped in bright red splotches onto his white shirt. He didn't even blink when the bottle crashed against the wall behind him. There wasn't a sound in the room but the Haitian's rasping breaths as he finally leveled his weapon. Cody and Billy were about to dive in opposite directions when suddenly the loud gasping ceased, leaving the room bathed in silence. Caught like two rabbits in the glare of a hunter's light, the men froze. For a moment, the gunman just knelt there, not breathing, looking like a macabre work of art in the gallery of the damned, his revolver still aimed straight ahead. Then his eyes lost their focus, and with the gun still extended, he fell face forward onto the floor.

Cody and Billy barely had time to exhale when Michelle screamed. The remaining Haitian had his arm around her and was dragging her toward the doorway to the street.

The restaurant had a high ceiling and there was a balustrade, which ran around the entire room, leading to a pair of French doors that accessed an outside dining area. The outside area was directly above the entrance, overlooking the tree-lined street below. Travis was standing near the stairs to the upper walkway when he saw the Haitian grab Michelle and begin to pull her toward the entrance. She was kicking and screaming so much that her antagonist failed to see Travis climb to the walkway, moving toward the outside balcony. They were in the foyer, struggling, when Travis raced above them and out onto the alfresco dining area. The Haitian finally brought his machete to Michelle's throat, drawing a touch of blood. "Stop now, bitch, or you die here!" he growled in a vicious baritone. She drew a quick, frightened breath as the blade touched her skin, and gave in. He began to pull her through the foyer and out to the street.

Travis was standing directly over the entrance, knowing that they had to come out right below him, but he wasn't sure quite what to do. If he leaped on the man, he might cut her throat as they struggled. It was then that he noticed the orchids growing in heavy, decorative cement pots every few feet on the ornate balcony. He picked one up with both hands and positioned himself over the doorway. In seconds he heard scuffling and their heads appeared below him. The Haitian held her close. There was little distance between them, but there was little choice. Leading the man below by just a fraction of a second, Travis dropped the heavy pot. The cement vase struck him squarely on the head, breaking in two, the pieces crashing onto the pavement. His legs buckled and he almost went to his knees, arms dropping momentarily from Michelle. She immediately rolled away from him. Most men would have been out for the count, but he was a big, hard man. As the Haitian straightened up and shook his head to clear it, Travis leapt from the balcony and they both tumbled to the pavement. For a fellow who had just been soundly bashed, the guy was quick. He was on his feet in an instant, and as Travis rose, the Haitian swung his machete. Travis ducked as the blade whistled just inches above his head and clanged into one of the cement columns that supported the balcony. Before his assailant could swing again, Travis rushed in under his arm and tackled him, driving him back toward the street and into the side of a parked Peugeot. Travis slammed the man against the car so hard the fellow's arms flailed out and he lost his grip on the machete, which went flying over the hood of the car. Travis didn't give the guy a chance to recover. He straightened up and hit him with a hard left jab, then followed it with a walloping right roundhouse that broke the man's jaw. As the Haitian's knees sagged, Travis grabbed him, spun him around, and drove him through the passenger side window in a shower of broken glass.

Billy and Cody had just come through the doors of the restaurant as Travis put the finishing touches on his opponent. He looked over to see if Michelle was all right when suddenly there was a screeching of tires in the street and Cody yelled a warning. Travis saw the glint of a gun barrel in the car racing past the restaurant. Michelle stood, open-mouthed, about ten feet from him, as the driver of the car pointed his automatic weapon. Travis took two steps and dove, catching the woman waist-high and knocking her over the hedge by the entrance, onto the lawn on the other side. Billy and Cody had already thrown themselves flat as the spray of bullets redecorated the front of the building. The car screeched past and continued on down the street, out of sight.

Travis found himself on top of Michelle, their noses nearly touching as they lay in the soft grass behind the hedge. Their eyes locked. A moment passed, and Michelle whispered, "I think the danger is over now."

"Yeah, I know," murmured Travis. "Too bad."

Cody called to them. Travis stood up and helped Michelle to her feet. Together they reentered the restaurant.

Pierre was being helped to his feet by the maitre d' as they walked into the dining room. Michelle ran over and hugged her father, quickly checking the bruise and small cut on his head where he'd been struck. Pierre took her hand away and looked over at Travis and his friends. "Robert here tells me that while I was out you performed some sort of American cowboy circus act, throwing knives and shooting people?" He nudged the dead Haitian on the floor with his foot. "Saving the day just like one of those dreadful John Wayne westerns."

Travis smiled at the description.

"I am also told," Pierre spoke more seriously, "that you saved my life, and that of my daughter also. There are no words, monsieur, in French or English that can convey sufficiently my gratitude for protecting my daughter and myself. Let it suffice to say, if there is anything that you need while in my country, anything at all that is remotely within my power, it is yours." He stuck out his hand then. "Monsieur Christian, you may call me Pierre, and while you and your friends are in Port au Prince, you will do me the honor of staying with us in our villa. It is but the smallest of ways I can find to repay you. Perhaps we can assist you in some fashion, in the research of your book."

Travis hesitated. "It's really not necessary, we have a hotel."

"Nonsense. I simply won't accept your refusal. You must allow an old man some dignity."

Travis looked at Cody and Billy. Cody just shrugged. Travis exhaled and smiled. "Very well, we accept your generous offer."

They could hear the police sirens in the distance as they moved toward the door. Pierre glanced back at the man in the center of the floor, then over to Cody. "You killed him at over twenty feet with a backhanded throw of your knife, eh? That's really quite impressive. I knew a man in the French Resistance who was that good."

Cody grinned modestly. "I only wounded him. Billy finished him off when he scared him to death with the bottle."

Pierre looked puzzled as the rest of them laughed.

Billy leaned over and put his hand on Pierre's shoulder. "I guess you had to be there."

"I was," said Pierre, "but I guess you had to be conscious."

They spent an hour with the Haitian police. Pierre Dubonnet's influence was sufficient to make the questioning brief and the explanations acceptable. When it was over, they piled into Pierre's big Mercedes and drove away. A half-hour later they were at the gates of his villa, overlooking the bay. The gates opened automatically and they rolled up the long, tree-lined drive to the front of the house. It was a large but tasteful affair, done in white brick, with a Spanish barrel-tiled roof. They exited the car and walked through the columned veranda to a pair of huge mahogany doors, which were opened immediately by a servant. A few minutes later they were all settled into the large, comfortable living room. Travis and Michelle had quite casually managed to find themselves seated together on a leather couch across from the others.

After drinks had been served, Pierre stood and offered a toast: "To new friends. May your enterprises here be an unrivaled success. And to John Wayne, wherever you are."

As everyone laughed, Travis studied the Frenchman for a moment. He was a small, spry man in his late fifties, early sixties. He had a prominent nose, and wore a trim mustache and goatee that, like his hair, had turned an elegant gray. His eyes were bright blue as were those of his daughter, and carried the same mischievous sparkle. But beyond the humor, Travis saw determination and strength. He remembered how quickly the older man had risen and gone for the gunman when his daughter was insulted. He was a man used to luxury, but it was Travis's guess that he had earned it.

During the course of the evening, the conversation ranged from literature, including, of course, Cody and Billy's book, to Pierre's history and how he came to Haiti.

When the war in Europe ended, he was twenty-five years old. His family had been in the wine business, owning vineyards in the Bordeaux region of France for over thirty years. The vineyards and the business had been totally devastated by the war. The Germans had killed his father and mother. He sold his share of the holdings to his brother, and with six thousand francs in his pocket he set out to see the world.

In 1947, while sailing in the Caribbean, he discovered Haiti. He fell in love with the lush land, the delightful climate, and the bright, carefree people of the countryside. He saw the fields of sugarcane that seemed to thrust effortlessly out of the ground. He remembered the war and the shortages of sugar.

He sold his sailboat and bought three hundred acres of land that included an older home. With the last of his money, he purchased equipment for the business. In the process he met another cane grower, a fellow Frenchman, and the man graciously shared with Pierre the mechanics of the business. The people of the region got to know him, and he them. He treated everyone who worked for him fairly and often labored in the fields along with the Haitians, or shared a glass of sugary rum with them in the evenings. He succeeded where others had failed, and in time, his holdings grew.

Pierre took a sip of his drink. "Eventually I returned to France to find a wife. Again fate smiled on me and I discovered a lovely lady who married me and we returned to Haiti. Two years later, Michelle was born." He smiled as he looked over at his daughter. "Michelle was educated in the secondary schools of Haiti but we sent her to college in the U.S. She returned four years later with a degree in economics."

The conversation also worked its way around to the evening's incident at the restaurant, and its political ramifications. In somber tones, Pierre explained the present problems of Haiti and the newest development concerning Nyakang, the voodoo priest attempting to purge Haiti of any modern influence.

"He's using ancient voodoo rites as a catalyst to stir the superstitious fears of the people and unite them against outside authority of any sort. He wants to bring Haiti back to some sort of traditional Garden of Eden, where everyone lives on nuts and berries, and the most technologically advanced tool is a shovel. He wants a violent purge of all Westerners and Europeans, just like Boukman Dutty in the slave uprising two hundred years ago.

"At first, everyone thought he was just a crazy *houngan*, but his influence is growing and he's beginning to use terrorist techniques on the upper class. You saw for yourself tonight. It's rumored he has a secret hiding place in the caves of Tortue, but no one knows for sure. He's like a firefly on a moonless night. He is seen only when he wants to be."

Travis nodded, realizing that the timing of their project was a little less than perfect. While hunting for their treasure, they would have to keep a serious eye out for a homicidal voodoo priest, as well as the authorities.

As the conversation moved around the room, Travis struggled to appear casual and keep from stealing too many glances at Michelle. He found himself wishing he could just take her hand in his—a strange sensation for a fairly committed bachelor. She would catch him every once in a while, and the look she returned carried no disappointment.

About midnight, the last of the drinks were finished. Pierre bade them goodnight and they were shown to their rooms. Belongings had been sent for from the hotel. There was a polite but lingering touch of hands and eyes as Travis said goodnight to Michelle.

Once inside his room, Travis, tired as he was, found he couldn't sleep. The excitement of the evening, the gunfight, the incredible girl, and the disquieting feeling of recognition had overloaded his mind and it wasn't ready to turn off. He opened the French doors in his room and walked out onto a balcony that ran completely around the upper floors of the house. He was standing by the rail watching the full moon duck in and out of the gray cotton-candy clouds, painting their edges in soft silver, when a quiet voice spoke from behind him.

"It's beautiful, isn't it?"

He turned, startled, to find Michelle standing there.

"I couldn't sleep. I was standing over there by the rail when I saw you come out."

He smiled, surprised and pleased. "Yes, it is beautiful. I couldn't sleep, either."

She moved next to him without the least hint of shyness. They were almost touching. Travis felt his pulse quicken to the beat of a six-minute mile.

A passing cloud cloaked the moon, and as they were enveloped in the warm darkness of the Haitian night, she spoke again. "You and I experienced a strange *déjà vu* tonight." She brushed her hair back with one hand and turned to him. "Had I been strictly a good Catholic I would have either denied it or been frightened by it, or both. But I am a child of Haiti as well, and I know there are many things in this world that can't be explained with a dash of holy water and a Hail Mary." The moon broke free of the clouds at that moment and cast its light across her. Illuminated by the pale glow, she was like an alabaster statue in a Greek garden. "Tell me, Travis Christian, that you sensed it too when our eyes touched."

He looked down at the girl with the moon in her eyes, and his hands rose to her shoulders. A sensation of timelessness wrapped around them like a crystal cocoon. In the space of a single heartbeat, faded images like old photographs in a tattered album flickered at the edge of recollection, whispering memories they knew only by emotion. Slowly, he drew her to him, and she came willingly, turning her face up to his, parting her lips ...

At breakfast the next morning, Cody was discreet enough not to ask Travis where he had been when he went to get him just after dawn and found his room empty. A blind man with a head cold could have sensed the electricity between Travis and Michelle. Travis's friends politely ignored it, as did Pierre.

The Frenchman studied Travis as he talked. The big American was intelligent, fairly good looking, and certainly no coward. His daughter could do worse.

As they ate, Pierre informed them that a car and a driver would be at their disposal and that he would arrange an appointment for them with the Minister of the Interior in the afternoon to clear their project with the government. They thanked him between mouthfuls of fresh ham and eggs, hot scones, and a variety of fresh fruit that would have made Carmen Miranda envious. Michelle and Pierre had an appointment with their attorney in Port au Prince that morning, but they all agreed to meet back for an early supper.

Breakfast complete, Pierre called the Minister of the

Interior and got them in at two o'clock. Then he and Michelle bid them adieu and took the Mercedes into town.

Michelle had told Travis he would enjoy Henri, the driver/interpreter she had chosen for them. She was right. At two o'clock sharp, their car pulled into the driveway. The driver didn't beep the horn as most drivers would. Travis, Cody, and Billy were in the living room when they heard the car pull up. A few seconds later they heard a raspy saxophone's rendition of *Havana Daydreamin'* float across the yard

Everyone came out to find Henri sitting on the hood of the car, pulling a soft, bluesy melody from his tenor sax. As soon as he saw them he jumped down, threw his saxophone in the front seat, and scrambled around to open the back door of the car. He was a skinny little fellow, and his bright red shirt and baggy blue pants practically hung off him. He had a fuzzy halo of curly, black hair, chocolate-colored skin, and huge, expressive eyes, which sat above a wide smile crammed full of square, white teeth. He hopped over, bobbing his head in sort of a short bow while carrying on a continuous stream of one-sided conversation. "Hey, morning morning, big bosses, I be your excellently good driver, mon. You call me Henri. Henri know every place in Port au Prince, mon! Henri know every very cool place in Haiti! You just say where to go and Henri get you there quick!" He pumped everyone's hand, then ushered them into the vehicle, a late model four-door Volvo. Cody told Henri to take them to Government Square—the Ministry of the Interior. Henri bobbed his head three or four times. "No problem, mon, no problem. You late, Boss? You be late, Henri drive excellently fast, run over any stinkin' body in our way!" He smiled that big square-toothed smile while looking back in the mirror at Cody.

Cody shook his head. "No, we're not late, and don't run over anyone. Just drive normal."

Normal to Henri was Richard Petty on amphetamines. Travis finally had to reach up and grab him by the shoulder. "The important thing, Henri, is that we get there alive, okay? Now, slow down a bit."

"Okay, Boss, okay," Henri said as he slowed down to a comfortable speed—one which bank robbers might use to elude police.

While he weaved in and out of traffic, Henri talked at about the same speed as he drove. "Hey, Boss, you like music? Henri love music! 'Specially American music—play very excellent sax, mon. Someday Henri get to U.S. of A. and become famous musician, get stinkin' rich, have a plenty fast car and many American girlfriends with big breasts!" They all chortled at Henri's specific goals. Henri waited for them to quit chuckling, then called back at them while looking in the rearview mirror. "Hey, Bosses, maybe Henri take such good care of you and you like Henri so much you buy him ticket for U.S. of A. You tell immigrations peoples Henri be distant cousin." Henri looked at his arm and then back at them and smiled. "Much distant."

They arrived early at the ministry. Henri plopped himself on the hood of the car with his sax, while they went up the stone stairs and into the building. They found their way to the office on the third floor and entered through a large, elaborately carved door. An attractive secretary announced them and they were ushered into a large, expensively furnished room. Across the room, behind an oversized solid mahogany desk, sat Louis Jacques Riche, Minister of the Interior. He was a tall, lithe man, dressed in an expensive Brooks Brothers suit. His skin was the color of the desk, rich and dark, his features narrow, sharp, and his attitude somber but not necessarily unfriendly. "Welcome, gentlemen," he said in a rich baritone as he came around the desk to shake hands. "Monsieur Dubonnett spoke highly of you all in our brief conversation this morning. Please, be seated. How can I be of service to you?"

Cody fielded the question and began by introducing his friends, then describing the book they were writing, explaining their desire to research the topography of the island of Tortue as well as the actual location of the original village. In the process, Cody opened his briefcase and produced the letter of introduction from his editor friend in Key West. The minister read the letter, then questioned them as to the other books they'd written. Cody answered honestly that this was their first full novel. Monsieur Riche leaned back and put his fingers together under his chin for a moment, then looked at Billy. "May I see your outline, the outline of the novel? I would like to see how it will reflect upon Haiti at present. As you said, it spans three hundred years."

Billy was taken aback for a moment, but he was quick, and barely missed a beat. "Well, yes, I suppose that's not unreasonable." He was not at all sure where he was going when Cody spoke up.

"I have it, Billy, you put it in my briefcase last night."

"Billy looked over, trying his best to conceal his surprise. "Oh yes, that's right. I forgot."

Cody opened his briefcase again and handed the minister a folder. "The book is estimated at four hundred pages. There is a breakdown of proposed chapters and the first chapter is complete, to give you a feeling for the context."

Riche took the manuscript. Billy and Travis sat open-mouthed.

The minister put the papers on his desk and opened the folder. Looking up he said, "Gentlemen, if you will, allow me a few minutes to scan the information. Please smoke if you wish. May I offer you coffee?"

They declined, and the minister, with a nod, began to read. As Riche turned the pages, Travis looked over at Cody and raised his eyebrows. Cody just leaned back in his chair and smiled.

Ten minutes later, minister Riche looked up. "It appears a legitimate enough literary enterprise, Mr. Cody. In fact, it's actually quite entertaining. I hope you'll send me a copy when it's published."

"I would be most pleased to do so," replied Cody, smiling.

The Minister eased his chair back. "I will see that you are provided a letter from this office giving you freedom on the island of Tortue. You may run into a government patrol there, as we are doing an investigation in that area. Present your papers and do not antagonize them, and you will be fine. One word of caution: We are experiencing some minor problems with a rebellious voodoo priest in that locale. He's somewhat of a violent character, so stay close to your sailboat in the evening. That would be my advice."

Cody tucked his manuscript into his briefcase and after shaking hands all around, the minister escorted them to the door and instructed his secretary to prepare the proper form for them. Twenty minutes later they were headed down the stairs of the building, permission in hand.

As they walked, Travis turned to Cody. "Okay, how did you pull that off up there, with the manuscript?"

Cody grinned. "You should know me by now, Travis.

I'm the closest thing there is to a grown up Boy Scout: I'm always prepared. I paid a writer friend of mine in Key West to do me up a little outline and story, just in case."

Travis just shook his head. "William J., you're amazing."

"That I am, lad. That I am," replied Cody with a grin.

The Minister watched from his window as they got into the car and drove away. He let go of the blinds, walked to the phone, and buzzed his secretary. "Elena, get me Colonel Juele."

The secretary dialed the number with just a touch of discomfort. She hated thinking about the Colonel, let alone talking to him. Of all the people in Haiti, including President-for-Life Jean-Claude, Colonel Juele was the one man you never wanted to displease. He was head of the VSN—*Le Voluntaires pour la Securite Nationale*, a militia originally established by Papa Doc to protect his regime. They now worked for Jean-Claude, his son. Their common name was the Ton Ton Macoute. They were vicious, cruel, and brutal. They had license to do anything to anyone in the name of security, and the parameters of security were continuously stretched to satisfy the situation with the Ton Ton Macoute.

Minister Riche lit a cigarette as he waited for the connection, tilting his head and blowing the bluish smoke toward the ceiling. "Colonel? Yes, Riche at the Ministry of the Interior. Yes, thank you, it has been a while. Colonel, I have a situation that might bear a little attention. We have three Americans who have requested permission to spend some time on the island of Tortue, ostensibly for the purpose of researching a book they are writing. One of them, a William Cody, has been in and out of Haiti a number of times. Our intelligence sources suspect he might be a smuggler." He paused for a moment, listening. "Mmmmmm, what a coincidence. I see, very well then. I'm pleased I followed my instincts and passed it on." He paused again. "Thank you, Sir. Just doing my job. Yes, yes, you too."

Smuggling was not an uncommon practice in Haiti. Some of the more sophisticated organizations even had arrangements with certain government officials. But if you were playing without permission, you were fair game, and if caught, your goods would be sold and the profit divided amongst those who discovered you. For some time, Riche had used his position to his advantage. He and Juele had worked together before.

Riche hung up and took another drag from his cigarette. One of the colonel's sources, a marina manager, had already brought these men to his attention. It seemed the American government was interested in them also.

At VSN Headquarters, Colonel Juele put down the phone and rose ponderously from his seat behind the desk. He wasn't a tall man, perhaps five feet, eight or nine inches, but he was built like a tank—a walking refrigerator. He weighed two hundred and twenty-five pounds and most of it was muscle. He had legs like tree stumps and arms larger than a woman's waist. He was an impressive sight to begin with, but he was made absolutely startling by the fact he was a French/Haitian albino. His head was shaved and shone like a billiard ball, and he had the heavy, blunt features of a boxer—all sculpted from pale pink clay and splashed with dark freckles. The hair on his arms was sparse and yellow-white. He had small, mean eyes with black-ice pupils that were surrounded with the reddish-violet iris typical of albinos. Fear and pain were his specialties. He enjoyed his work and it showed in those eyes. He wasn't just arresting-looking—he was frightening.

Juele walked around to the front of his desk and leaned against it, deliberating for a moment, deciding how best to deal with this situation. After a moment or two, he reached for the phone. He had a captain whose work he appreciated. The man was intelligent and almost as conscientiously brutal as the Colonel himself. He decided to turn him loose on this. He dialed the number. "Captain Tousant, Juele here. Come to my office at your earliest convenience. I have a project for you."

Winston Magruder arrived at La Bouganvilla about the same time Travis and his companions were meeting with the minister. The desk clerk informed him, "They gone."

"Gone where? They just checked in!"

"Gone," said the clerk, deadpan.

Magruder took out an American ten-dollar bill. "You remember where 'they gone' to?"

The clerk's personality changed when he saw the money. "Oh yes, yes. Now I remember good," he said, reaching for the bill.

Winston snatched it back. "Talk first!"

"They stay now at Dubonnet Villa. Driver come for bags last night."

"Where's the Dubonnet Villa?"

The clerk took out a phone book and scribbled an address from it. "Give this to taxi."

Magruder reluctantly gave the man the tenspot and strode angrily out into the heat and the glare of the tropical noonday sun. *Damn it anyway! I just friggin' found them and now I have to find them all over again.* He decided he was going to camp out on the Dubonnet's lawn if he had to, but they weren't getting away again.

Henri raced through the crowded streets of Port au Prince and returned his charges to the villa, miraculously not killing any pedestrians in the process. On the way back, he kept up a steady stream of conversation, telling them what a "excellently good number one guy he was." If they needed it, he could get it, or he knew where it was and could take them to it. He even invited them to the Haitian nightclub where he played sax. They politely declined, saying they'd had enough of Haitian nightclubs for a while.

As they pulled up to the gates of the villa, no one noticed the vehicle at the end of the street, or its quiet, observant occupant.

That night at dinner, with haunting wisps of Henri's saxophone drifting gently on the evening breeze, they told the Dubonnets about their driving "adventure" with the little Haitian, and their meeting with Minister Riche.

"I, personally, have never had any problem with Riche, but I don't entirely trust him. He seems to be a man who lives above his means," said Pierre.

Billy nodded. "A man who lives above his means is faithful only to his purse."

Cody smiled when he heard that. "Reminds me of the old axiom on the difference between a man and a dog."

"Which is?" asked Travis.

"You can't 'buy' a dog."

"Speaking of services," Michelle said, looking across at the three men. "You could probably use a guide on Tortue, and certainly an interpreter. I recommend that you take Henri with you." She saw the looks on their faces at the mention of Henri. She smiled. "There is only one poor road on the island and almost no vehicles." They visibly relaxed. "He's loyal as the day is long and he speaks English well, which is a big plus. He can help with carrying equipment and such. Besides, he's a Haitian. He can get co-operation from the people that you couldn't hope for. If you promise him a ticket to the States when you're done, I imagine he'd kill for you as well."

They all nodded, agreeing. "Thanks," said Travis, "that's a good idea."

"I'm also going to supply you with a guide who knows Tortue front and back."

"Terrific," said Travis. "That would be a big help. Who's this? One of your people?"

"Yes," said Michelle, smiling. "Me."

Travis broke the stunned silence. "You? What do you know about Tortue?"

"Everything. Our plantation is on the very northwest corner of Haiti. Our property borders the channel between Tortue and mainland Haiti. I was a bit of a tomboy when I was younger. By the time I was fifteen, I was sailing my own little sloop over to Tortue. Several of us, children from the local plantations, would get together and spend weekends over there, fishing, camping, exploring, and treasure hunting."

At the mention of treasure, the men's interest became somewhat more acute.

"Did you ever find anything? You know ... treasure?" asked Cody casually.

"Oh, lots of old bottles and a handful of artifacts, including a few coins, but never any serious treasure. Though I'm quite sure there's some buried there somewhere."

"I'll bet there is," said Billy, catching a look from Travis.

"Anyway," Michelle continued, "there isn't much about Tortue I don't know, from its history to its present layout. I don't know why exactly, but the island has always held a fascination for me. I became sort of a Tortue buff." She looked over at Billy and Cody. "Ego aside, I'm quite sure I can be of some assistance to you and your book, in one fashion or another."

Travis looked at Michelle, then over at Pierre. "This is great! I mean, I'd love to have Michelle with us, but what about this crazy zombie priest? It could be dangerous."

Pierre shook his head and smiled. "Monsieur Christian, my daughter is twenty-five years old. I have long since given up trying to 'tell' her anything. If she wants to go, she will, dangerous or not."

"Well?" said Michelle as she turned back to the three to them. "What do you say? Do I get the job?"

Travis took a breath and looked over at Cody and Billy. They realized that this was going to complicate matters somewhat, and they would have to tell her the truth. But it seemed safe. Besides, she might prove to be a big help on the island.

Travis turned from Cody to Michelle. For a second he paused, then grinned. "Why not?" He raised his glass of wine. "To adventure. To Tortue."

They all raised their glasses.

After dinner, Pierre explained that they would be going back to the plantation Sunday, two days hence. They decided that he and Henri would drive up while Michelle and the men sailed the boat around to a little bay a half a mile from their home. There they could take on fresh fruits and vegetables, then sail around to the northern side of Tortue in a few hours.

Later that evening, Travis and Michelle stood hand in hand on the balcony as the full moon rose over the dark green hillside and the sound of the cicadas filled the night air. They stood in silence—gazing out at the bay where the moonlight glimmered on the steel-colored water and a hundred thousand flickering lights from the city blanketed the surrounding hills.

She leaned against him and he put his arm around her, drawing her close, touching her forehead with his lips. There was a natural ease between them, a comfort usually only purchased with time and experience. Yet combined with this contentment was the fierce passion of new love. It was a pleasurable contradiction.

Bathed in the soft glow of the moon, the lovers sighed, grateful for the gift of fate that had allowed them a few bars of harmony in the music of their lives.

That same moon, however, touched another soul that night, as he squatted near the jagged mouth of a cave in the hills of Tortue. And he was less than happy.

Chapter Six

Nyakang sat and stared into the flames of the fire. Three of his men were dead, a fourth captured. Nothing was accomplished. His target, Dubonnet, had survived, as had his daughter. He turned to the frightened messenger. "Go!" The man, anxious to be dismissed from the darkness that lay around the *bokor*, put his head down, eyes to the ground, and backed away into the jungle. Seconds later, Nyakang could hear the slap of the man's feet as he dashed down the trail. He smiled evilly at the man's fear, and spat into the flames.

In time, he would have his revenge on the Americans who saved Dubonnet, and he would have the Frenchman as well—all in good time. They were together in one basket now, and the word from his watchers in the Dubonnet household was that the basket was moving in his direction. He would exercise patience. It was one of his virtues. It had been necessary to his survival, patience and control. He had not always been Nyakang, the Night God.

Born Nathan Seville, the seventh child of a waterfront whore in Port au Prince, his childhood itself had been an exercise in survival. He watched his hopeless mother die of tuberculosis. He saw his sisters sold into a system that bartered their flesh because there was nothing else to sell, and there was never enough money to buy their souls back once their feet had touched the path. His two brothers were small and weak—they drowned in a system that never even knew they existed—they succumbed to sickness and disease and were swept away. Nathan's desire to survive became more savage with each tragedy he witnessed. With each trauma experienced he became harder, stronger.

His mother, when she was around, blamed their plight on the rich Europeans who controlled Haiti, and the "lackeys," as she called the light-skinned blacks who helped them. Nathan watched the Europeans and Americans in their big cars, and the fat Haitian officials who helped them steal his country, and his hate grew.

He was ten when his mother died, but her death made little difference. He was already on his own, a street urchin surviving on odd jobs here and there, stealing to make up the difference. He was a big child, and in the ghetto that was rare. But there was something else about him, a fierce cruelty, a primal savageness—a quality of power rarely seen in one that young. It caused everyone, even many of the adults, to give him a wide berth.

Two things took place in Nathan's life that shaped his personality and directed his destiny. One, as mundane as it seemed, was that he was befriended by a man who owned a butcher shop at the edge of town and given a job. He worked for the man for a little over a year. One of his jobs while in the butcher's employ was to kill and dress the animals they sold—sheep, goats, chickens, and the occasional calf. It was then that he discovered his taste for bloodletting, and his affection for the knife. It wasn't long before he realized that he loved the feel of the knife as it bit into flesh, the gush of hot, sticky blood, and most of all, the look in the animal's eyes. With this revelation, and the cancer of violence he carried in his soul, he soon graduated to a more exotic level of killing. The first time it was in a bar. It was over a woman, and it was over in an instant. The other man had a bottle and swung it at him. Before he realized it, Seville had drawn the knife he carried and plunged it into the man's stomach, driving it up and ripping it out. His assailant looked up, shocked, still holding the bottle at his side, aware instantly of the irreparable damage done inside him—knowing that death, uncompromising and non-negotiable, was but a few breaths away. Nathan stood there panting, his pulse racing, knife in hand. There was no fear, only pure, unadulterated excitement. He realized then that nothing, and no one, could make him feel as exhilarated as he felt at that moment when he ripped the essence of life from another human being with the blade of his knife.

That was the first time he had killed, but there had been others since. Many others. It was his murderous urge that finally drove him from the city and into the countryside.

In a fit of anger, he killed a girl one night because she wouldn't please him in the fashion he desired. She had been the daughter of a policeman. The ensuing manhunt, rare for Port au Prince, forced him to leave, to seek the anonymity of the country.

The local farmers were stupid people, peasants, and he had no trouble stealing from them or intimidating them enough to give him what he needed. But he wanted more than sustenance. He needed a place of refuge.

Two weeks after entering the hills above Port au Prince, he was caught stealing a chicken from a small village. The farmers rose up in unison and chased him into the jungle, brandishing their machetes and shouting. One or two he could deal with, but eight or ten were not good odds, so he dropped the chicken and ran. This time, however, they did not stop at the edge of the clearing, as the others had. These men followed him down the narrow path, running hard, intent on having him. It took fifteen minutes of heart-hammering flight to lose them, and he had to break from the main trail, heading into the tangled jungle to do so. When finally he could no longer hear them, he stood panting in the midst of the gloomy, gray-green jungle and looked around. He was no longer sure which way he had come in, or how to get out and avoid the village. He paused and leaned against a vine-covered tree, catching his breath. Then, taking direction from the afternoon sun, he began to walk. An hour later he broke into a clearing. The sun was setting now, lengthening the shadows of leaf and vine. The jungle rested in that eerie stillness of evening as the sun relinquished the world to the moon, and its creatures paused in quiet reverence, observing the change. As he stepped out from the thick foliage, he saw a hut, built from bamboo and thatched with palm, at the rear of the clearing. A few scrawny chickens pecked aimlessly at the brown dirt around the hut, and on the other side of the clearing was a small stand of corn, just ripening.

At least I can eat well here, he thought as he moved up to the shanty.

Approaching the door, he noticed strange symbols drawn in the flat, hard earth near the entrance. The indentations had been colored with a dark brown liquid. He was no stranger to that substance. The hairs on the back of his neck stood up, and he walked around the symbols rather than striding boldly over them.

Reaching the entrance he paused, and putting his hand on the threshold, stuck his head into the warm twilight gloom of the hut. There, on the dirt floor, was a sleeping mat, the remains of a small fire, and a bamboo table. On the table were several candles, an incense tray, and a human skull. Affixed to the walls around the hut were gourds, the dried skins of animals, lizards, and frogs. Leather pouches bulging with mysterious contents dangled from pegs. One of the tallow candles on the table burned, its flickering light shifting the gloom back and forth, giving the room a mystical sinister quality.

He was standing there, surveying the room, not altogether anxious to enter for some reason, when he heard a swooshing sound followed by a loud crack next to his ear. Startled, he jerked around to find himself facing a small, wizened man with a black rawhide whip in his hand. The man's skin hung in wrinkled layers. His hair was short and graying. A handful of slightly pointed teeth canted in his mouth like tobacco-stained stalactites. But it was his eyes that captured Nathan. Those cold orbs shone like beacons from a lighthouse on a distant, barren shore. Nathan had never seen such intensity in another's eyes. They gleamed with malevolent energy. They shouted forbidden knowledge—they claimed dominion over the darkness in man's soul.

His hand went to the knife and he drew it. The creature with the wizened face smiled, and quicker than Nathan would have thought possible, the whip snapped again. There was a stinging slap on his hand and his knife went flying, burying itself point first in the dirt a dozen feet away. Recovering from his shock, his anger rising, he took a step toward the old man.

In a cracked and ancient voice, like the croak of an old tree frog, the man spoke. "Now that you have arrived, do not cause me to take your eyes to teach you manners. I could teach you to see without them, but it would be a painful, delaying lesson for you."

The old man flexed his arm and the whip rippled with life, like an angry snake. He stood in front of Nathan, unconcerned. Nathan stopped, taken aback by the situation. It was always he who had struck the uncertainty, the fear. Here, for the first time, this ancient gnome had reversed the situation. His anger flared again and he took another step. The whip snapped again. The tip of the whip struck just above his right eye, on the eyebrow. He cried out, raising his hand to his face, certain his eye was gone.

"That was your last warning and your first lesson. I do not tolerate stubbornness," croaked the old man. "You will obey or life will become a painful experience, and I have at my disposal many varieties of pain." As he spoke, he smiled strangely, raised his arm, and dropped the whip into a tall, woven palm basket next to him. Nathan couldn't believe it. The stupid little man had just given up his only weapon. He tensed for a rush when the gnome, face still slashed with that ugly smile, nudged the basket with his foot, knocking it over. From the darkness of the basket's narrow mouth something moved, something hissed angrily. Suddenly a dark triangular head appeared, with two malicious obsidian eyes, followed by a thick, black-scaled body. The huge serpent slowly uncoiled and began to slither toward Nathan.

The man blinked his uninjured eye in disbelief, which rapidly changed to horror as the snake crawled closer, rearing its head, opening its pale mouth and hissing at him. It mattered little at this point whether the whip was still in the basket—although he could see no sign of it. The apparent metamorphosis was too much for Nathan's superstitious nature. He stumbled backward against the side of the hut, his eyes wide in terror, his mouth moving, making small, incoherent sounds as the snake moved within inches of his legs. The old man snapped his fingers, mumbling a string of strange words, and the serpent stopped. The creature arched upward, its head a good three feet off the ground. It opened its mouth again, exposing inch-long needle-like fangs, and hissed one last time, those terrible eyes riveted on Seville. Reluctantly then, it turned and retreated into the basket, leaving Nathan crushed against the bamboo wall, his chest heaving.

The old wizard righted the basket and reached into it, retrieving only an inert rawhide whip. "Pain has many forms," he said quietly. "You do not have to be cut to bleed."

Such was Nathan's introduction to Ona Taz, wizard, sorcerer, *bokor* extraordinaire, proprietor of the darkness in the spirit of man.

Nathan stood pressed against the hut, struggling to bring himself under control, as Ona Taz spoke again. "I have known that you would come to me for years. I have known for days now that the end of your journey neared. You struggle now with your fate as you struggle with the hatred in your heart. You must learn to use the elements that are part of you as vessels to carry you to your desires, not as obstructions to your destiny. I will show you how to use your anger and the violence in your soul as a whetstone to sharpen your knife, as an impetus to focus your thrust at the enemy."

Nathan moved slowly away from the bamboo at his back, staring at the old man. "Why? Who are you? How could you know I was coming?"

The *bokor* smiled. "You have watched but you have not seen. Do you think you just stumbled onto me?" he snorted. "If I did not desire your presence, the jungle would have swallowed you whole and spit your bones out. Your remains would have grown green with mold, and you would have faded from the earth like last night's moon. You are here because you seek change, in yourself and for this land. You think first of yourself now, but that will change. You understand the roots of your anger but you are like a child who cannot control its bowels. You must learn to void yourself when you command it, and not simply when you feel the need.

"You have come to me because it is your destiny to transform this country, to cleanse it, to teach its people to be strong and independent again, not pawns for the greedy Europeans. You will lead the people as we chase the defilers from the land with our machetes, as our ancestors did two hundred years ago!

"I can teach you not only command of yourself, but command of the elements around you. I can invest in you the ultimate power of control over your fellow man. I can show you how to suck the *ti bon ange*, the willpower, the character, from another human soul and put it in your pocket; how to summon the *loas* of the elements, the spirits of fire, water, wind, and war; to draw the force of *pwin* to execute your will and make others powerless before you, to talk to the dead. I can give you all the wonders of the darkness, and together we can return Haiti to its people.

"My knowledge and power are great, but I am old and frail of body." Then he smiled evilly. "But not that frail yet, as you have seen. The task ahead, however, requires youth and endurance. I need someone with strength, singularity of purpose, and most of all, a willingness to learn. The rewards are many, but the path you will travel is harsh and dangerous. You have been chosen as the recipient of the black candle. Only you can determine if you are strong enough and worthy enough to take it from me."

Again Nathan asked, "Why me?"

"I am a sorcerer, not a god!" shouted the wizard. "I do not have all the answers. Be satisfied in the knowledge that you have been chosen."

The small man paused. "Sit!" he said, pointing to the

dirt by the wall of the hut. Nathan hesitated, not used to being told what to do. "Sit, I said!" the *bokor* commanded fiercely, and his whip quivered. Nathan quickly complied, then leaned against the hut. The older man squatted on his haunches like a forest gnome and stared at Nathan with eyes like black, sacrificial pools. Then he spoke again, in that same hoarse voice that sounded like gravel being crunched underfoot.

"Two weeks ago, as I sat in the darkness of my hut, Ogoun, the spirit of fire and war, the blacksmith god, came to me. I was directed to prepare the metal for the knife that would cut the cancer from our land and free Haiti. You are the metal to be shaped into the blade of revenge. You are the future of Haiti. Are you brave enough to accept the challenge?"

Suddenly Nathan realized that, throughout his life, he had carried the manifest destiny of this moment. His anger, his hatred, his compelling desire for revenge against the Western/European influence and its lackeys ... It had all been preordained that he would come to this place and time.

Nathan gazed at the *bokor* with a strange new look in his eyes. He nodded, solemnly, respectfully. "Teach me."

The old man smiled in satisfaction, and the lessons began.

The sorcerer was powerfully talented in the black arts. There was no one equal to him in Haiti. There was perhaps no one equal to him anywhere. He had guarded his secrets jealously and had not displayed his talents for the sake of recognition, as others had. He was not well known, but he was dangerously evil and as ruthless as any *bokor* who had ever breathed the salt air or watched the night moon rise over the hills of Haiti. He had practiced his art and hoarded his knowledge to one end: to crush

European domination and lead the Haitian people back to the old ways.

He began by introducing Nathan to the *loas*, the deities of the voodoo faith, in ceremonies that ranged from serene, almost delicate, to loud, terrifying spectacles of communion where Ona Taz served as the *cheval*—the horse to be mounted by the *loas* and the spirits of the dead. Later he taught Nathan the ability to command the *loas*, the use of *pwin*, the magical force summoned to execute the will of the sorcerer. He taught him the use of potions and powders and poisons, and finally he taught him spells.

Nathan's apprenticeship lasted three years, and in that time his knowledge of the black arts and his malevolent talent grew daily. He became a dark sponge, greedily sucking up the science of evil.

As he graduated past the initiate stage, his power became frightening. He had learned to focus his energy. The hatred and the rage that festered within him were no longer obstacles, they were kindling for the fires of his obsession. He was no less cruel a man than he had been, but he was far more dangerous. He had learned to cut without a knife.

Finally, near the end of his apprenticeship, the young sorcerer was shown his past. It was then that he came to fully understand his obsession for revenge and his hatred for those who bled his country. He knew exactly who he was, and where he was going. In the ceremony Ona Taz performed, he learned who he had been.

They sat quietly on the floor of the hut. The sun had just fallen below the tree line. It would be dark soon.

Ona Taz, his eyes gleaming like pools of black metal, stared at the apprentice before him, "You have come far, Child of the Night. You have learned much here in the present. Tonight you will learn of the past, and how the threads of past existence weave together to form the tapestry of this life. Though my practice of the ancient arts differs somewhat from the voodoo in the hills of this land, there is between us a common foundation. We have all grown from the ancient root and we share the shade from the four branches of the great tree of Voodoo.

"First and foremost, in our philosophy of communion with spirits, those of the elements and those souls passed from this earth. We also share the power of ceremony and the value of ritual, potions, powders and spells. We celebrate the joy of life and the pleasure of revenge with equal fervor—and binding it all together is the knowledge of the continual passage of the soul through the portal of life, time and time again.

"It is this continuous return of the spirit to new flesh, and the weight of responsibility each return carries, that you will come to understand tonight."

Ona Taz traced a cabalistic design in the dirt floor with a stick. He took a powder from the pouch at his side and sprinkled it on the runes while whispering an invocation to the gods. His words were ancient, but the meanings were no longer confusing to the younger man. Nathan was given a gourd containing a potion concocted by the old *bokor*. Nathan drank. It was warm and thick as fresh blood, and as bitter as jealous rage. Nathan drank it all and set the gourd down. Ona Taz handed him a tallow candle from the table. Its single flame threw cold shadows across the room. Nathan placed the candle in both hands, held it a foot from his eyes and began to study the flame. The old man picked up his *asson*, his sacred rattle, filled with the dried vertebrae of snake, and began to shake it with a slow cadence.

Nathan watched the flame of the candle flicker and

dance atop the greasy, yellow candle. He was suddenly aware of the rainbow of colors in the aura surrounding it. The flame began to grow brighter, broader, and as it did so, the aura expanded to maintain its parameter. Soon the flame engulfed his vision. The soft colors of the halo encircled him. The room had disappeared. He had become part of the aura. The light of the candle flickered and beckoned, and he stepped into the flame.

He saw a man, a giant black man, dressed in the clothes of a past century. The man stood on a secluded knoll on the northern plain of Haiti under a huge banyan tree. It was night and lightening flashed in jagged arcs across the rain-filled sky as the man raised his hands and shouted to the sea of dark faces before him. The sensation Nathan experienced was not unlike that of some dreams, where you are the main participant and an onlooker simultaneously. He could feel the wind on his face, heavy with the promise of rain, the sensation of power experienced by the man, the fear and the electricity in the crowd around him.

The man bellowed forth a strident supplication to the gods. A sacrifice was offered. Once again the man shouted to the crowd in a powerful, fervent timbre, and the seeds of rebellion were planted in the fertile earth of that pain-filled land, nurtured by freshly spilled blood.

The scene changed and he saw a land ravaged by the maturity of that same revolution. The dark hills were afire with burning plantations. Flaming fields blushed the clouds and reddened the sky at night. Ash filled the air and covered the sea, and the fiery spectacle could be seen a hundred miles away. The carnival of horror continued for weeks as a huge wave of rage-inflamed, rebellious slaves rolled across the land. Thousands of whites were driven from their homes and killed, falling prey to those they had brutally mistreated for so long.

Nathan watched as this same man rode the crest of the wave, his fiery oratory and his powerful magic the cornerstones of the rebellion. Then he watched the man die—captured by the French—and tortured horribly. He felt the searing pain of the glowing irons as they stuck to and burned through his skin, hissing as they sucked the moisture from his flesh. And finally he felt the rough caress of the hangman's noose as it tightened round his neck.

At some point, with startling revelation, he realized he was watching himself. He was experiencing the accounts of his spirit, his *ti bon ange*, in another time. He knew intrinsically that the man he watched was Boukman Dutty, charismatic leader of the Haitian revolt in the 1790s.

When he returned from the flame, he found Ona Taz sitting in front of him. "You understand the demands of your soul now, Child of Africa. Soon my work ends and yours begins."

That night, in a second ceremony that not only marked his coming full circle, but also recognized the completion of his apprenticeship, Nathan was given his name. As angry daggers of lightning tore great patches of fabric from the dark sky and wind lashed the tiny hut, pulling at the thatch with greedy fingers and causing the bamboo to grate and creak, a ritual was conducted in which the old Nathan was buried and the new man, thé *Neg Guinee*, the child of Africa, was born. The new child's name was Nyakang, Night God—God of Darkness. He, Nyakang, would cause darkness to fall on the usurpers of his land, and in that night he and his people would come to repay the debt of suffering visited on them for 400 years.

Nyakang stared into the flames of the fire at the mouth of his cave, remembering that distant ceremony, and a mirthless smile touched his lips. Much was changed since destiny had taken him to the old *bokor*.

When he was given his name, and Nyakang felt the infusion of its magical power, he knew at that moment he was stronger than Ona Taz.

He knew it was time to begin his journey into history. He would strike out now and set in motion the legend that would be the nexus of his control over the superstitious people of Haiti. He had begun to fabricate a story of how his powers had come to him, a captivating tale of communion with the gods and of divine gifts bestowed.

Such was the coldness of the two men's personalities that, in the three years they had spent together, there was really no bond between them other than that of mutual hate and the dream of revenge. As Nyakang's power began to blossom, the powerful egos of the two men spawned even more of a gulf between them. The situation was further exacerbated by Ona Taz's eventual realization that, although he had always assumed he would stand by Nyakang's side and be venerated as mentor, it was not part of his apprentice's plan at all.

The day of resolution finally came, as Nyakang prepared to leave.

Ona Taz went to draw water from the creek one morning and as he returned, he found Nyakang packing the old *bokor*'s powders and potions in a *mancote* straw bag. The big man reached for the *bokor's asson,* and put it in the bag. He spoke, not even looking up: "There is nothing else you can teach me, old man. I go now."

Anger flushed the older man's face. "You can go when you please, but you leave only with the knowledge I have given you, not with my possessions, you ungrateful peasant."

Nyakang looked up from his rummaging with a brutal smile. "I will take whatever I want and there is nothing you can do about it."

Ona Taz reached for the whip at his side, but as he did so, Nyakang rose swiftly and slammed the small man with a straight-arm, knocking him out the door of the hut, sending him sprawling in the dirt of the yard. The *bokor* lost his whip as he tumbled backwards. Nyakang stepped forward and picked it up.

Ona Taz rose to his feet, his face contorted with anger. "I will teach you now, never to—"

Nyakang simply stared at him. He raised his hand slowly and dropped the whip into the woven basket at the side of the hut. Both men stood stock still, eyes locked, as they challenged each other's power. The hot morning sun glazed their skin, and small, clear rivulets of sweat began to wind their way down the wrinkles of the old *bokor's* face. A moment later, in the basket there was a rustle, and a hiss.

The viper's head appeared at the dark mouth of the frond container. The serpent rose up and slithered effortlessly to the ground, moving into the clearing between the two men. Immersed in their struggle, hands clenched at their sides in concentration and rage, neither man spoke. The snake hissed, and those terrible eyes turned toward Nyakang. The creature glided slowly, almost uncertainly, toward the younger sorcerer. Nyakang showed no sign of fear, but he broke the silence as he whispered ancient, powerful words. The snake hesitated, then stopped. The great triangular head of the viper swiveled slowly toward Ona Taz. Once more the younger man muttered an incantation. The creature hissed angrily, changed direction and slid forward with purpose. The old *bokor's* eyes grew wide, his concentration broken as the snake came at him. He mouthed a few syllables in an ancient tongue, but he was already stumbling backward, his hands coming up. As it reached Ona Taz, a full half of the obsidian-colored reptile rose off the ground, its back arched. The sorcerer grabbed the snake just below the head just as it opened its opaque maw and spit a great stream of venom into the man's eyes. Ona Taz cried out as the acid-like poison ate into the soft flesh of his eyeballs. He threw his hands into the air, trying to dislodge the viper that had now wrapped itself around his wrist and was twisting up his arm, toward his neck. He stumbled about, flailing, screaming, trying to pull the snake from him while clawing at his ruined eyes at the same time.

Nyakang watched as the serpent worked its way up his mentor's arm and began to coil its hard body around the man's neck. As it squeezed, Ona Taz's screams became strangled gurgles. The man's eyes bulged, his face darkened and his tongue protruded from a crooked mouth. His strength was fading now, and the head of the snake broke free from his grasp. It reared back in triumph and struck him in the face, burying its fangs in the flesh of his cheeks over and over again. The *bokor* grabbed feebly at the reptile, his body performing on willpower alone. Finally, when the poison struck his heart, the old man shuddered and opened his mouth to scream, but there were no words left for Ona Taz. His knees buckled, and silently he collapsed to the dirt.

Nyakang walked over and looked down at the blind, dead eyes of the man on the ground. He snapped his fingers. The snake slithered off the corpse and coiled at the young *bokor's* feet.

Nyakang lifted his eyes from the fire and gazed at the dark jungle around him. It had been a long path from there to here, and there was still a distance to travel. But he was closer, much closer to his goal. His name was spoken in hushed tones around evening fires in the hills and villages from Cap Haitian to Port au Prince. His assassins had their targets, and one by one they would strike. This first failure angered him, but he was not discouraged. If it had not been for the Americans, he would have succeeded. He would be patient. The gods were bringing them to him for retribution. He knew from his spies that the Americans and the girl were leaving for Tortue tomorrow; they were expected to stay as long as a month. In two weeks there would be a full moon and another initiation ceremony, and they would need a sacrifice, perhaps more than one. The gods could be greedy.

Chapter Seven

The sail from Port au Prince to the northern tip of Haiti took a day and a half. The winds were light and the waters around them sparkled clear and bright as the sailboat nudged its way through the gentle waves. The four of them, Michelle and the three men, fell into a natural harmony. They were all well read and well traveled, and they all seemed to have that rakish, acerbic wit which made conversation both a challenge and a pleasure.

Sitting in the cockpit, they bantered and laughed as the boat heeled gently from the touch of the wind. The men told outrageous adventure stories, and Michelle appeared appropriately impressed, although the tales sounded to her as if they came from the pages of *Soldier of Fortune*. Michelle sunbathed on the deck and admired the grace of the seabirds floating above them. The men admired Michelle as she sunbathed. She divided her attention among them and teased with all of them, but there was never any question to whom she belonged.

On the afternoon of the second day, Travis and Michelle sat on the bow of the sailboat, legs dangling over the side, leaning over the stainless steel railing as they watched a small pod of bottlenose porpoise keep pace with the boat. Cody was in the stern at the tiller and Billy was below, taking a nap. Salt spray misted their tanned bodies, providing some relief from the warm tropical sun, and there was just enough breeze to ruffle their hair. She was still staring at the dolphins as she spoke. "I don't think I've really thanked you for what you did for my father and me the other night in the Chez Caribe."

Travis grinned. "As far as I'm concerned, you have."

She smiled and gently cuffed him on the arm. "I wasn't thanking you then. In case you didn't notice, that was for me as much as it was for you." Then seriously she said, "No, I really am beyond grateful. You were amazing."

There was pensive look in Travis's eyes for a moment and he spoke without looking at her. "I'm not as amazing as you think. I don't know that you'll understand this—I'm not sure I do—but most of my life I've felt like a very average guy with a soldier of fortune trapped in his psyche. Most everything I've ever done that was the least bit daring scared the crap out of me. I did it because the soldier of fortune insisted. Learning to fly, combat in Vietnam—I always seemed captured somewhere between the terror and the triumph."

"It's hard for me to imagine you being afraid. A guy with muscles in more places than most people have places—a fellow who shoots a pistol like Wyatt Earp."

Travis couldn't help but smile at her description but there was no humor in his eyes. He turned to her. "I'll tell you something that almost no one else knows—except maybe Cody. I have a terrible fear, a fear of dying—maybe not so much in the midst and confusion of battle, caught up in the fray and shoulder to shoulder with comrades, but dying alone—going out totally alone. I used to have nightmares in 'Nam—nightmares of my 'copter going down and being trapped inside alive and watching the VC coming out of the jungle—being enveloped by an avalanche of terror in the last moments. I've carried that baggage for as long as I can remember. All I know for sure is, dying alone terrifies me."

She took his hand, gazing at him. "Only fools and madmen are without fears. Each of us is frightened of something. It's how we confront that fear that changes us for better or worse, in this life and the next."

"Thanks," he said sincerely. Then he grinned again. "Well, now that you know my deepest secret, my crowning imperfection, do you have any flaws you'd like to tell me about? Now would be a good time."

She shook her hair back and looked at him as the corners of her mouth curved upward. "Nope. I'm perfect."

That evening they sailed into the small bay abutting the hills of the plantation. The house, visible from the water, sat nestled against the base of those hills. They took the dinghy in and walked up the road to the driveway. As they entered the drive, there was no doubt that Pierre and Henri had arrived. They could hear the riffs from Henri's sax drifting across the garden, the soft, silky notes carried along by the fragrance of hundreds of blooming flowers throughout the grounds.

The house was surprisingly modest, perhaps only three thousand square feet. It had a white stucco exterior with another barrel-tiled roof; very similar to something you might see in the Mediterranean. A large, manicured lawn adorned with countless fruit trees and colorful flowers surrounded it.

They were greeted enthusiastically by Pierre and Henri then given an opportunity to freshen up before supper, which was served on the patio overlooking the bay. During dinner they discussed their plans, or those that could be discussed over dining. They had decided to spend about three weeks on Tortue. The sailboat would serve as a base of operations and they had ample camping gear for forays into the island. If they needed more supplies they could always return to the plantation, a half-day sail.

The main crop of cane had been harvested and Pierre assured Michelle that he could manage things without her for a while. The after-dinner conversation finally wound down and, as the following day would begin at first light, everyone opted to retire early.

The next morning, a brilliant Caribbean dawn found them loading fresh fruit and other perishables aboard the sailboat. By eight o'clock the supplies were stored and everyone was on board. They upped anchor and waved goodbye to Pierre on the shore as the breeze snapped the canvas full and the sailboat skipped out of the bay, into the channel.

During the four-hour trip to the northern side of Tortue, they sat Michelle down and told her the truth. As it was absolutely impossible to do otherwise, Henri was made party to the explanation as well.

When Billy finished with the slightly abbreviated version of the story he had told previously in the bar, Michelle sat back and exhaled softly. Then she looked over at Travis.

"I don't know which I feel most, anger at not being told sooner, being lied to, or excitement."

"Let the excitement win out, honey," said Travis. "There was never any question about telling you, it was only a matter of when. There was no point in telling you and your father something that could compromise his position in the Haitian political community. You needed to be told alone and, my feelings aside, we needed a chance to determine how well you would fit in with us before we told you."

Michelle looked over at Travis and her eyes held that mischievous sparkle, but there seemed to be a touch of clear acrylic to them. "Listen, Mr. Christian, if you want a relationship with me, there can be no lies."

"It's a deal," responded Travis, employing his most contrite look. "Won't happen again."

Cody glanced over at Henri who was sitting there with an unusually serious look on his face. "What's wrong, buddy?"

"Henri doan like no stinkin' voodoo priests, mon. Henri want to keep his *ti bon ange* inside his head!"

"Don't worry, Henri, we'll take care of you."

"Humph," muttered the little Haitian, totally unconvinced. "That plenty bad *bokor* eat white man's Jesus magic for breakfast. Doan even get stomach ache!"

"If my Jesus magic doesn't work, I'll see how he digests buckshot," Billy declared from the rail.

"I'll make a deal with you," said Travis. "You stick with us and if we find the treasure, we'll buy you a ticket to the U.S. of A."

The Haitian grinned a buck-toothed smile at that, his spirits brightening visibly. "For ticket to U.S. of A. Henri give his *ti bon ange* to stinkin' *bokor*. Henri be American zombie sax player!"

As they sailed, the sun reached its zenith, then fell off toward the horizon. The winds kept the boat at a steady seven knots and by three that afternoon they sailed into the small bay, bordered by granite cliffs on one side and a white sandy beach on the other. As they entered the bay, a stillness fell over the crew.

It was Billy who broke the spell, pointing ahead. "The original village of Tortuga lies over there, just beyond that stand of coconut trees. Many of the stone foundations to the old homes are still there."

Travis found himself locked in the strangest of sensations when he studied that shoreline and those granite cliffs. He couldn't figure out why, but he thought there should have been a bell ...

Michelle gazed past the coconut trees to where the remains of the village lay. "I would like to show you the ruins," she said, almost to herself. "They give me the oddest sense of a peace and comfort most of the time. But there are other times when I feel uneasy—like I just have to get out of there." She shook her head, embarrassed slightly by her confession.

They dropped anchor about a hundred yards off shore and took the dinghy in. In the few remaining hours of daylight, they explored the shoreline, taking the small path to the top of the granite cliffs and looking out over the bay, then returned to the beach to walk briefly through the ruins of the old village.

As they walked, Travis felt himself drawn toward the far end of the time-razed town, but night was falling and there was no time for any serious exploring. Agreeing that it would be best to return in the morning, when they had more light, they paddled back to the sailboat for the evening.

Several of the locals from the fishing village, about half a mile down the beach, watched their arrival. One in particular paid close attention to the *blancs* as they paddled ashore. With an unpleasant smile he turned and trotted away, up the trail toward the hills.

The sun set, blushing the cottontail clouds on the horizon with soft pink and orange. The half-moon crept from the sea and took its place among the summer stars.

After supper they all sat around the cockpit topside, gazing at the brilliant heavens and talking of Tortue—its history and its treasure.

Travis was staring at the fading shoreline. "What I would give to be able to drop three hundred years for just ten minutes and see what this place was really like—to walk though that village one time."

"If you talk to people about it, you'll discover that almost everyone has a place and a time that they are strangely drawn to—an era that captures them," said Billy. "Doesn't matter if they're a Holy Roller or a Hare Krishna, there's someplace on the globe they've never been, that, for an unknown reason, fascinates them. This is my place and time. The Caribbean has intrigued me since I was a child."

The little Haitian shifted the sax on his lap. "Henri never been there, but he have great love for Miami Beach."

Everyone smiled. "I think that's more of a current passion than a distant one, Henri," said Michelle. She eased back in her seat. "Tobinsky, the Russian poet said it best—*Have you never, in all of your travels, come upon that hauntingly familiar landscape, that curiously captivating scene of mountain, desert, or tropical isle, which struck such a note at the core of your being that you stood there, enthralled, wrapped in gossamer threads of distant recollection? And the mere sight of this landscape soothed your soul like a healing balm, as a voice deep inside you cried, "I'm home again.""*

Billy lit one of his small, black cigars, exhaling off the stern, toward the shore. "Yeah, that's it in a nutshell." He gazed out at the darkening island. "I know that treasure's out there. I know inside the deepest part of me that it all happened just the way Esquimelin described it." He looked around at the others. "And we're gonna find it. It's not a matter of if, but when."

The evening progressed and the conversation waned as the moon changed from gold to yellow, and finally to a pale lustrous silver, hanging over them like the last bauble on a mobile in a baby's crib.

Finally, worn from the early start and the excitement of the day, they each sought their bunks, enjoying the small fantasies that drifted through the last of their consciousness as sleep found them. That night Travis experienced the first of his dreams.

It was short, and not as rich in detail as it was in sensation. He saw himself aboard an old sailing ship. He felt the spray mist across the bow, its salty wetness glistening on his bronzed skin. He looked about at the hard, sun-darkened faces of the men around him—pirates one and all—buccaneers. He briefly studied those faces. There were those he thought he recognized, not so much by countenance as by some ageless kinship. The sensation was fleeting yet profound, inexplicable. Their faces bobbed to the surface of his memory for a moment like a submerged log carried by the torrent of a rain-swollen river, only to disappear again, irretrievably, before he could place them.

They were preparing to attack another ship. They hid near the gunnels, out of sight. There was a pistol shot that signaled the attack, and they surged over the side, throwing grappling hooks and firing into the startled faces of their foes. He vaguely sensed a huge man at his side, an African. He leaped to the deck of the other ship, his cutlass slashing, and through the smoke, the cries, and the blood, the huge black man never left him—the man was *always* at his back. The images faded and gradually shifted to another scene heavy with fear and remorse. He stood over the body of a mortally wounded friend. The terrible certainty that death had finally found him was almost overwhelming. He was alone, and they were coming at him ... The dream dimmed, the characters became shadows and he awoke, his heart hammering, sweat soaking his pillow.

It was unlike any dream he had ever experienced. It was so vivid, the sensations so real. Even awake, he could still feel the sun burn his back and smell his own anxious sweat. The dry metallic taste of fear coated his mouth like sawdust and pennies. He lay awake for an hour before succumbing to a restless sleep plagued with ancient, strangely familiar images.

After breakfast the following morning they unloaded some of the supplies they would need for the next few days—camping gear, a metal detector, cooking equipment, etcetera. They also took to shore the small Mo-ped that they had tied on deck. Tortue had one poor but negotiable road that ran around the edge of the island. There was a ferry that came across the channel from the mainland once a week, on Wednesdays. It docked on the far side, facing the big island, for half an hour, allowing passengers to disembark and picking up those who wished to return to the mainland. Once they were situated, Cody was going to return to Port au Prince via the ferry and a bus, then fly back to the States for the plane. Because the following day was Wednesday, he wanted to get everything set so he could make the ferry and return as quickly as possible. With any luck he figured to be back Friday.

While they got themselves organized, Cody and Michelle took the Mo-ped and, at her direction, went to look at the airstrip, to make sure there would be no problem getting in. It was only a couple of miles from where they were anchored. There was a dirt trail that led to the main pot-holed road, taking them to the bulldozed gravel strip. As they neared the strip, two large hills rose out of the jungle behind it, and Michelle found Cody slowing down, staring at the hills and the narrow pass between them. They had nearly slowed to a stop when she tapped Cody on the shoulder. "Are you all right?"

Cody started, nodded slowly. "Yeah, yeah, I guess. I

looked over at those hills and the damnedest sensation came over me—"

"A sadness and a sense of loss," she said, interrupting him.

He stopped the motorcycle and looked back at her. "How'd you know that?"

"It's done the same thing to me. The first time I saw those hills, several years ago, I sat and cried for ten minutes. I don't know what, but I think something very sad took place there a long time ago." With the smoke from a distant fire in her eyes, she paused and gazed again at the pass. "I have often wondered if I might not have been there when it did."

She shook her head sharply, as if breaking the spell, and pointed. "That's the strip, dead ahead."

Cody glanced once more at the two hills, strangely touched for a man who believed more in the here and now than in the hereafter. "Who knows," he whispered, almost to himself. "Who knows." Then he revved the cycle slightly and, without speaking, they continued on their way to the runway.

Back on the beach, Cody informed Travis that the strip was workable and that he would have Billy drive him around to the ferry in the morning. He omitted his experience with the hills. It felt too personal, too difficult for him to describe comfortably.

They decided to set up a day camp on the beach near the ruins of the village, at least until Cody got back. They would still sleep in the sailboat at night for now. Tents were erected, one for Travis and Michelle, one for each of the others. Michelle and Henri assembled a cooking fire pit while the men dug a latrine. By one o'clock, everything was pretty much in order, so they decided to explore the old village.

They were walking through the vined and overgrown ruins, speculating, digging a bit here and there, when they reached the stone foundation of what must have been a small cottage, about three-quarters of the way through the village. Two of the walls had been worn away by time. One wall rose up about a foot, and the other stood perhaps three feet high. The surviving walls were connected, forming an L-shape. Travis felt an almost magnetic emotional attraction. As he stood in the center of the cottage's remains, looking around, he felt Michelle take his hand. They stood there, wrapped in a cocoon of vague recollection, captured by emotions they didn't understand. Yet they only had to look at each other's eyes to know that the sensation was shared. As if Travis had served as the catalyst for a distant memory, Michelle started, drew a deep breath and released his hand. Slowly, hesitantly, she moved to the tallest wall with a smoky, faraway look in her eyes. She knelt by the ancient, mortared rock and ran her hand over the base of the wall, near the ground. Gripping one of the rocks that extended out from the wall she pulled. When it didn't budge, she tugged again. When it still didn't move, she went to the one next to it and pulled again. Travis came over and knelt by her as she tried a third rock, and it shifted slightly. She tugged at it again and, to his surprise, the rock slid from the wall. She paused and looked at Travis, anxious, confused, almost frightened. Slowly she reached down, putting her hand in the opening. Feeling an object, she grasped it and pulled it out. There, in her hand, was a dusty old apothecary jar with a pewter lid, but that was the least remarkable part of the find. Folded inside the jar was a small book of some sort.

The others gathered around her. She carefully opened the jar and gently removed the leather-bound book. Due to the jar, and the enclosure of the rock wall, it was remarkably preserved. The leather was dried and hard, but just pliable enough to be straightened out. The pages inside were very brittle, but still legible.

Michelle held her breath as she read the first page, written in the old English vernacular of the time. The others leaned over her shoulder watching, waiting, wanting to know what it was they had found. She looked up a moment later. "It's a diary of sorts—the history of a handful of people who came to Tortuga from England in sixteen hundred and sixty-eight. It's written by a lady who was part of the group." Michelle exhaled softly. "Anne. Anne was her name."

"What an incredible find," Travis said.

Michelle gazed at the words on the open page. She wasn't comfortable with the dialect, but the phrasing seemed natural and easy. "I don't understand it. I don't know how, I just knew..."

Travis stood, taking her hand and helping her up as she reluctantly closed the book. "It's getting late, and we've got a full day tomorrow. Let's go back to the ship and have supper. Then we'll all have a drink and you can read to us."

Dinner was a hasty affair, some canned stew and fresh vegetables, with mangoes from Pierre's orchards for dessert. The conversation revolved mostly around Michelle's find. There was an anticipation in the air that even the most stoic of them could not deny. Each of them with, of course, the exception of Henri, had undergone a recent experience beyond the realms of simple understanding and explanation. It was as if the curtain of time had been pulled back for a moment and in front of them lay a stage on which it appeared they had acted before, and there, veiled in the mists of faint recognition, were the shadows of fellow performers. By and large, their experiences were solitary in nature, but there seemed to be a common thread of time and place in them. The time up to now had been uncertain, but the place, they were all coming to realize, was there on the isle of Tortue.

When supper was complete and the dishes done, they gathered around Michelle in the cabin, like anxious children awaiting a bedtime story. She sat at the table with Billy and Travis. Cody lounged on a nearby bunk and Henri sat on the far side of the table. She looked around at them one time, cleared her throat, and began to read.

"In the spring of sixteen sixty-eight, I sailed with my mother and our servants from the English port of London. We were bound for Barbados, our home in the isles of the Caribbean ..."

As she read, they, like children of time, cast off the garments of this life and walked into the river of the ages, to be baptized by recollection.

She read for almost two hours. There was no way she could have stopped, had any of them wished her to do so. They all sat silent as tombstones, mesmerized by the tale of buccaneers, Spanish gold, rescue, and revenge.

The last entry was scribbled hastily and barely legible. "We are being attacked! Hundreds of Spanish assail the village at this very moment. Fire and smoke are everywhere. I can hear the desperate struggle of men in arms at the end of the village and it moves this way. I write these lines, afraid that they will be my last, afraid for my child not yet born, and my man. I pray, dear God, preserve us."

Tears streamed down Michelle's face as she read, choking out the last few words. When she had finished there wasn't a sound in the room. She closed the book to a stunned, emotionally impregnated silence.

Travis and Billy just sat there, tears brimming their eyes. Cody stared at the floor, afraid to look up, but he spoke in a quiet, faraway voice. "They didn't make it, did they? At least not many of them."

"I think the girl survived," said Michelle in a small voice, understanding now, for the first time, her affinity for the isle of Tortue.

"Yes, I think she did, and so did Will, of course," whispered Billy. There was a boat ..."

"The boat was in the tide waters behind the hills," said Travis quietly. Billy and Cody looked up. Travis hadn't even seen the two hills and the pass. Travis looked over at them, his face etched with the confusion of impossible recollection.

"I don't know how," he said, "but I remember." He took a deep, ragged breath. "I've always considered myself sort of a Presbyterian Buddhist—I liked the strength and conviction of Christianity, but was drawn to the serenity and seemingly logical explanation of life offered in Eastern Religion. I felt that Karma— reincarnation—was a viable possibility, yet I had, by no means, accepted it as fact. But here tonight, as Michelle spoke, I swear I remembered. It's vague, and it only comes in brief glimpses, but it's not my imagination. And last night I dreamt of taking the Spanish ship, just exactly as it occurred in the book." He paused, choked with emotion, and looked up at the ceiling. "Dear God, can it really be that we were here, far and away in another time?" He turned to Cody. "You and I—I believe we died here."

"Yes," said Cody.

It was as if the dam that held the river of time had been breached. They were all aware that through some sort of celestial alchemy involving fate and circumstance, it appeared they had been cast together once again, to fulfill a destiny that had begun over three hundred years ago. The purpose of it all was yet uncertain, but the fact that it was taking place no longer seemed an arguable point. It was an astounding, staggering revelation. Its width and depth were almost too broad for simple understanding and acceptance, yet the evidence of recall lay before each of them. Undeniable and irrefutable, it spoke of past existence, and of a life shared before, in that very place.

With the extraordinary events of the evening, there was little sleep to be found that night for anyone. The morning sun diffused the previous night's bizarre experience somewhat and they set about the day's projects with vigor. But anchored in the lee of their thoughts was the enduring knowledge that they were part of something far more significant than a simple treasure hunt.

After breakfast, Billy and Cody left for the ferry. It was due to arrive about ten, and it was nearly an hour's trip around the island by Mo-ped. Because of the ferry's infrequency, Cody couldn't afford to be late.

After they'd left, a slightly subdued Henri helped Travis unload some more of the metal-detecting equipment from the boat. When Travis asked why he was so quiet today, Henri looked up from the box they were unpacking. "Henri see some plenty spooky white man's Jesus magic yesterday. Henri no want to see past. Henri no want to see future. Henri like it now! Henri think you all *blanc houngans!*"

The trip by Mo-ped took Cody and Billy through one of the two villages on the island. They waved to the locals as they passed by. A few waved back half-heartedly, but most just ignored them.

"Same reaction I got before," said Billy. "It's like they don't want to know you, like they're afraid to know you."

When they reached the landing for the ferry, they found it had already arrived. Those who had been aboard had already disembarked and a handful of people with straw baskets and cloth bags were boarding for the trip to Port de Paix on the mainland.

The two men shook hands. Billy wished Cody a safe trip, then turned the Mo-ped around and headed back. Cody walked up the ramp onto the crusty little freighter. Finding a seat on the benches that lined the gunnels, he gazed out over the water, the odor of unwashed bodies and diesel fumes assaulting his nose. It bothered him little, though. He was lost in the experiences of the last week or so. He had wanted an adventure, and up to this point he hadn't been disappointed. His musing was interrupted slightly by the sight of a white man in a small outboard motorboat, beating his way through the waves toward Tortue. The boats passed within a hundred yards of each other, but the man never waved, never even looked over. His attention was occupied with the navigation of the boat through the swells.

The fellow looked vaguely familiar. Cody wanted to say Key West, but his look at the man had been fleeting and it was so unlikely that he just shrugged and returned to his thoughts.

Winston Magruder hated boats. He always got seasick. But there was no other way around this, so he threw up over the side and kept going.

When William Cody and his friends had left the Dubonnet's villa, Winston phoned, pretending to be with the American Embassy, claiming to have a message for them. He was informed that they had left for Tortue. He went back to the hotel for his gear, hopped in his rental car, and headed for the northern coast.

Magruder needed a way on and off the island at will. If they found the treasure and were preparing to leave, he'd have to be able to get back to the mainland in a flash to notify his people in the States. So, he rented a little skiff from a marina in Port de Paix, and, packing his camping gear, took off for Tortue.

Having done some research on Tortue and its history, Magruder knew that the old village lay on the far side of the island. He figured he'd work his way around until he spotted the sailboat, then back off a mile or so, come ashore, and hide the boat in the mangroves. After two hours of banging from swell to swell and throwing up everything but his lower intestine, he spotted the sailboat. He immediately turned toward shore and found a sandy spot sandwiched between two thick stands of mangroves. He pulled the boat up, mostly out of the water, cut some branches to cover it partially, then grabbed his gear and took off along the shoreline. As he walked, the grimace he had carried for the last two hours faded, and he began to smile. He was closing in on his prey, and he was out of that piece-of-crap fiberglass bathtub.

Captain Tousant and three of his men had been flown in and dropped off at the gravel strip two days before. They had watched the arrival of the sailboat from atop the granite cliffs, then moved cautiously back into the jungle to their camp as the occupants of the boat disembarked for their afternoon of sightseeing. Later the next day, they watched Cody pace off the airstrip. The captain smiled. Colonel Juele was right, there was more here than just a commonplace research expedition. Something was going on, and he intended to be right there when it happened.

Unaware of each other, the clandestine observers gathered around Travis and his group like vultures over a fresh kill. It was August 1, 1980. Off the coast of Africa that morning, a huge, poorly formed weather system began to coalesce. Gathering strength and definition, it started its inexorable movement westward across the Atlantic Ocean, toward the Lesser Antilles, as the big storms of late summer do.

Chapter Eight

When Billy returned from the ferry, they packed sufficient gear for a day's hike and finally began their search for the third bag of coins—the one that would hold the final clue to the treasure. Neither in a practical or preternatural sense had the veil of time been lifted sufficiently for any of them to see the location of the cache. There was, however, a collective certainty felt by all of them that, when it was right, the doors of time would open. For the time being, they accepted the earthbound challenge of the search enthusiastically, and, packing a couple of hand-held metal detectors along with the coin containing the last clue, they trekked off into the hills.

The group chose a path on the east side of the old village that led into the interior of the island, perhaps a half a mile from the curiously emotive twin hills.

They had been walking for about an hour when Billy, in the lead, paused and pulled the beaten coin from his pocket. "Let's refresh our memories on old Will's prose—perhaps it'll help." He read the last clue out loud again as they walked.

"Stand on the lip of God's green table, here on the isle of the sword. Find the moon as she crawls from the sea amid the season of the storm.

"When the glow of God's great lantern has finally been cast, it touches a tree that stands like a frigate's mast, there in the clearing below.

"Fifty steps west in strides that are bold lie the coins and the clue to the Brotherhood's gold."

"Well, there're two things we can be sure of," said Travis. "We're definitely in the season of the storm, and the tree that stands like a frigate's mast is long since gone. That was three hundred years ago. There have probably been ten major hurricanes through here since then. What we're going to have to find is God's green—" Suddenly his words faded. As Travis had been speaking, they had stepped from the jungle path into a clearing. There before them, maybe a quarter-mile distant, stood a hill with almost vertical sides, covered in lush green foliage. The top of the hill had suffered a substantial geological amputation at some far-off point in time. It was as if, in some distant dance of creation, the foot of God had come down squarely on the very crest of the hill, squashing it as flat as a tabletop.

They all stood there. No one said a word. For a moment they just stared at the vision borne in the passages of a pirate's prose.

"Well, there's your table," said Michelle quietly, not taking her eyes from the hill.

Billy and Travis just nodded, still staring.

Henri just shook his head. "More stinkin' white man Jesus magic. You all just a bunch of *blanc houngans!*"

That broke the spell enough for Travis to look over and smile at the others. "Come on, we've got an appointment with a lost tree."

They realized as they approached the plain in front of the hill that they had a sizable task before them. The area was scattered with stands of Australian pines, Scottish pines, Mahogany trees, and a hundred other varieties of trees, shrubs, and bushes. This, combined with the fact that the tree they were looking for no longer existed, made it a formidable challenge.

They paused, slightly overwhelmed, and Travis turned to Billy. "Where do we start? Do you feel anything? Do you have any ideas?"

Billy thought before answering and took a deep breath, closing his eyes for a second. He opened them and gazed across the plain. "It has changed here," he said quietly. "Storms."

Travis nodded, having already deducted this, but said nothing so as not to break Billy's concentration.

The small man shook his head slightly. "I'm not really sure, but I feel a pull toward the hill. I think what we're looking for was closer to the table than the jungle. I think we should work the detectors around the larger stands of pine trees in the area adjacent to the hill." Then, with more certainty, he nodded. "It was a pine tree that Will mentioned in the clue—a big pine."

The group walked to the base of the hill, deciding to take a break in the shade it offered and have a bite to eat, while considering the best approach to the task ahead. They ambled over to the sloping side of the tabletop and sat down beside a huge, rounded boulder that jutted partially out of the gravel and dirt on the side of the hill. As they ate the sandwiches that Michelle had prepared, Travis leaned against the boulder, listening to the conversation and speculation, adding a word here and there. He closed his eyes for a moment, head against the hard granite, and suddenly found himself relaxing for the first time in several days, succumbing to a strange sense of tranquility.

After lunch, they started with a stand of trees about a hundred yards out, to the far left of the table. Travis took one detector through the trees while Billy worked the perimeter with the other. It took about two hours of continuous sweeping to satisfy them that there was nothing in the area. They moved to the next large cluster of pines, toward the center of the clearing, and began again. Another two hours elapsed before everyone was convinced they were in the wrong area. By then it was late afternoon and time to return to the boat. There was still an hour's trek back.

As they reached the edge of the jungle, Billy looked back across the clearing, to the Table of God. Still staring he spoke: "It's out there somewhere—not just the last bag, but the treasure." Then he turned to the others with that crooked smile. "We'll find it. Tomorrow's another day, and we'll find it."

They made supper on the beach, then sat around the fire listening to soft melodies from Henri's sax. The sun crashed into the horizon with typical Caribbean splendor and shadows lengthened. Night obscured the jungle and darkened the waters in front of them, leaving only the strip of white, sandy beach vaguely visible. They were just packing up, preparing to take the dinghy out to the boat when, faintly, on the wind, they heard the drums. Travis looked over at Billy, who stood dead still, listening. An involuntary shudder touched his back, and when he looked up at Travis there was fear in his eyes. There was also anger. "He's out there tonight, and he knows we're here."

Nyakang stood in the center of the circle and felt the drums take him. He let the throbbing, almost discordant beat crawl inside him. His senses sucked in the angry rhythm and let it build like rising waters against a failing levy. Sweat poured off his body in rivulets from the heat of the fire, the night, and the expectation, slicking the palm that held the knife aloft. Finally, when he could stand it no longer, when the dam of violent need burst inside him, he cried out loud, and the knife fell.

He ran his finger across the flat, wet blade, then brought it to his tongue. He tasted the salty warmth and thought with sweet anticipation of the coming full moon and the *blanc* woman on the beach.

During the treasure hunters' search that afternoon, Magruder from one side and Captain Tousant from the other, watched them continuously. Observing them sweep the area with the detectors, the Captain, who knew the history of Tortue well, began to think about treasure. Maybe they knew something that the others before them hadn't. He would report to Colonel Juele via the radio tonight and see how he wanted this handled.

Back on the boat, as they prepared for bed, Travis turned on the marine radio. The past few evenings had been so filled with the excitement and revelation, he had simply forgotten. The news he received was not good. There was a tropical depression forming about 800 miles east-southeast of the Greater Antilles. If it continued its present course, the storm would strike the Dominican Republic and Haiti in less than three days. Travis wondered to himself as he fell asleep if that was why he was beginning to get that old uncomfortable feeling of impending misfortune.

The following day, Travis, Michelle, and Billy returned to the pine tree plain, while Henri took a walk down to the local village to see what he could find out. They spent five hours searching, and exhausted all but two small stands of trees in front of the hill.

Magruder and Tousant noted their efforts.

Captain Tousant had contacted Colonel Juele the night before.

"You remain hidden and you watch," said Juele. "If

they discover anything of value, whether it's drugs or treasure, you contact me immediately. I will take a launch around with a platoon of my Leopards. Together we will relieve these tourists of their burden."

When the weary treasure hunters returned to camp that evening, Henri had supper ready. While they ate, he told them about his visit to the village. "Somethin' spooky goin' on here," Henri said. "Them damned stinkin' natives scared very much shitless. Everybody act like they got juju man hidin' in closet. Nobody want to talk. Everybody act like Henri got stinkin' bad disease. One ol' lady talk to Henri. She so old Henri think she just no more afraid of nothin'. Anyway, she say people been disappearin'. Somebody go to get water, no come back. Some guy wake up, his wife be gone from hut. Mostly girls, young women be disappearin'. Everybody very much scared. That ol' lady say she think bad *bokor* out there."

Henri's news was not really news, but it was still disconcerting. That evening the group packed up early and headed off to the sailboat before it was completely dark. That night, Travis's dreams of ancient visions were crowded with images of a large, black snake.

The next morning at ten o'clock, Cody buzzed the beach in the big twin-engine Beechcraft. They all waved from the beach and they could see him returning the wave from the cockpit. As Cody turned toward the airstrip, Billy grabbed the Mo-ped and took off to get him.

Cody was waiting by the plane when Billy arrived. The blond-haired man stood gazing at the twin hills behind him, but the sound of the motorcycle brought him around and his look changed to a bright smile when he saw his friend.

Billy pulled up and got off the Mo-ped. "How was the flight down?" he asked as they shook hands.

"Piece of cake. Tail winds and good weather all the way."

Billy walked over and ran his hand along the plane's fuselage affectionately. "Lord. A Beech C-45, my favorite. I flew one of these back and forth from the islands for three years while working for that cargo company in Miami. Man, you just gotta let me fly this while we're here."

"No problem, we'll take her for a spin around the island later." Cody locked the plane and they headed back to camp.

Travis had taken a handful of lobster off shore that morning in a quick dive, so the group had an early lunch of those with baked potatoes and fresh fruit from the island. When lunch was completed, they decided to walk back to the strip for a quick ride in Cody's plane. From there they would head back to the table and begin sweeping the last two stands of trees in front of the hill.

During that morning, the depression Travis had been watching was upgraded to a tropical storm.

It was only about two miles from the camp to the strip. The beautiful, silver airplane sat patiently on the gravel runway. Big, twin 450-horsepower engines jutted proudly out of each wing on either side of the metal and glass cockpit. With nearly a 2,500-pound useful load and a cruising speed of close to 200 MPH, she was a hard working lady of infinite grace, classic lines, and forgiving nature. As Cody put it, "You can push her and she'll take it. You can treat her rough when you need to and she'll never let you down. She's at her best when she's giving you her most, like a fine horse or a good hooker."

They had all been walking toward the plane while Cody was speaking. When he finished, they realized that Travis had stopped behind them. When Cody and the others turned around, they saw Travis standing there, staring at the twin hills.

Cody didn't say a word. He simply walked back to his friend and put his hand on his shoulder. Their eyes met for a moment, then both men turned to gaze at the pass between the hills. Finally, Travis inhaled deeply and sighed, nodding slightly.

Wrapped in the soft silence of recollection, the two men began to walk toward the plane again, the others falling in quietly beside them, understanding all too well.

When they reached the plane, Cody unlocked the sliding cargo doors saying, "I brought a little toy to help us get a real bird's-eye view of the island, to give us a little perspective."

There was a metal framework in the cargo area of the plane—an open-air cockpit of sorts, connecting an engine with a propeller in the back that operated vertically like an airplane, but with a set of rotors on top like a helicopter. The rotor blades had been disconnected and lay beside the device. The rest of it was small enough to be lifted in and out of the cargo doors intact.

"It's a gyrocopter!" explained Cody with a flourish. "Runs on pennies, flies slow enough to get a good look at the terrain below, and you can land and take off in less than a hundred feet." As the others just stood there, amazed at the contraption, Cody encouraged them. "Come on, help me get it out. I'll give you a demonstration!"

Twenty minutes later, they had the gyro out of the

plane and the rotors installed. They pulled it out onto the strip and Cody put on his leather aviator cap and goggles. He fired up the little two-cycle engine, got the rotors moving, and got in.

"Sounds like a sewing machine on bennies," said Billy.

Henri looked over, shaking his head. "That one plenty stinkin' crazy white man. Them little blades stop them turns, that fall out of sky like coconut out of tall tree!"

Cody gave them a thumbs up and threw the gyro into gear. As it moved forward, the rotors picked up speed, and seconds later Cody was skimming effortlessly over the airstrip. He pulled the controls back and the device, which looked like something that the Wright brothers and Rube Goldberg might have built, lifted up like a metal insect and sailed out over the water. Cody swung it around and brought it back fifty feet over their heads. Then, turning sharply, he set it down a hundred feet from the Beechcraft. As the rotors quit turning, the others gathered around.

"Pretty nifty, huh?" said Cody, smiling.

"Yeah," replied Travis. "You're gonna have to teach me to fly that. I think I'd like it."

Henri "humphed." "Henri rather play musical chairs with sharp sticks dan fly dat stinkin' thing!"

When Travis stopped laughing he said, "Okay. Let's take a quick ride in the Beech, and maybe we'll see something from the air that we haven't been able to spot from the ground. Then we'll head over and sweep the last section of trees in front of the hill."

The plane had seats for a pilot and co-pilot up front, with one more set of seats directly behind those. The rest had been removed for cargo. Cody took the controls and Billy sat to his right. Henri and Michelle took the two seats behind them, with Travis sitting in the aisle between, holding the seats for support. Henri was quiet. It was his first plane ride. He was sweating more than the weather dictated, and his hands shook as Michelle showed him how to fasten his seat belt.

Billy and Cody went through the start-up procedure and both engines fired on command. Cody turned the plane around and taxied back to the end of the strip, about 400 yards down from the twin hills. He turned to Billy. "You want to take her up?"

"Sure thing!" Billy settled himself into the seat with a wiggle and hollered over his shoulder as he pushed the twin throttles in. "Hang on, everybody, here we go!" As the engines roared and the plane picked up momentum, Henri moaned and crossed himself, willing at that point to try even the white man's Jesus magic to protect him.

Billy applied a little right rudder to keep her centered on the runway and eased back the controls when they reached optimum takeoff speed. The nose came up gently and they broke free from the earth. He threw the gear up, removed the ten degrees of flaps, and pulled the plane toward the sky. Cody noted that his control of the airplane and his procedures were perfect. He had been watching carefully, prepared to take over at any moment. They had never flown together before, and although Billy claimed he was an extremely qualified pilot for this plane, Cody couldn't be sure until he saw it. Pilots have a reputation for being notorious talkers when it comes to experience and experiences. They make fishermen seem like amateurs.

Cody relaxed and let Billy fly, and fly he did. He took them up to four thousand feet and put the plane into a slow spiraling circle, giving them an excellent view of the island below. When he neared the ground, he put it into straight and level slow flight and ran the length of the island at two hundred feet.

For the first few minutes, Henri sat with his eyes squeezed shut, mumbling a combination of Latin verse and voodoo incantations. Gradually, though, he began to open his eyes, and toward the end of the flight he was actually enjoying himself. The others picked out the two villages and the ferry dockage and got a bird's-eye view of the table hill and the plain they were searching. As they made a pass on the far coast, just east of the ferry, Travis noticed about two dozen large, canoe-like boats pulled up out of sight in the mangroves. He wondered what would bring that many Haitians from the mainland to the island of Tortue.

Billy finally swung the plane around and brought it back to the strip for a perfect landing, taxiing up behind the twin hills and shutting down the engines.

Cody turned to him and put out his hand. "You can fly my plane anytime you want."

Billy beamed at the compliment.

As soon as everyone was out of the plane, they picked up the metal-detecting equipment, shovels, and picks, and headed for the table. It was two o'clock, and they still had a few hours of daylight in which to search.

The path from the plane to the table led them through the pass between the two hills. It was just as Billy had described it long ago at the bar in Key West. The residual emotional aura around the pass was so dense it was almost tangible. Travis paused once, certain he had heard the shouts of men, and the clash of steel.

Twenty minutes later they reached the clearing in front of the table and went to work again. There were but two stands left to search. They were small, to the point of being insignificant, and directly in front of the hill. Travis pointed to the one on the left, and they began. An hour later, they were nearing completion of the first one when Billy, who was just on the outside of the trees, signaled that he was picking something up. It was a fairly strong signal and it was deep. Travis grabbed a shovel and two feet of dirt later, the shovel struck metal.

As they clawed the dirt away, they realized immediately that it wasn't the bag of coins. It was steel, flat and wide, with a deteriorated wooded handle. Next to the first one, they discovered a second, exactly the same—two battle-axes. They dug around the axes and carefully lifted them from the ground. It was then that they noticed the bones underneath. As Travis lifted the two axes from the ground and brushed the dirt from the heavy, battle-scarred blades, he was physically shocked by sensation. For a split second, he saw the huge African again, at his side and at his back, and he knew who was buried there. As he put his hand into the hole and gently, almost lovingly, touched the bones below, he saw the glint of a single gold coin, beaten flat and wide. It must have been laying on the axe heads and been shifted by the digging.

He brought the coin from the hole and held it to the light. He spoke quietly, reading the inscription etched in the gold: "It says, 'In life he was never far from his captain's side, and death has changed that little.'" Billy took a deep, shaky breath and looked at Travis, who simply handed him the coin.

With the gold piece in his hand, Billy spoke again: "I think Will buried him here, near his captain, as sort of an eternal guardian. He knew it was what Joba would have wanted."

Travis carefully laid the battle-axes back on Joba's remains and gently filled the hole. When it was done, they all stood around like those gathered at a funeral and, in a sense, it was. They were paying homage to a long departed friend, a singularly courageous individual who had given his life for his companions three centuries before.

By the time they had completed the impromptu ceremony, the sun was working its way toward the treetops at the edges of the clearing. The last stand of pines would have to wait until morning.

From a nearby hill, Captain Tousant put his field glasses down and wondered why they all looked so sad at the finding of a gold coin.

That night, after supper, they sat in the cockpit of the boat and discussed their plans for the next couple of days, while being serenaded by Henri. The talented little Haitian sat on the bow and twirled out soft, raspy melodies as he played to the stars, and the nearly full moon.

Before bed, Travis listened to the marine radio once again and realized they had a problem—his name was Allen. It was the first storm of the season and was showing promise of being a monster. As of noon, he had been declared a Category One hurricane. By evening he had risen to Category Two, packing winds of nearly 100 MPH. The storm was located 600 miles south-southeast of them, and was moving with one of the fastest ground speeds ever recorded. If the hurricane continued on its present course, they would have to leave the island the day after tomorrow. The following morning would be too late. There was barely sufficient time to get the sailboat out and back to the mainland, and in reality it was probably just as safe here, in that tight little harbor, as it would be anywhere else. After a discussion, they agreed that they would search for the treasure all the next day. The following day they would begin to transfer all they could from the sailboat to the plane, leaving the island no later than sunset that evening.

The group bade each other goodnight, retiring to their individual bunks, leaving Michelle and Travis alone in the cockpit, staring at the moon as it reflected off the quiet, dark water. He put his arm around her and she snuggled against him, sighing in a sensual, contented way. They shared the forward cabin, but the close quarters of the sailboat restricted romance. Their time together, other than that, had been limited. Her face against his chest, she spoke softly, but seriously. "You know, the excitement of this search, the finding of the diary—it's all been a wonderful experience, and I know that treasure lies waiting for us out there somewhere. But even so, there's a small part of me that wants to be gone from this island, to be safely away from here with you. Treasure or no treasure, I can't say I'll be disappointed when we lift off that strip in Cody's plane. There's a part of me that's terrified I might lose you again, before we've had a chance to live, and to love."

"Not to worry, sweetheart," Travis soothed, stroking her hair. "We're going to find that treasure and be out of here before there's a whisper of wind from Allen. Trust me, I don't want a repeat performance of our last experience here. I'd much rather spend the rest of my days sipping piña coladas with you and watching the kids play on the beach."

She pulled away slightly and looked up at him. "Kids?"

"Why not?" he said. "When we find the treasure we'll be rich enough to afford them."

She giggled in that low, sensuous way that took his

breath, and nestled against him. "I love you, Travis Christian. It took me a long time to find you again, and you're not getting away this time."

"I love you too, darlin'," he whispered.

Chapter Nine

By the time the first rays of the morning sun had breached the darkness surrounding the island, everyone was up and dressed. A hasty breakfast of cinnamon rolls was washed down with rich Jamaican coffee, and when it was light enough to see the path, they headed out toward the pine tree plain. There was only one stand of trees left to check. Their plan was to give it a quick going over, then move to the perimeter of the hill.

They had been working for a half hour and the sun was just cresting the treetops when Billy, in his sweeping, noticed a large circular indentation at the edge of the pines. He knelt for a moment and looked at it, running his hand around the crumbling edges of the circle. Suddenly he realized that it was the remains of a huge tree. All that was left now was the deteriorating base, rotting its way back into the earth. But at one time it must have been an enormous tree. He rose from the base of the tree like a man in a daze, yet there was purpose and direction to his movements. Fifty bold strides ... The others had stopped what they were doing and were watching him. He halted at the end of fifty paces. The sun was at his back. He smiled and swung the detector in an arc in front of him.

Nothing.

The smile fading somewhat, he moved forward another three feet and passed the machine over the ground, sweeping to both sides.

Still nothing.

Billy backed up a half dozen feet and tried again. The silence of the machine mocked his intuition. *I was just certain,* he thought to himself. *Certain.* Puzzled, he turned to call to the others, casually bringing the head of the detector around as he did, and it suddenly sang like the bells of Saint Mary's.

The disintegrating leather pouch and the coins that it held lay less than two feet below the surface. There was that same silent awe as before when Billy handed them to eager hands around him. Again, the coin he wanted was near the bottom, and one of the last to come out. His hand shook slightly as he pulled it free and brushed it off. The others stood around him, waiting. He turned the coin to the light and read aloud.

"'When the late summer sun rises out of the sea, shimmerin' 'cross the crests o' the trees, its gilded caress touches those now at rest 'neath a secreted pirate's dream.

"'A round shot fired from the cannon of God lies planted in Mother Earth's wound. And there 'neath the gash lies the Brotherhood's gold sealed in a buccaneer's tomb.

"'Hold fast, matey, with the new sun behind ye, and walk the beam of a brigantine to the great granite round shot of God.'"

When Billy finished, they all turned toward the base of the hill, less than another fifty feet from them. The morning sun had just crested the trees of the clearing, painting the hill with bold, golden strokes. There, directly before them, protruding from the hill like a great gilded cannonball, was the round mass of granite they had picnicked beside the day they began their search.

The revelation, the realization, struck almost simultaneously as Billy raised his arm and pointed with complete certainty. "There lies the bloody round shot of God, and the treasure of the Brotherhood!"

Everyone stood in stunned silence as Travis

whispered, "Jesus!"

Cody bent over and picked up his shovel. "Let's go," he said. "I have to see." Grabbing their picks and shovels, the others followed. It had been a long time in coming and they, too, had to see.

Travis dug the point of the pick in around the sides of the boulder while Cody, Billy, and Henri cleared away the rubble with their shovels. They were giddy with excitement. There was not an ounce of doubt in any of them, only the prickly pleasure of anticipation. They knew, one and all, that the treasure was waiting for them. It was their destiny.

When they had cleared sufficient dirt and gravel to get the point of a pickax behind the stone, Cody took the other pick and both he and Travis wedged the points into the back of the rock, levering the granite ball loose from the gash in the hill. Slowly, the big stone began to move, grating from its pocket in the hillside, reluctant to relinquish its guardianship of a treasure it had protected for three hundred years.

Finally, with one concerted effort from Travis and Cody, the stone broke its bond with the earth and rolled ponderously to the side. Both men stood up and stepped back. For a moment, no one moved. They all just stood there staring at the dark, jagged wound in the side of the hill.

Travis's pick dropped from his hand and he moved slowly forward, the others following. Only Henri stayed on the outside, shaking his head and muttering something about not "goin' in no stinkin' cave."

The sun had just risen over the trees behind them and the tendrils of light shone directly into the opening, diffusing the darkness, illuminating the cave with a soft, smoky aura. Silent as monks, one by one they entered.

The vision before them would be burned into their memory for the rest of their lives.

Old Will, with a flare for the dramatic, had opened all the chests when he left them. He felt the two friends he left there should be able to see the booty around them. In the center of the dirt floor there were two mounds, side by side. On each grave lay a cutlass, its blade nicked from battle, but its steel sharp and bright. On one grave, next to the sword, lay a single gold coin attached to a thick gold chain. The wealth of Midas, a buccaneer's dream, lay around the mounds. Chests filled with gold coins, gold and silver jewelry encrusted with precious stones, stacks of gold and silver bars, and fat leather bags stuffed with uncut emeralds. The emotion of recollection and the visual impact of the treasure were staggering, almost overwhelming. Once inside the cave, no one moved again. The only noises were the gasps of astonishment and the sound of quickened breaths as they echoed off the hard granite walls.

Billy moved forward first, the impact of recall inundating him like a ground swell in a summer storm. Kneeling at the graves, he took the two swords and the coin that lay atop the mounds and, turning, stood before Travis and Cody.

"My friends," he said in the most quiet and respectful voice, part of him here, and part locked in distant memory, "I don't claim to understand the workings of God, and I've got no idea why we were chosen for this. I am certain, for no other reason than simply because I remember—the bond that exists between us is not new. We've been comrades in arms before, and these," he said, looking at the swords he held, "long ago, belonged to you." He held them out. "They're yours. They served you well. I'd like to return them to you now."

Travis and Cody grasped the hilts of the cutlasses, and lifetimes blew away like leaves in a gale. Seas misted before huge wooden bows. Yellowed canvas snapped taut on hewn wooden spars. The sound of steel on steel clashed in their ears, along with the roar of cannon, the smell of powder, the smoke in the air, the screams of the wounded, and the cries of the crew as they shouted time and time again, "For the Brotherhood! For the Brotherhood!" The three of them looked at each other and the room crackled with electricity of memory and emotion.

Billy turned to Travis. "Three hundred years ago you wore this coin around your neck, given to you by the men of this island. You gave it to me to hold for you. It's my pleasure to return it to you now."

They held each other's eyes as Travis took the coin and the chain from his friend's hand. The morning sun reflected off its edge as he raised the coin and saw the Brotherhood's emblem etched in the gold.

The warmest of smiles crossed his face as he looked up at his friends. He wanted to reach out and crush each of them to his breast. He wanted them to know that he would carry this moment in his heart, not just for a lifetime, but forever. Travis knew then that, truly, they were all children of time, and that within this circle of life, this confusing, uncertain continuum of space and ages, some things are forever.

"Michelle," he whispered, as he gently took her hand. "Billy, Cody," he said, turning. "Come, let's have a look at what we left ourselves a long time ago."

The treasure was staggering. It wasn't King Tut's tomb, but there was more wealth there than they had to worry about spending in a lifetime. There were uncut emeralds the size of golf balls, stacks of ten-pound gold and silver ingots, chests of solid gold coins, and stone-encrusted jewelry. With the price of gold and gems at an all-time high, it didn't take long for the value to stagger the imagination.

As the sun rose, they began to lose light in the cave, so they carried a box of gem-encrusted jewelry outside. They set it by the boulder and, there in the light of the morning sun, examined the treasure that had been destined for the court of Spain over three centuries ago. As the group inspected the almost incalculable wealth in their hands, they discussed the scheme for getting their riches off the island and into the States before hurricane Allen hit and changed all their plans.

It was decided they would begin the transfer of the treasure to the plane immediately. There was a considerable amount of bulk to deal with, but the weight was the real problem. They estimated there was over 1,500 pounds of treasure to be transferred. There was almost a full tank of fuel on the plane, Cody having refueled when he cleared customs in Port au Prince. Those factors, along with the weight of the passengers and pilot, had the plane somewhat overloaded. Cody figured he could get them into the air all right, but the other problems were manpower and time. Each chest required two men to carry it and there were at least a dozen chests and crates. It was nearly a half-hour walk to the plane from the cave—an hour round trip for two men. It was late morning already. The best they could hope for was to complete half the transfer before nightfall and the other half on the following morning.

Travis cut some saplings and made two stretchers for carrying the chests. Tying a chest between the poles, with a man at each end, they were able to maneuver their newfound wealth with minimal discomfort. Henri and

Travis took one, Billy and Cody the other. Michelle carried the two bags of emeralds that they had transferred to the canvas bag in which she had originally carried lunch. They had to travel to the western end of the pine tree plain, then through a small stretch of jungle, across the clearing in front of the twin hills, up the slope, through the pass, and down the other side to the plane. It made for a long and tiring afternoon, but profitable— very profitable.

With little more than a couple of breaks for a drink of water, they worked until the setting sun touched the top of the table. They still had five chests to transfer. There wasn't any way they were going to finish before dark. Reluctantly, the treasure hunters picked up their equipment and headed back to camp.

The walk back to the beach was a euphoric procession. They had done it. They had found the treasure! Lord, they were pleased with themselves.

Captain Tousant was already on the radio to Colonel Juele. When he described the remarkable discovery, Juele was skeptical. "Are you sure? Are you positive it was a pirate treasure?"

"Colonel, I have my field glasses. I saw the jewel-encrusted gold! I saw the chests of coins! They had bags—*bags*—of uncut emeralds! I watched them transfer it for easier carrying."

Juele's face broke into a satisfied smile as he listened. "Very well, Tousant, I'll take your word for it. This is what you do: Maintain your surveillance of them. I'll be there first thing in the morning with two-dozen soldiers. We'll fly to Port de Paix tonight and take a launch from there at first light. Meet us a quarter-mile east of the fishing village, but keep a couple of your men on them at all times. Instruct your men to shoot out the tires of the plane if they look remotely like they are thinking of leaving. Do you understand?"

Magruder sat back against a tree, took his hat off, and wiped the sweat from his forehead. He stared in stunned disbelief at the chests of treasure as they emerged from the cleft in the hill. *Sweet Jesus! There were millions, millions of dollar's worth of treasure there! Just one of those chests and he'd never have to work again.* He had to catch himself, put the brakes on those kinds of thoughts. *These people were thieves. They were stealing a treasure from Haiti and planning on secreting it into the U.S. without a thought of legal process or taxes. He was an authorized guardian of the financial security of the United States of America. His job was to stop them!* There, that was better. He was all right now ... Tonight he'd pay a visit to their campsite, find out what their game plan was. As he went over his plans for the evening, he watched them open another chest of solid gold coins. "Sweet Jesus!" he moaned again.

That night, the small group of tired but ecstatic treasure hunters broke out the champagne and celebrated the full circle of their lives and finding the treasure. Even Henri was beside himself. He was going to the U.S. of A. They had even promised him enough money for an excellently fast car. He'd have to find the big-breasted women on his own.

As they sat around the campfire, just a little giddy from the good champagne and great fortune, Cody's little brass bell tinkled.

Cody always covered himself three ways to Sunday. He said that he never took chances—he took calculated risks, with contingency plans and constant perimeter checks. As to perimeters, Cody had taken a piece of monofilament fishing line and run it about ten feet inside the border of the jungle that surrounded three sides of the little horseshoe-shaped clearing of beach where they had set up camp. The line ran from tree to tree, about a foot off the ground all the way around the clearing, then back to camp. Cody had hammered a forked stick into the sand in the center of the campsite, tied a little brass bell to the line and hung it on the stick. Anyone approaching from the jungle and not paying attention would kick the almost invisible line, causing the bell to ring.

When the bell tinkled, the conversation in camp stopped for a second. It tinkled once more, sharply, then went quiet. Cody immediately picked up where he had left off in the story he was telling, but while he spoke his eyes caught Travis' and delivered another message. A few seconds later Travis stood and stretched, saying nature was calling and he'd be right back. He walked off, down to the beach, while Cody continued his story.

Magruder had felt his foot catch something as he moved in on the camp, but it was dark now and he couldn't tell what it was. *Probably one of the million or so clinging vines that grew on the ground and in the trees on this miserable bloody island,* he thought. He couldn't wait to sew this up and get back to civilization, take a shower, and sleep in a real bed again. This camping-out crap was for the birds. He itched everywhere from all the friggin' bug bites, he smelled like a goat in heat, and he hadn't eaten a decent meal in days. But he was closing in now; soon he'd have them. He'd just get a little closer to the clearing so he could hear what they were saying.

A few moments later, he heard something behind him. But before he could turn, he felt the barrel of a gun in the small of his back. "Not a move. Not a single move," a voice growled. "You do anything other than breathe fast, you're dead. Now come up slowly, with your hands over your head."

Magruder's stomach felt like he'd just dropped twenty floors in a runaway elevator. He did as he was told and felt himself expertly frisked. His short-barreled .38 was quickly removed from his belt. "Move!" the voice said, emphasizing the point with the gun barrel against his back again. He walked forward, out into the clearing and the camp. The others around the fire looked up to see the two men come out of the jungle. As Magruder got close to the others, he saw that they were smiling slightly, and he hazarded a quick glance back as the harsh voice commanded him to stop.

"Crap," he said to himself. The guy behind him had pushed him out of the jungle with a friggin' stick! He didn't even have a gun until he took the pistol. Travis came around, holding Winston's revolver, and stared at him hard.

"Suppose you tell us who you are and what the hell you're doing here?"

"Suppose you go to hell," Magruder said, getting some of his courage back. "I don't have to tell you squat."

The big man stared at him a moment longer. "Give me your wallet," he said.

"I ain't giving you anythi—" started Magruder, but he was interrupted by the sound of his own pistol being cocked. The man brought the pistol up to Winston's face, then lowered it to his crotch. "I'm going to count to three. One—"

"You wouldn't't!"

"Two."

"Okay! Okay!" yelled Magruder. "You can have it! You can have it!" He pulled the wallet out of his back pocket and tossed it over. Travis caught the billfold deftly and flipped it open, glancing at the identification card, then up at the man. "Special agent for the IRS? What are you doing—" He caught himself, realizing.

Magruder smiled. "Yeah, you're right, we've been on you all along." He glanced around at all of them. "I've been watching you for days. I saw you find the treasure! How do like them apples, huh?"

"Not so well, I admit," replied Cody, standing up and coming over. "But like they say, it ain't over 'til the fat lady sings."

"The problem now is what do we do with him?" asked Travis, looking at the group, then glancing back at Magruder.

"Well, we can't let him go," said Cody. "He must have a way on and off the island. If we let him go, we're screwed."

Magruder smiled at that, and the others knew Cody was right. "We could shoot him and bury him on the beach," Billy piped up. "Or bury him on the beach at low tide, with just his head sticking out, like in the old days."

Magruder blanched and took an involuntary step backward, until he saw the others smiling at Billy. "You wouldn't do that."

"We might," said Travis. "We have our interests to protect, and as you've seen, we have quite a lot of interests." Travis looked at Magruder. "Come here and sit down." Travis paused, looking at the identification card again. "Mr. ... Magruder," he said, waving the gun at one of the big logs sitting near the campfire, "have a seat."

Winston slowly complied, wondering what was coming next.

Travis walked around in front of him and looked down. "Tell me ... Winston, do you have a family? Kids?"

"No, just me."

Travis nodded. What do you make a year, Winston?"

Magruder hesitated, then shrugged and answered, "about twenty thousand, plus benefits."

Travis cocked the gun and aimed it at Winston's head again. "I could kill you now and solve all our problems. You know that, don't you?"

Winston gulped and nodded silently.

"Or maybe I could make you an offer you couldn't refuse."

"Whaddaya mean by that?"

"Do you really like your job, Winston? I mean, is it the end-all to beat-all for you?"

Magruder thought about the question. He liked his work now pretty much, but he hated being low man on the totem pole. He didn't like the way the other agents treated him, or any newcomer for that matter. He had to admit that there were a lot of assholes in his business. "I guess it's all right. Why?"

"What if I offered you the freedom to change professions if you wanted. Maybe enough freedom for a condo on Miami Beach, a new sports car, and, say, a hundred thousand to live on, until you figured out who you wanted to be when you grew up? A man like you, with your abilities, should have his own business, maybe your own detective agency. Basically, Magruder, I'm giving you a couple of choices: You can be rich or you can become a missing person. Which sounds best to you?"

"You realize that you're attempting to bribe a government official?"

"Do you realize that I'm going to tie you up, lower you over the side of the sailboat tonight, and let the sharks eat you while we sleep if you give me the wrong answer?"

Magruder thought about it a second longer. "I think I

like the rich choice better."

Travis smiled for the first time. "You're showing signs of promise."

Magruder pictured the condo on Miami Beach, and he too smiled for the first time.

Travis continued, "Okay, this is the deal. You stick with us now. You go back on the plane with us. If Cody does his magic act and gets us in safe, we'll fill your pockets with gold coins and emeralds and send you on your way. At that point you can keep your job or quit, your choice. If you're considering double-crossing us after you're paid, let me tell you how that works. There'll be five of us to testify that we paid you off to get us into the country. First off, you'll never be able to cash in coin one, with the way they'll be watching you. Secondly, your reputation will be shot. You'll be lucky if they let you chase delinquent accounts. You'll never be trusted again. That's if they don't simply cashier you out as a bad risk and an embarrassment to the agency. You know as sure as I'm standing here, that I'm right, Winston. If they catch us when we land, you can simply tell them you went undercover to gain our confidence. You'll probably be a hero. The way I see it, you can't lose."

Magruder smiled again. That was the same way he saw it.

"Now for the bad news," said Travis. "We're trusting souls but we're not stupid. Until we get in the plane and underway, we're going to have to keep real close grips on you. We'll have to tie you up overnight, and you're going to have to tell us where your means of transportation is as well."

"No, problem," said Magruder. He had crossed the threshold of decision with less difficulty than he would have expected. He had seen the wealth these people possessed. Why shouldn't some of it be his? It beat the hell out of being shark bait. He was already trying to decide what kind of car he wanted. "I've got a boat about a mile from the village. I'll show you in the morning."

Travis looked over at the others and smiled. The unexpected event had resolved itself nicely—especially for Magruder. With better than ten million dollars in gold and jewels they had, a couple hundred thousand for insurance was cheap.

An hour later, they were all aboard the sailboat. Magruder had been bound hand and foot and laid comfortably to rest on the extra bunk. The others had retired to their individual berths. With the astounding events of the day, sleep was once again difficult to come by.

The full moon rose from the sea and its pale glow touched the sailboat and the water. The gentle ebb and flow of the tides whispered secrets to the beach, and the night breeze hushed as it listened.

Chapter Ten

A half hour after sunrise, everyone was dressed and breakfast had been dispensed with. Overnight, hurricane Allen had remained true to its course and was steadily increasing in strength. Estimated time of arrival on mainland Hispaniola was early the following morning.

They had conferred over breakfast, deciding to split up in order to maximize efforts in their last few hours, before relinquishing the island to the oncoming storm. Travis, Billy, and Winston would go back to the cave and complete the removal of the treasure. Michelle and Cody were to break camp and unload the easily negotiable valuables from the sailboat, taking them by Mo-ped to the plane. As they all stood on deck, preparing to depart in the dinghy, Travis turned to Cody and Billy.

"Listen, I don't know why, but I'm getting a terrible case of heebie-jeebies. Something isn't right out there, and I think it's coming our way. If I didn't know this feeling so well, I'd say I was being paranoid, what with Magruder showing up and the storm and all. But that's not it. I'm sure that's not it. This warning system has kept me alive too many times for me to ignore it now. I think we should break out the guns."

Cody didn't even question Travis. He simply turned around, went below, and opened up the secret compartments. He pulled out Travis's M-16, Billy's shotgun, and his own Thompson, as well as extra ammo for all. Travis turned to Magruder, patting the agent's .38 revolver in his belt.

"Winston, if we have a problem, I'm going to give this back to you. But for now, I'll hang on to it."

"Okay by me," Magruder replied amiably.

Before closing the lids on the secret compartments, Cody glanced at the grenades and the C-4 hidden there, making a mental note to be sure to pull those out today, on one of the trips to the plane. With that taken care of, they headed toward shore in the dinghy, beaching the small boat and walking to camp.

It took Travis and his companions an hour to get back to the table, and for the next few hours they transported the last of the treasure to the plane.

Cody and Michelle completed the transfer of the essentials from the sailboat and were waiting under the wing of the Beechcraft when Travis and the others showed up with the second-to-last load. They had but two more small chests and they would be finished. Cody told them he needed to do a good preflight and check the engines before taking off, so he stayed with the plane while Travis, Magruder, and Billy agreed to go back for the last of the cache.

While they were preparing to return to the cave, Michelle realized that she had left her diary in the sailboat. She decided to take the Mo-ped back with Henri while the others completed their respective tasks. As Michelle started to leave, Travis turned and called her over to him. Taking her hands, he said, "Listen, you get that diary and get right back, okay?"

She drew back, looking at him. "Travis, I won't be gone an hour. What's wrong?"

He took a quick breath and exhaled nervously. "I've still got that uncomfortable feeling of sugar ants crawling up and down my spine. I'm just damned near sure that all the excitement isn't over, and I want you close if there's a problem."

She smiled. "I love you, too," she said. "I'll be careful, and I'll be right back."

Travis chuckled and relaxed a bit. "Yeah, okay." Then he pulled her to him and kissed her. "I do love you, you know," he whispered.

"Yes," she said softly, "I know."

Half an hour later, as Travis and his companions neared the mouth of the cave, they saw movement in a stand of pines about seventy-five yards from them. Suddenly, a handful of soldiers emerged about fifty yards to their left, by a large granite outcropping. The men, in camouflage fatigues, spread out and raised their weapons. Colonel Juele had arrived with two dozen of his hand-picked men and had decided there were to be no survivors to argue possession. Dodging the first few rounds from the soldiers, Travis and Magruder scrambled for cover behind the big granite boulder at the mouth of the cave, while Billy, who had been walking in front of them, ducked into the cave itself. Travis shouldered his M-16 and clipped off six rounds. Two soldiers fell to the ground in the clearing and the others clambered back to the safety of the rocks behind them. They began to return fire. As Billy opened up with the shotgun from the cave, the soldiers hidden in the pine trees began shooting. Travis and Magruder were boxed in, caught in a crossfire. The boulder no longer offered much protection. As the two dashed for the mouth of the cave, a round caught Travis in the upper arm. It only grazed him, but the shock cost him his grip on the rifle and it clattered to the ground as he ran. He turned to go back for it, but was discouraged by half a dozen bullets as they kicked up the earth in front of him. Travis and Magruder fell into the cave, their backs against the wall on either side of the small opening, as bullets slapped the ground around the entrance.

Billy looked over at Travis as he checked the gash on his arm. "That's the friggin' Haitian military out there! And it doesn't look like they're terribly interested in negotiation! Does everybody in the bloody Caribbean know about this treasure? Did we take out an ad somewhere that nobody told me about? 'Wanted, anyone without conscience who wants to be rich. Meet on Tortue for your share of treasure belonging to a group of very naive people.'"

Travis laughed despite the pain. "They didn't tell me about it either."

Magruder moved over and, without a word, cut the sleeve back on Travis's arm. Taking the cloth, he bound the wound. Travis nodded thanks as Winston worked. In the meantime, Billy hazarded a quick look outside the cave. What he saw wasn't encouraging. The two groups of soldiers were closing in. He managed one round from his shotgun before being forced back inside by a barrage of fire from the oncoming men. "Well, boys," he said as he leaned against the wall and put another shell in the shotgun, "they're coming for us and I, for one, plan to make 'em pay just a little."

Travis took the revolver from his belt, flipped open the cylinder, and checked the loads. Then he looked over at Billy. "Doesn't look like we have a lot of options."

"No, it doesn't, buddy."

Travis turned to Magruder. "In just a few seconds, Billy and I are going to roll out of here shooting. If it's gonna happen, I want to be in the sunlight. There's just a chance we may confuse them long enough for you to slip out and make a run for the jungle. It's a slim chance, but it's better than none at all, and that's what you've got if you stay with us. We'll do our best to cover you. Good luck, Winston, and I'm sorry we got you into this."

Winston couldn't help but smile, even though he was certain he was going to die. "That's a strange thing for you to be saying to a man who chased you all this way with the intent of arresting you and ruining your life."

"Yeah, well, maybe so," agreed Travis, "but I somehow suspect that if things would have worked out differently, you would have become one of us, not one of them."

They could hear the shouts of the soldiers now as they neared the cave. With a final nod to Winston, Travis turned to Billy. "Ready?"

Billy nodded tensely.

"Okay, on the count of three. One. Two—"

It was then that they heard the whirl of the rotor-blades coming over the top of the hill.

While pre-flighting the plane, Cody heard gunfire in the direction of the cave. On foot it would have taken him a half-hour to get there—too long to be of any help. He looked over at the gyro. Five minutes later he was in the air.

As he neared the clearing, he could hear the gunfire increasing. He didn't know who it was but he was gut-sure they were after his friends. That made them fair game. He rose over the hill and saw the two groups of men in camouflage uniforms firing at the mouth of the cave. He glanced down and saw Travis's M16 lying on the ground near the entrance. A cold lump of fear hardened in his gut when he saw that gun. Travis would never leave his weapon if he were all right. Cody's eyes went hard as he jammed the controls forward and the 'copter dropped into a stomach-lurching dive. "Paybacks are a bitch," he muttered through clenched teeth.

Both groups had bunched up and were no more than fifty yards from the mouth of the cave when the gyrocopter, like an angry metal dragonfly, leapt over the hill and swept down on them.

Most of the men, having never seen a gyro before, stood there in gaping astonishment at the whirling contraption and the goggled pilot. Cody zoomed fifty feet over the top of them, holding the controls with one hand while pulling pins from grenades with his teeth and dropping the deadly bombs on the men below. The grenades exploded dead center in the two groups of men—thousands of razor-sharp pieces of shrapnel shredded flesh and bone for a hundred-foot radius, killing or disabling half of the soldiers on the first pass. The wounded screamed and thrashed, men dropped their weapons and stumbled blindly around in the smoke and dust. But William J. Cody wasn't done. He cranked the little machine around in a neck-snapping turn and brought it down to ground level for a second pass. This time he cradled his trusty Thompson in his arm and opened up on the confused and disoriented soldiers who had survived his first assault. There weren't many who survived his second.

When the men in the cave realized what was happening, Travis tossed the pistol to Magruder and he dashed out, snatching up his rifle, firing at the remaining soldiers. Billy was right on his heels, covering him with the shotgun and Magruder followed, firing wildly into the melee. Cody barreled by them, not twenty feet off the ground, as he completed his second pass. He smiled broadly at the sight of Travis and waved his weapon from the open cockpit, then tore the sky open in another wrenching turn and climb.

In just a few minutes it was over. A few of the

soldiers made the jungle, the rest lay dead in the clearing. Cody had just begun to feel that they'd pulled it off, when one of the surviving soldiers stopped and turned at the edge of the clearing. He aimed at the man in the sky who had foiled his plans and opened up with a burst from his automatic rifle. It was pure luck, but three of those rounds struck Cody's propeller and engine, just as he had reached an altitude of about 300 feet. The wooden propeller shattered. Cody immediately shut the engine down, and vertical movement ceased. Reacting instantly to the loss of power, Cody threw the 'copter down at the ground to keep the rotors turning and supplying lift. When he was sure he had a sufficient lift factor, he set up a glideslope taking him over a large stand of mahogany trees, and into the plain beyond. There was a fairly bad vibration somewhere, but everything seemed to be holding together.

What Cody didn't know was that one of the bullets had smashed into the bolts that held the shaft for the rotors in place, badly damaging them. As he made his approach, the vibration in the shaft finally broke the bolts. Fifty feet over the stand of mahogany trees, the shaft twisted, screamed, ground to a halt, and the rotors stopped turning. Cody might as well have been flying a rock.

Travis watched in horror as his friend, the man who had just saved all their lives, plummeted from the sky in the silent metal skeleton.

The big man just inside the foliage at the edge of the clearing smiled as he saw the 'copter go down. Pausing just long enough to bind the wound on his leg, he began working his way through the jungle. As he limped, the pain fed his rage. He would have revenge on the rest of them, too. Yes, he would ...

Cody and his gyro tumbled out of the sky into the center of the stand, striking a huge tree, breaking limbs and snapping branches like match sticks, burrowing into the heart of the thick limbs until the craft slammed against the trunk itself. After striking the enormous trunk, it dropped, grating and twisting, another fifteen feet, coming to a jarring halt as the frame caught in the fork of a branch fifty feet above the ground. The heavy limb creaked, giving downward a foot or so, and a small fracture appeared where it joined the trunk, but it held for the moment. All was silent in the green labyrinth of trees and vines, the creatures stilled by the sudden, chaotic invasion of man and machine.

In the eerie stillness that followed, with a sound like that of heavy cloth ripping, the branch that held the gyro succumbed to gravity and began to crack.

Travis was already running before the machine struck the jungle, with Billy and Magruder close behind. Seconds later he had reached the stand and was tearing his way through the thick undergrowth, searching the ground and the canopy above for Cody and his vehicle. He reached the broken limbs and the scattered pieces of the 'copter in time to look up and see the big branch begin to crack. The gyro would have probably plummeted down at that point, had it not been for a sizable branch from a nearby tree. The great limb that held the craft snapped, but before it gave completely, it came to rest on a slightly smaller one that had grown out from another tree underneath it. The lesser limb bent and held, though it was obvious from the weight of the 'copter and the bowing of the branch that this was temporary at best.

Ignoring the danger, Travis was halfway up the tree by the time the others got there. He was ten feet below Cody when, with a labored groan, the bough supporting the gyro cracked most of the way through, putting all of its weight on the limb below. He only had seconds ... Travis scrambled up the trunk, limb to limb, until he was next to the bent and mangled machine.

Cody lay thrown forward over the controls. His left arm hung loosely at his side, his forearm bruised and swollen—most likely fractured. Blood trickled down his face from a cut on his forehead. He was unconscious, but he was breathing. Travis wanted to call to him but he was afraid that he might come to and move, causing the tenuously balanced machine to slide off the branch and plunge to the earth. Quickly, Travis crawled out on a branch only a couple of feet above the 'copter. By laying flat on the limb, he was able to reach down to Cody in the gyro. As he stretched out to undo Cody's safety belt, the damaged bough creaked again and gave another six inches. Travis held on to his branch with one hand while working the clasp on Cody's belt with the other. The position of Cody's body and the pressure he exerted against the belt was making it nearly impossible to undo the clasp. Travis struggled frantically, stretching until his shoulder muscles ached. He pressed and pulled on the buckle wildly, drawing breaths in panicked gasps between clenched teeth. There was a continuous creaking, and a slow, inexorable downward movement of the bough that held the gyro. It was going ... Travis cried out as the limb gave, jerking and pressing maniacally on the belt and buckle that trapped his friend. Just as the limb finally yielded and the craft began to slip downward, the safety latch snapped free. The big branch popped like a gunshot and cracked free of the tree, taking the twisted, metal machine with it as it crashed through the foliage to the ground.

As the gyrocopter slipped away toward the earth,

Travis reached out and, with a desperate grab, caught the collar of Cody's shirt, pulling the small man free of the plummeting machine.

Travis now lay stretched out prone on a limb, fifty feet above the ground, holding on with one hand, while below him dangled a full-grown man, held tenuously by his shirt collar. Travis was a powerful fellow, but he had made a quick grab for Cody and had managed a poor grip at best. If he didn't do something quickly, he'd lose him. Below, Billy was on his way up. But he'd never make it in time.

Travis lay on the branch, catching his breath and gathering his strength, terrified that he might fail his friend. For a second, he looked down at Cody, dangling bloody and helpless below him. Just then, Cody regained consciousness. His head wobbled back and his dazed eyes looked up at Travis. "Whatcha doin' up there?" he muttered almost incoherently.

Travis couldn't help but smile. "It's a long way down this tree, and I thought you might like some help."

Cody smiled, secure in the knowledge that his friend had him. "Yeah," he mumbled, "pretty bad landing."

Travis clenched his fist around the cloth of Cody's collar and squeezed with every ounce of strength he had, burying the fabric into the palm of his hand with his nails. The muscles and tendons of his powerful arm rippled, petrified with exertion, as if carved from the hard wood of the mahogany tree itself. Slowly, he began to ease back off the limb, toward the trunk. He was not going to lose his friend. He simply refused to. The world could shift on its axis and shake the mountains around him into the sea—it wouldn't matter. He was taking his friend down out of that tree. Travis swallowed his doubts, overcame the pain and the panic, and his arm became granite. There was nothing at that moment more important than his partner's life, and nothing was going to take that man from his grasp.

In slow, decisive movements, he pulled himself along the limb as he moved back toward the huge trunk with Cody suspended in his grip. When he reached the trunk, in a Herculean effort borne of mind more than body, he pushed himself up from the branch with one hand and hauled his friend up and over the branch with the other. By the time Billy finally reached him, Travis sat straddling the limb with his back against the trunk—drenched with sweat, his chest heaving. Cody was draped over the branch in front of him like a dead cowboy over a horse. Travis still gripped his friend's collar.

Billy smiled at Cody, who was just on the verge of consciousness. "You hang in there, buddy," he said. "We'll have you out of here in no time."

Cody, dangling over the branch, nodded slightly. "Good," he mumbled. "Need an aspirin."

For the next ten minutes, the two men carefully worked their friend down out of the tree to the ground. When they reached the safety of the jungle floor, they cleaned his head wound with Billy's handkerchief and bound his forearm. It wasn't a bad fracture, but it was painful nonetheless. They made a splint with a small piece of aluminum from the gyro and Cody's belt. Other than the two obvious injuries and a handful of bruises, there seemed to be nothing else seriously wrong. The branches of the tree had cushioned the 'copter's impact. Had it struck anywhere else on the flat plain, they would have been burying him.

Michelle had heard the gunfire in the distance as she and Henri were rowing back from the sailboat. The direction told her it was probably at the treasure site. For the moment, she didn't know what to do. They could race for the cave, but the trouble could be over and Travis gone before she got there. They could head back to the plane, which was most logical, but then she'd have to wait for news ... Her intuitive fear of losing Travis had blossomed into outright panic and she was terrified. She struggled with her indecision as they quickly rowed for the shore and beached the boat.

They had just reached the camp, returning for the Mo-ped, when from out of the dark green shadows of the jungle stepped Nyakang. A perverse smile touched his face when he realized his good fortune at finding the girl alone. He pointed and, melting out of the charcoal gloom of the trees around them, came his minions.

Henri picked up a heavy piece of firewood and turned to face his assailants. Putting Michelle at his back, he whispered tensely, "You run, Missy, you run now!" But she never had a chance. The circle closed behind them as she turned, and they were trapped. Slowly, in a silence congested with violence and hate, they closed in. Clubs and knives in hand, they reached for the woman and her small protector.

As terrified as he was, Henri stood his ground, striking at them wildly and spitting curses, but there were simply too many. He managed to knock down two before he heard Michelle scream from behind him. A big Haitian with wild eyes and skin the color of coal had dashed in and slapped Michelle with an open hand, knocking her to the ground. When Henri turned to help her, a tall man wielding a club leaped in and struck him down. Before he could recover, they fell on him, their knives and clubs rising and falling in terrible cadence.

Michelle screamed and tried to crawl to her companion, to stop the cruel punishment, but she was slammed into the sand by a foot in the center of her back, knocking the breath from her. Before she could recover, a burlap bag was thrust over her head and her hands and feet were bound. Seconds later, she was tossed over a muscled shoulder and carried away, leaving her brave friend in the clearing, his blood pooling in the sand.

For the next hour and a half she was jostled and bounced, being traded from shoulder to shoulder until the group reached its destination. When they finally stopped, she was dumped onto the damp earth of the jungle and left. Blinded by the burlap hood, her hands and feet numb from the excruciatingly tight bonds, she lay in a silence broken only by her own raspy breathing. Afraid, alone, and devastated by the loss of Henri, she cried for the courageous little Haitian who had sacrificed himself to protect her. He had been part of her household for a dozen years. He was more than an employee—he had been a friend. And in the end he had put her safety above his own, as only a true friend would do. She lay on the warm, damp jungle floor and silently suffered the loss of her petite Henri, while the sun set and the full moon rose.

Cody was stiff and sore, but ambulatory. Shrugging off their offers of assistance, he rose to his feet. "I'm okay, I'm okay. We've got to get moving, it's getting late. I want to be out of here before it even smells like a hurricane." Looking at his arm in the makeshift sling, then over to Billy, he spoke again. "You're going to have to fly us out of here now, Billy. Travis is a great pilot, but you've got the hours in that kind of plane. He doesn't."

Billy nodded. "No problem, man. Piece of cake."

They headed back to the cave, got the last two chests of coins, tied them to the stretcher, and moved out. Half an hour later they were back at the airstrip. It was six o'clock. Michelle and Henri were nowhere to be seen.

Travis had been jittery the whole way back. When Michelle wasn't at the plane, he was looking for the panic button. They checked inside the aircraft, then yelled for them, but it didn't appear that they had returned from the campsite.

Travis turned to the others. "I'm sure something has happened. I'm going looking for her. I'm—"

"We're going with you," Cody interrupted.

Travis looked at his friend, grateful for such a companion, but shook his head. "No, buddy, you stay here. You've got a fractured arm and probably a mild concussion—you're in no condition for it. You stay and guard the plane. I'll take Billy and Magruder."

"He's right," agreed Billy. "We've got a serious investment in this now. I don't want to come back and find that somebody has relieved us of it. You hold the fort; we'll go find Michelle and be right back."

Outnumbered, Cody reluctantly agreed. Travis grabbed a couple more magazines for the M16 and Billy stocked up on ammo for his shotgun. They gave Magruder his pistol. Travis looked over at Cody and nodded. "See ya soon." Then he turned back to Magruder and Billy. "Okay, let's go."

Cody watched them trot off down the dirt road to the beach, then he sat down against the wheel of the plane, in the shade of the wing and waited.

Twenty minutes later, the trio had reached the beach and the campsite. Travis saw the little Haitian lying in the sand at the edge of the clearing, as if he were asleep ... Moving closer, he could see the red trail in the sand that Henri had left as he crawled after those who had taken Michelle, collapsing near the edge of the jungle. Billy and

Magruder covered Travis as he knelt next to Henri and gently rolled him over. The little man's arms were badly lacerated from fending off the knives. He had a stab wound in his side, and had lost a small piece of his ear. His face and head were battered from the rain of blows from the clubs. He had lost a great deal of blood, but miraculously, he was still alive. As Travis rolled him over, he came to and looked up.

"Travis, Travis," he whispered hoarsely, reaching up feebly. "Henri so sorry ... Henri try to protect Missy Michelle but they beat and stab poor Henri."

"Who? Who took her, Henri?"

"Bunch a stinkin' natives," replied Henri, trying to spit, but lacking the strength. "Henri think it was big *bokor.*" He closed his eyes for a moment, drifting on the edge of consciousness, then opened them again. "Big nasty basatard, big muscles, scary eyes ..." He faded and lay limp in his friend's arms.

Billy nodded emphatically. "That's him, Travis. That's the son of a bitch!"

Travis laid Henri down gently, then stood and looked at the others. "I'm going after her. You get Henri back to the plane and get him taken care of."

"You can't go alone!" cried Billy. "You won't have a chance."

Travis patted his M16, with a mirthless smile. "Yeah, I will. Henri's going to die if he doesn't get attention now. There's plasma, bandages, and pain killers in the kit on the plane."

"You don't even know where they've taken her!" Billy started to protest. But at that moment, just as the sun was disappearing over a horizon that darkened with the promise of storm, the drums began.

They all stood silent and still, listening to the

discordant rhythm carried faintly on the rising wind. "I do now," answered Travis. "Take him back to the plane, see to him. Come after me if you want—I won't be hard to find. Just follow the drums." Travis turned to Magruder. "This isn't your fight, Winston. Just get Henri back to the plane, that's all I ask. You can wait for us there."

Magruder paused for a moment, then looked up at Travis. "In the last twenty-four hours, watching you people, I've witnessed more honest-to-God friendship and the responsibilities that go with it than I have in my entire adult life. Travis, if I'm in this for a penny, I'm in it for a dollar. If it's all the same to you, I'll be coming along with Billy when he goes looking for you."

Travis smiled and extended his hand. "Welcome to our side, Winston." Travis threw the bolt of his weapon and looked once more at his friends. "Take good care of Henri. I'll see you soon."

"You can take it to the bank," replied Billy, as Magruder nodded.

After Travis had disappeared down the trail, they placed Henri in a blanket from the sailboat and, carrying him between them, they set out hurriedly for the plane.

The sun had set and night was falling on the jungle of Tortue. Travis ran along the darkening trail, following the turns that led toward the drums. The moon rose above him, bright and cold like quicksilver, casting soft, smoky streamers of luminescence through the canopy above. Around him, the night creatures called tentatively to one another, welcoming the darkness. Travis ran on, following the ragged, tempestuous rhythm of the drums. As he drew closer, he began to hear the voices; the high, ethereal chanting of the damned. He had been alternately running, then walking, for over an hour. He was in the center of the island, east of the table and the plane. He was close. Cautiously, he moved in.

Chapter Eleven

Michelle could hear the subdued murmur of voices around her. The light that diffused through the porous weave of the burlap told her that night was approaching.

Her hands and feet had long since lost their feeling, and fear lay like a hard, cold stone in her stomach, leaving her mouth as dry as dust and her pulse quickened. She could not shake from her mind the image of the voodoo priest and the terrible sacrifice Billy witnessed. Nonetheless, she held on, praying for deliverance, and for the safety of Travis and her friends. Suddenly there were footsteps coming toward her, and the harsh, guttural voice of Nyakang banished the stillness. Rough hands rolled her over and tore the hood from her head. Above stood half a dozen men and three women, the giant voodoo priest in the forefront. He shouted a command and the women knelt with knives in their hands. Michelle cried out as they grabbed her and sliced the bonds, cut away her shirt, then stripped her. When she thrashed and tried to twist away, one woman put a knife under her chin and drew blood, "Stay still, whore," she hissed, "or the cutting will begin early!"

While she lay naked and afraid, the women rubbed her body with a pungent-smelling oil. Though none but the women touched her, the men watched. Through the dusky gloom, she could see their eyes, filled with vicious passion—angry need.

As Michelle was being rubbed with the oil, she smelled the sweet smoke of the fire. The kindling had been torched and the hungry flames licked up around the huge logs that formed the bonfire. As the light faded completely and darkness stole in, the drums began. Soft and timorous at first, like nervous fingers, the softly insistent hypnotic rhythm crept in and closed about her, and the cold moon rose in the heavens.

Another fierce command from Nyakang brought a single woman carrying a gourd. In the gourd was a thick, bittersweet liquid the color of dried blood. They held her head and forced the contents down her throat. She gagged on its warm vileness and the excess spilled down the sides of her face, onto her chest. She choked and gasped but still they forced the remainder into her unwilling stomach.

They all drew back and watched her for a moment. She felt the effect of the drug in seconds. She began to relax, her limbs diffused with anesthesia. Mind and body succumbed, surrendering to the narcotic, and apprehension melted. The warm jungle floor felt good against her naked body. She was overcome by a sensation of detachment and weightlessness. She could see the full moon pulse above her through the trees. She was sure she could soar up into its pale luminescence if she could just spread her wings ...

Looking down at her, Nyakang nodded, and quietly they all left her to prepare for the ceremony. There was no need to guard her anymore.

As the footsteps of her captors faded into the distance, reverberating like summer thunder to her expanded senses, Michelle performed one last consciously rebellious act. She turned and retched, purging her system of as much of the foul brown liquid as she could. Then she spread her wings and flew into the moon.

As Travis desperately sought the path to the drums, their intensity began to increase. Charged now with the jagged cadence of violent promise, they fed his panic. Every part of his being screamed that time was running out.

The drums had grown louder; he was close. He forced himself to calm down. Travis realized that he had to temper his emotions with intelligence now. He had to succeed for her to survive. He moved off the path and into the jungle, creeping silently through the underbrush, moving toward the drums and the voices. He could hear the haunting, cacophonous melody, the decadent harmony, as the intensity of the voices rose and fell with the rhythm of the drums. The melody was beautifully vile—as wickedly alluring as a comely but diseased whore. It tugged at him, urging him, seducing him. It was then, before the voices consumed him, that he reached into his shirt. From around his neck he pulled a string. Tied to it was a pair of soft plastic earplugs. They had been a gift from Billy. He had given a pair to both Travis and Cody, just on the chance ... He ripped them from the string and shoved them deep into his ears. A wave of control washed over him as he was graced with silence.

Michelle awoke from her drug-induced journey to find herself tied to a bamboo platform of some sort. She was stretched out, her hands tied behind her head at one end of the table, her feet tied together at the other end. She was staring at the immense yellow moon suspended directly over her. She was sedate, but no longer as sedated as she had been. Still, the trembling cadence of the drums and the chanting voices seduced her senses, drawing her into quiet pools of lassitude. She gazed up in sweet lethargy and watched the building winds whip dark clouds across the craters of the moon.

There was a man with a knife next to her now.

Michelle's rational mind knew that she should be afraid, but the soft, satiny cocoon of indifference around her insulated her from the terror. He was bringing the knife down now, across her chest, above her right breast. As he drew the knife across pale skin, the scarlet brightness of blood and pain seared her senses, breaking the hypnotic spell, giving license to her voice, and she screamed.

Travis was close to the clearing when, even through the earplugs, he heard the high, piercing scream. It jolted him like an electric shock. *Michelle!* Rushing forward now, abandoning all caution, he quickly reached the edge of the ravine.

He looked down on the same hellish torch-lit scene that Billy had witnessed months ago. A circle of glistening, ebony bodies undulated to the ragged rhythm of the drums. The bonfire in the center rose and licked at the moon through the hole in the flame-blushed parasol above, while the giant man in the center raised his knife again over Michelle. Travis raised his gun, aimed, and pulled the trigger.

Unfortunately, the report of the M16 coincided with the thud of a rifle butt against the back of Travis's skull. He had been spotted by one of Nyakang's armed guards who were protecting the perimeter of the ceremony. The rifle stock slammed into him just a fraction of a second before he pulled the trigger, throwing his shot off. The bullet hammered the ground in front of Nyakang's feet, and everyone stopped. The drums fell silent, the dancers drew back, and Travis tumbled down the embankment into the ravine, unconscious.

After leaving Henri with Cody, Billy and Magruder took out after Travis. They were half a mile away when they heard the shot. "That's Travis's M16," yelled Billy. "I know that sound. Come on, let's go!" They trotted for the next ten minutes along the moonlit trail. Suddenly, the drums that had fallen silent began again. Billy's caution kicked in. "Okay, we're close now, so we slow down and move in real quiet." They eased off the trail and into the safety and obscurity of the jungle, but they stayed with the path as they worked their way silently toward the drums. Moments after leaving the trail, they saw the guards standing in the path, armed with rifles. When the guards started moving toward them, Billy whispered, "Wait 'til they get past us, then we'll take 'em quietly from behind." Unfortunately, they never got the chance. Magruder, just a little nervous at the prospect of fighting a man in the dark, shifted just slightly as the men came up the trail. One of them spotted him and started to bring his gun up. Winston had him covered, but froze when the moment came to pull the trigger. Just as the guard's gun leveled on Magruder, Billy's shotgun roared twice, and the two men were jerked off the trail into the brush by the impact of the rounds at close range.

Winston turned to Billy, shame coloring his face. "I ... I'm sorry. I just—"

Billy just patted him on the shoulder as they knelt there in the jungle. "It's okay, Magruder," he said as he stood up, facing him. "It happens to a lot of people the first time. I've got a gut-level feeling that before the night's over, you're gonna get another chance."

Billy was talking and hadn't noticed the third sentry as he moved quietly up the trail, pointing his weapon at the small man's back. Fortunately, Magruder, who was still kneeling at the edge of the path, spotted him. This time there was no hesitating. The man was about to kill his friend. He raised his pistol, aiming right behind Billy, and fired three shots. The guard on the moonlit trail jerked and danced as the slugs hammered him, firing a burst of his own weapon into the treetops as he fell. Billy swung around, his gun ready, to find the dead man staring at him, not fifteen feet away.

Billy looked at the Haitian, then back to Magruder. A touch of a smile played over his face. "Told you you'd get another chance."

Winston stood up and took a deep breath. He glanced once more at the dead guard, then over at Billy. "Let's get going."

"Right you are. Winston ..."

"Yeah?"

"Thanks, partner."

Magruder nodded, deadpan, and headed down the trail, but as he turned, Billy saw the moonlight play off the small, proud smile on his face.

As they headed toward the drums, Magruder grabbed the automatic rifle from the man he'd just shot.

Billy and Magruder were about to ambush the guards when Travis regained consciousness. He found himself tied to the trunk of a huge rubber tree at the edge of the clearing, perhaps thirty feet from the bonfire and the altar. His arms were pulled up above his head and his hands were tied together, bound to the tree. His feet had been left unbound, but with his hands so tightly fettered above his head, his legs were useless.

Nyakang stood beside the altar, knife in hand, eyes glistening with malignant power, blue-black body gleaming with oil and sweat. He nodded, pleased, as Travis came to and focused on the altar and Michelle.

Nyakang was no fool. He had thirty armed men in the jungle surrounding the clearing. No one succeeds at insurrection without precaution and forethought. He was not going to be surprised by a government patrol in the midst of a ceremony, and tonight was an extremely important one.

He was initiating twenty *houngans* and their most revered acolytes—the priests and priestesses of the most powerful voodoo societies in Haiti. Their followers would be his now—their power and control his to wield. The word was spreading. Soon the uprising would begin ...

Nyakang smiled malevolently at the man tied to the tree, straining at his bonds. Tonight, the gods would feed twice.

Travis put the pain in his head aside and focused on the scene in front of him. The *houngans* and their acolytes, clothed in bright-colored ceremonial robes, their dark skins oiled and shining, moved in a writhing semicircle behind the voodoo priest. He stood poised beside the altar, his knife raised just above Michelle. The giant *bokor,* smiling wickedly, put the point of the blade against Michelle's shoulder and drew it down an inch, painting another bright red line on her skin. The drums stepped up their tempo. Quietly at first, like the distant cry of a wounded animal, the dancers behind the priest began to moan. Their bodies started to sway, slowly melding with the hypnotic meter of the drums.

Panic clawed at his insides as Travis strained against the ropes that held him. But just as the *bokor's* knife began to descend again, the sound of gunfire reverberated through the jungle, startling the dancers and breaking the spell. Travis heard the solid thump of Billy's shotgun, followed by pistol shots and automatic rifle fire. His friends were coming, but they were badly outnumbered. Once again the mood of the ceremony was shattered. Nyakang's eyes hooded in anger. He pointed toward the gunfire and shouted a command. Immediately, the armed guards surrounding the clearing took out after the intruders. Nyakang swung around to the initiates. He snarled another order and pointed. They, too, followed the guards, grabbing up their machetes and ceremonial knives from their belongings at the edge of the clearing. Billy and Magruder were about to be attacked by over sixty men and women, armed with machetes to automatic rifles. Travis was concerned for them, but he had his own problems.

Nyakang stood in the clearing by the altar, flanked by his two personal bodyguards—hard, brutish-looking men wielding wickedly sharp machetes. Other than them, the clearing was empty. The fire cracked and popped in the silence of the ravine, casting flickering shadows into the surrounding jungle.

As Travis glanced about for something, some way to free himself, Nyakang looked over at him and spoke: "You waste your time struggling. Tonight your fate is here, at the edge of my blade. You and your woman will be the first of the defilers to feed my gods. You will be the first in a lineage of pain, first in the long line of retribution for three hundred years of suffering and misery. In moments, your friends will be dead. I will have you watch as I cut the life from your woman, and after I have taken her *ti bon ange*, it will be your turn." With that he reached down and ran the blade along Michelle's arm. She cried out as the point of the knife broke the skin and Travis struggled maniacally against his bonds. It was then, when his panic and fear had reached an apex, that he heard a booming baritone voice inside his head and sensed a powerful presence beside him.

"Prepare yourself, my captain," the voice said, *"your moment comes!"* Travis ceased his struggles, shocked to the point of immobility. *It's not possible*, he thought. *It must be a trick of the voodoo priest...* Yet, somehow, he knew the voice. Beyond a shadow of a doubt, he recognized that voice. Again he heard the baritone rumble, and felt the presence of Joba standing next to him. He could suddenly see, in

his mind's eye, the giant African with his enormous, corded muscles and smoldering yellow eyes. The voice spoke again: *"Now, in this life, as before, Captain, I am here with you. Long I have watched over you, as I said I would, though you were unaware. It has been my voice you have heeded without understanding, in times of danger. Your moment comes now. Remember all your weapons, Captain."* It was then that Travis felt the solid hardness of the derringer that he had stuffed in the top of his field boot before leaving the plane.

Nyakang was looking at him strangely, wondering why his prisoner had quit struggling so abruptly and seemed so preoccupied.

Travis felt the bonds at his hands tense up, as if gripped by a giant hand.

Again the voice called. *"There is no strength greater than the knowledge that you are never alone, no force stronger than your belief in the power of spirit. Where there is faith, anything is possible. Now, my captain, as you once told me in the hold of a sinking ship—pull! Pull, if you want to live!"*

Suddenly Travis felt charged with primal energy. For the first time in his life he was absolutely certain of the width and depth of spirit surrounding and protecting him, and the certainty of survival surged through him like an electric current. His muscles knotted as he bore down on the ropes that held him. His eyes shone with a bright confidence and he vibrated with a sense of power he had never before experienced.

Travis looked up at the *bokor*, not thirty feet away, and locked eyes with him. Veins bulged on the American's neck and temples; his muscles trembled and rivulets of sweat poured down his face. Finally, the rope, weakened by age and the dampness of the jungle, could no longer stand the pressure. At its weakest point, it gave, snapping like kite twine as Travis stumbled from the tree.

Nyakang and his two guards gaped in slack-jawed disbelief, shocked by the spectacle of the man suddenly breaking free of his bonds and stumbling at them. Overcome by superstitious fear, the two guards took a step backward as Travis pulled the remaining rope from his wrists.

Nyakang recovered quickly, and shoving them both forward, shouted, "Kill him! Kill him now!" The two guards hesitated just long enough for their captive to reach down and pull the derringer from his boot. They were moving forward, machetes raised, when Travis rose up and shot each of them once in the chest. Both lumbered into the dirt like charging rhinos, trembling in death throes at the *bokor's* feet.

Nyakang took a step forward and hurled his knife. Travis threw himself to the side as the knife whirled by, ricocheting off the trunk of the tree behind him and burying itself in the dirt on the far side of the clearing. As the American turned to face Nyakang, the *bokor* removed his whip from his side. He held the supple black leather rolled into a coil, the braids of the weapon shining like scales against the firelight.

"You have interrupted my plans enough tonight," hissed Nyakang. "Now, bear witness to the power of darkness." He surprised Travis by bringing the whip up and slipping it into a tall woven basket next to the altar, mumbling incomprehensible words and passing his hand over the narrow mouth of the container as he did so.

The action was confusing, but it mattered little to Travis. He took a couple of deep breaths and marshaled himself for a rush at the man, but the *bokor* just smiled and casually knocked the basket over. At first Travis thought his eyes were playing tricks on him. He blinked and wiped the sweat from his face. Slowly, from the mouth of the frond container came an enormous triangular head. Cold, malignant eyes focused on him as the reptile opened its venomous yellow mouth and hissed. In seconds it had arched itself downward and slid from its lair. The snake was as shiny black as obsidian and easily eight feet long. Its hard, rippling body was a thick as a man's arm. It moved with a terrifying sense of purpose as it reared up off the ground, its head weaving, hissing at Travis from fanged maw. The creature's head rose nearly four feet off the ground as it slithered toward its prey. Involuntarily, Travis stumbled backward against the tree as malevolence incarnate glided forward, targeting him with merciless eyes. There was a part of him that would have run pell-mell into the jungle had it not been for Michelle, tied to the bamboo altar.

Travis steeled himself as best he could and stood his ground. Searching desperately for a means to combat this hideous creature and forcing back the panic that was trying to consume him, he spotted one of the dead guard's machetes lying a few feet to the right. The snake was no more than a dozen feet away. Its head was weaving slowly, hypnotically, and its shining, desolate eyes locked on Travis. As he faced the reptile, Travis found himself transfixed by those iniquitous sable orbs. Suddenly, he felt a numbness begin to spread out from his spine. A paralysis of exquisite, irrepressible horror began to engulf him, containing him as surely as if he had been swallowed by that translucent maw. His legs weakened. In seconds, his limbs felt too heavy to lift. Those two terrible chips of obsidian were consuming him. His panicked mind shouted commands that his body refused to obey. With his will trapped like a June bug in a jar, Travis felt the threads of sanity slipping ...

The firelight danced off glistening ebony scales as the

snake reared its head and hissed with obscene delight, tensing the muscles around the poison glands at the back of its throat, preparing to squirt its venom ... But just before the reptile drew back and loosed the acid-like contagion, Joba called again.

Strong and forceful, the booming voice kicked down the doors between two worlds and slammed into Travis's consciousness with the momentum of a freight train. *"Captain! Captain! There is no magic greater than your belief in yourself, no force stronger than your own conviction. Your greatest weapon is your faith. He who made the mountains and the sea and breathed life into man is far greater than this evil charlatan and his parlor tricks! Trust in Him! Trust in yourself!"*

Suddenly he felt the touch of a huge hand on his shoulder, and with it once again came an infusion of power and energy. The floodwaters of panic receded, leaving his senses and his resolution crystal clear. The Lord that Travis prayed so little to, had provided him with the gift of faith, delivered by a soul hundreds of years departed from this earth, a soul who had returned to traverse the veiled border of the two worlds solely for the love of his captain, because some things are forever ...

An instant before the snake spat its poison, Travis tumbled to the right, rolling over and coming up on his knees with the machete in his hand. The deadly stream of spittle passed over his shoulder and splashed against the tree. The snake twisted around. It hissed viciously and began to slide forward again. As Travis started to rise, his left hand brushed his pants pocket and he felt the heavy gold coin and chain from the cave. He quickly dug it out and shoved it forward, arms length from him. He held the chain, and the coin spun slowly, the firelight reflecting off its lustrous surface. The black, triangular head paused, weaving, as it studied the reflecting coin. The snake was less than six feet away. Suddenly, Travis flipped the coin into the air above the viper. Provoked by the quick movement of the coin and the glittering chain, the snake struck upward, stretching its long, muscled body. At that moment, Travis threw himself forward and swung the machete. The blade caught the reptile a foot below its head. The creature spewed venom into the air as the blade sliced through muscle and bone, severing the head from the body. As the knife cut the viper in half, Travis's momentum carried him forward and he lost his balance. He stumbled and fell, the machete flying from his hand as he broke his fall with his arms.

The snake lay next to him, its body writhing and twisting in agony while the mouth of the severed head, with its fangs extended, snapped open and shut like a horrible five-and-dime Halloween toy.

Michelle, from atop the altar, had been able to lift her head just enough to witness the drama. As Travis pitched forward onto his hands and knees, she saw Nyakang leap toward him. The *bokor* delivered two vicious kicks to Travis's ribs, knocking the breath from him as he collapsed face first onto the earth. Nyakang quickly seized the still-twisting body of the snake and pounced on Travis. Kneeling on the prostrate man's back, he looped the reptile's body over Travis's head and drew it tight around his neck. Before Travis had time to recover, he felt the pressure of the hard-scaled body against his larynx and his throat closed. Nyakang bore down, his oiled muscles reflecting the firelight like burnished mahogany. Blood and intestines gushed from the snake's body cavity, splashing both men as the sorcerer drew back with all his strength and crushed the still flailing, twisting creature against his victim's throat. It was a scene from one of Dante's nightmares.

As Michelle watched her mate being strangled, she struggled madly with her bonds. The rawhide that held her was wet and slippery from her sweat and was giving slightly, but time was running out for Travis.

Still gasping from the pain of the kicks, Travis flailed helplessly, face down in the dirt. With the giant *bokor* kneeling on his back, pressing him into the earth while strangling him from behind, he had no leverage—there was no way to fight back. While he still had breath in him, he rocked one way, then the other, reaching behind, trying to grab some part of the man who was slowly killing him. It was no use. He could barely reach the priest's oiled leg against his back.

Michelle watched in horror as she struggled, her breath coming in small, frightened gasps. She was witnessing the murder of her lover. He was dying in front of her and still she could not squeeze her raw and bleeding wrists from the wet straps. She began to cry in frustration as she fought to free herself, moaning fervently, "Oh, Travis, no, please, God, no, no ..." As she twisted frantically one last time, she thought she felt a pair of hands on the rawhide that held her wrists. Finally the leather gave, and with one last violent wrench, she yanked her hands through the strap. She glanced back quickly, anxious to see if someone had assisted her, but there was no one there.

Travis's windpipe had been choked closed, and he was reduced to small, helpless wheezes. His ears buzzed like a summer beehive and patches of darkness floated past his eyes. He was no longer a competitor in this contest—he was a victim, soon to be a casualty. He could feel himself being lifted to his knees as Nyakang raised him up from behind, still applying pressure. His enemy was prolonging the kill, enjoying the knowledge that his quarry was only moments from death, relishing the final moments. As Travis struggled to keep breath in his empty, tortured lungs, and his vision faded, he heard the voice one more time ...

"Hold on, Captain! Breathe! Breathe! Remember, where there is breath, there is hope."

Travis fought his fading sight and dragged in one small, wracked gasp. He was no longer moving now; he was concentrating solely on drawing in the desperately needed air, refusing to give up, postponing the end. Even so, as he tried for another breath, his constricted throat refused to allow even the smallest ration of air. The light faded and a dull red haze swirled in around him.

It was at that moment he felt the arms holding him jolt, as if shocked, then slowly fall away, releasing the pressure. Travis fell forward into the dirt, gasping, trying to draw air into his agonized lungs.

Still lying on the ground, he turned and looked up at the voodoo priest. The man stood above him, his feet spread wide, his hands at his sides, a look of profound surprise in his dilated black eyes. His expression was that of a man studying some distant, utterly shocking event, some desperately appalling, incomprehensible act. He took a staggering step toward Travis, then another. Almost in slow motion, he reached around at his back and grimaced, as if trying to scratch a dreadfully painful itch, turning stiffly as he did. It was then that Travis saw the machete buried between his shoulder blades, where Michelle had driven it. She stood behind the *bokor*, her face still filled with the rage of the moment and the horror of the consequence.

Nyakang reached back and grabbed the machete by the blade, his eyes wide with pain and exertion, and slowly wrenched the knife from his body with a bone-grating twist. He looked down at Travis and painfully began to raise his hand holding the bloodied knife, pointing at Travis, his eyes registering incredulous, inconceivable disappointment. He tried to speak through blood-covered, clenched teeth, but no words came. The only product of his effort was the blossoming of a pink froth at the corners of his mouth. Nyakang stood there staring at Travis with nothing more than sheer will power, refusing to relinquish his final vestiges of life force. Then, finally, as if it was simply too much effort to maintain the arm, it dropped loosely to his side, and with a deep, gurgling sigh, he collapsed, falling forward into the evilly consecrated earth of the clearing.

As the fire in the *bokor's* eyes burned to ash, onyx-colored clouds swallowed the moon and the malevolent, wind-gorged beast on the horizon forayed forth to the drumbeat of thunder. Born in the belly of the African ocean and nurtured to deadly intensity by the warm Caribbean sea, Hurricane Allen swept across the last few miles of churning ocean and slashed its way into the eastern coast of Hispaniola.

Chapter Twelve

Travis rose slowly, pulling the snake from around his throat and casting it to the ground. Michelle helped him to his feet. Turning to her, he could see the fear and the pain in her eyes. He was, at the same time, equally aware of her courage. He reached for his lady and she melted into his arms, drawing deep, jagged breaths and trying desperately to remain calm. She had suffered the horror of this evening without breaking, but more than that, she had put the terror and the pain behind her and saved his life. As Travis drew her to him, he had never felt more pride, nor experienced more love, for anyone in his life. She was companion, lover, and friend. She was forever.

After a moment, he gently drew her away. He took off his shirt and slipped it around her. She put her hands through the sleeves and buttoned it with a grateful nod. At the edge of the clearing they found her pants and shoes—claimed by one of the acolytes. They could hear the gunfire in the distance. Billy and Magruder were under siege. Travis could hear the thump of Billy's shotgun over the chatter of small arms fire. He looked up at the wispy stratus clouds racing by the moon. The wind was switching as the full fury of the storm approached. The tops of the trees had begun to yield, drawing with the wind toward the ebony mass on the horizon.

Travis glanced from the mottled, angry sky to Michelle. "We have a couple of problems. One is time; getting back to the plane before the full force of Allen smacks us. Secondly, and more immediate, is Billy and Magruder. I've got to go back and help them. I want you to take this trail—"

"Forget it, Mr. Christian," Michelle interrupted, "I'm not leaving you. If you're going back, I'm going back."

Travis smiled, nodding, "Okay, okay, I don't feel safe letting you out of my sight anyway."

"All right. What now?"

"I'm not exactly sure," he replied, looking around the clearing. "I need to draw that pack off Billy and Magruder, break them up. I don't know what—" He spotted a five-gallon can of gasoline near the edge of the clearing, used to light the bonfire at each ceremony. He walked over and lifted the can, shaking it. It was about half full; he popped the lid and put it up to his nose. It was gas, all right. Looking around the clearing once more, an idea began to form. There were a number of bottles around the periphery of the ravine. They had held the clear, strong "clarin rum" that often accompanied voodoo ceremonies. "Michelle," he called. "Quickly, find me half a dozen empty bottles."

Michelle brought the bottles and Travis filled them while they listened to the gunfire in the distance. "Hang on, buddy, hang on, I'm coming," he whispered as he topped off the last bottle. Ripping the shirt off one of the bodyguards, Travis tore it into strips, thrusting those down the necks of the containers. Then he turned them upside down for just a second, letting the gas soak the cloth. In the process of collecting bottles, Michelle discovered his rifle near the altar. The odds were getting better. Grabbing the M16 and the bottles, they started out of the clearing, but they hadn't gone ten feet when Travis jerked to a halt. "Hold on, Michelle," he said as he turned and dashed back. A few feet from the tree where he had been tied, he bent down and picked up the gold coin and chain. Closing his fist around it, he looked over at her, and she nodded. He stuffed it in his pocket and they were off, running down the path toward the gunfire.

Billy and Magruder had reached a small opening in the jungle where the trail split in several directions. One path led toward the pine tree plain and the table. Another turned toward the ceremonial clearing, and a third led back to the beach. There was a small embankment, maybe twenty feet high, near the trail that led toward the table. At the base of the embankment a huge tree had recently been felled for firewood. The branches were mostly gone, but the solid, three-foot-wide trunk lay against the soft earth like a club dropped by a careless god. It was there that they heard the angry cries of the pack surging down the path toward them.

"Sounds like we've got company," said Billy.

"Yeah," said Magruder. "This looks like as good a place as any to greet them."

The full moon broke through the clouds for a moment and lit the clearing like daylight. Crouching behind the tree trunk, the two men had no trouble spotting their targets as they came running out of the jungle. They waited until fifteen to twenty of them reached the clearing, deciding which way to go, then they opened up. Billy's shotgun barked out four quick rounds and Magruder sprayed them with the automatic rifle he had taken from the guard. They knocked down six or seven of them before the rest recovered and took cover in the surrounding trees.

Billy and Winston had drawn first blood. That was the good news. The bad news was, the continuous fire coming from the trees had them pinned down. They couldn't reach Travis, and sooner or later, they were going to be flanked. Then it was going to get sticky. Conserving ammo and firing just enough to keep their opponents at bay, they maintained a stalemate, but once their enemy worked through the thick jungle and came up behind them, it was going to be more like checkmate.

Billy sat with his back against the tree trunk, reloading. He turned to Magruder. "Listen, Winston, I think we're gonna have to take our chances and make a dash for the trees and the jungle. If we stay here much longer, they'll circle us and nail us from both sides. Whaddaya say?"

Magruder turned to Billy, as he too leaned against the log for a moment. "What do you say I cover you, and you go for the trees? With me keeping their heads down, you'll make it. If we both just get up and run, it's likely not to go so well. We'll be easy targets."

Billy paused, looked over at Winston with new respect in his eyes. Then he shook his head. "We go together, partner, or we stay together, that's how it is."

A small satisfied smile touched Winston's lips as he listened to Billy call him partner. "Okay, we go then. You ready?"

"No time like the present—on the count of three. One. Two—"

The jungle suddenly lit up in front of them.

As they neared the gunfire, Travis and Michelle slowed their pace and moved forward cautiously, keeping to the sides of the trail. Soon they could see the muzzle flashes in the trees ahead of them. By watching the flashes for a moment or two, Travis had a good idea where the enemy was concentrated. There were two main groups, one on each side of the trail, just into the jungle. They were using the big trees next to the path as cover. Travis was close enough to hear them shouting to each other in their harsh dialect.

He turned to Michelle, handing her the Bic lighter he kept for starting the gas stove on the boat. "We're going to get as close as we can—within throwing distance. Then you're going to light these as fast as I can toss them, okay?"

"It'll be my pleasure," she whispered fiercely, taking the gun and handing him the other bottles. Silently they crept up the trail, and when they were no more than forty feet away from the Haitians, Travis motioned to stop. He watched the muzzle flashes again, to be sure, then he set two bottles down. Holding three bottles by their necks in his left hand, he passed the fourth back to Michelle with his free hand. She lit it and as the greedy blue flames crawled up the gas-soaked rag, Travis stood and threw it as hard as he could toward the trunk of the tree that protected the men ahead. Without waiting for results, he handed back another, and Michelle quickly lit it. He threw another at the tree on the other side of the path.

The first bottle struck solidly and exploded in a blue-yellow fireball, covering the men next to the tree with its flaming contents. The second was equally effective, bursting into a searing, yellow flash, spraying liquid fire on all who crouched around the tree trunk. In seconds there was complete pandemonium. Three men who had received the brunt of the flaming bombs had become human torches, screaming and careening through the jungle as the fire ate clothing away and melted flesh. Several others, on the periphery of the explosions, danced around as the burning liquid devoured their hair and clothes. Travis quickly threw two more flaming bottles, and better than a dozen members of Haiti's newest voodoo society discovered their own little hell on earth. Flames ran down the trunks of the trees, licking branches, devouring leaves, lighting the clearing with a hellish glow.

Some of the acolytes panicked and ran into the clearing to escape the terrible fire. Billy and Winston quickly put an end to their panic. Michelle brought up the rifle and ripped off a half-dozen shots, discouraging any retreat back down the trail.

As the survivors melted into the jungle to recover and regroup, Travis, still holding the last Molotov cocktail, moved to the edge of the clearing and shouted, "Billy! Magruder! Where are you?"

"Over here!" Billy shouted as he rose up from behind the log, followed by Winston.

Travis turned back up the trail to get his lady and suddenly froze in disbelief—Nyakang lurched from the jungle behind her, machete in hand. The voodoo priest's chin and chest were covered with blood—a rich pink froth still covered his mouth and his eyes burned with a dull, unnatural light. He staggered mechanically toward her, machete raised, his countenance frozen in a macabre grimace. Michelle saw the look on Travis' face and turned. Completely unnerved, she screamed and stumbled backward as Nyakang's first swing barely missed her throat. She fell to the ground shuffling away as the priest, in faltering movements, gathered himself for a second strike. Michelle still held the rifle, but up to the moment she had been occupied with survival. Travis was too far away for a rush, so he did the only thing he could—he drew back and threw the bottle of gasoline. Nyakang raised up just as the bottle struck him solidly in the head, shattering, gashing his forehead and dousing him thoroughly with fuel. The diversion bought Michelle the moment she needed. She brought the gun up, pointed at the *bokor's* chest and fired three times before an ejecting shell jammed in the breech. Nyakang staggered backward from the impact but didn't go down. He stood there, weaving, staring at her with eyes that no longer belonged to this world. As he took a faltering step forward, Michelle reached into her pocket and pulled out the Bic lighter. Striking it, she touched it to the gasoline-dampened ground at the sorcerer's feet and scampered backward. The blue-yellow flames instantly licked across the earth and crept up the priest's leg. He gazed down, confused, almost fascinated, as the fire swept up his torso and finally those lost eyes registered terror as the flames engulfed him.

Travis had rushed to Michelle and was helping her away when a moan deep inside the *bokor* rose to a wail and he stumbled blindly at them, arms waving, the fire peeling his skin in strips, igniting his hair and searing his eyes. Enveloped by smoke, Nyakang collapsed to his knees and his arms dropped as the flames ate away at him. Gradually he folded, crumpling into a fetal position like a giant, grotesque doll, his flesh splitting and cracking as the inferno consumed him.

With a final look at the *bokor*, Travis and Michelle ran for the tree trunk while Magruder and Billy covered them. They made it to the log without incident, the main body of their assailants having fallen back, momentarily stunned. Injured and enraged, their pursuers were reorganizing. Travis and his companions had killed or wounded nearly twenty of them, but there were still over thirty out there—thirty creatures in that dark jungle whose covenant demanded revenge.

As they crouched behind the log, Billy turned to Travis. "We gotta get out of here, buddy. Dollars to donuts, they're not done with us, and I don't know about you, but I'm just about out of ammo."

Travis checked the clip in his rifle. He had less than twenty rounds. "Yeah, I see your point. Listen, the trail over there heads toward the table. If we push it, it's only fifteen minutes from there to the plane. If we can stay ahead of them, we've got a chance." Travis glanced around at them. Everyone nodded in agreement. "Okay, everybody, let's go."

Just as they stood up, two of Nyakang's guards burst out of the jungle behind them. The men had been quietly flanking them for the last few minutes. Magruder saw the gunmen first, having turned in that direction as he rose. The Haitians were already bringing their weapons to bear on the others. Winston shouted a warning but he knew it was too late. He threw himself against Travis and Michelle, knocking them aside. At the same time, he opened up on the two assailants, emptying his automatic rifle. Behind him, he heard Billy's shotgun bark, and the two men were jerked back into the jungle from the impact.

For a moment, no one moved in the smoky silence of the moonlit clearing. Travis rose slowly, helping Michelle to her feet. Travis reached for Winston's shoulder from behind, clasping it. "Thanks, Magruder, I may have to give you a bonus now."

"Don't think so," whispered Magruder, as he turned slowly around.

The first thing that Travis saw was the stricken look on his friend's face, then he looked down and saw the bright red patch spreading across Magruder's stomach, where the single round from the AK-47 had struck him. The bullet had torn through his large intestine, causing massive hemorrhaging. It had perforated his kidney as well, before lodging in the thick muscles of his lower back. Travis caught him as he collapsed, turning him gently and propping him up against the fallen tree.

Winston managed a wan smile as he looked at the

worried faces around him. "It's just a scratch," he whispered. "I'll be all right—in another lifetime." He shook his head. "Jesus, I'm starting to sound like you people." At that moment, they heard the angry cries of the minions a short distance into the jungle. Their leaders had worked them into a frenzy and they were coming again.

Winston leaned back and pulled the .38 caliber revolver from his belt, laying it on his lap. Then he looked up at Travis. "Get out of here, all of you. Get going! I can hold them for a while, give you a head start, otherwise you're all dead."

"Can't leave you, buddy," said Billy, kneeling next to him.

"Hell you can't!" rasped Winston. "You listen to me, and you listen good. I've never had anything I believed in, not in my whole goddamned life." He paused and grabbed Billy's arm as he was racked with a spasm of pain. Taking a breath, then expelling it slowly, he looked around at them all. "Everything, everybody let me down. I thought faith and friendship were just so much bullshit. But you people, you showed me that it was out there all the time. I discovered that the trick in having, is in giving ... I watched you people and I learned ..." He took Billy's arm again. "Are you really my friend?"

Billy paused for a moment and looked at him, then spoke softly. "Yeah, Winston, I am—you can take that to the bank."

"Then don't take this away from me!" Winston gasped. "You know damned well I'm not going to see Miami Beach again. I never made a difference to anybody my whole life. I don't want to die on some dark jungle trail, being dragged along like so much baggage. I'm gonna check out. I know it, and you know it. Now go, all of you, and let me do it with some honor. Let me make a difference, just this one time."

The creatures in the jungle had begun to howl now, like a pack of animals sensing their prey. They were nearing the edge of the clearing.

Magruder looked at them all one more time. "Go! Now, damnit. Please."

Billy put his hand on Magruder's shoulder, their eyes met and held, and at that moment, Mr. Winston Magruder entered the life circle of his new friends. In that eternal instant, the silken cords that would bind their spiritual destinies were intertwined.

Travis and Michelle knelt beside him. "This isn't the end of the show," Travis whispered. "It's only intermission. I'm somehow very certain I'll be seeing you again, my friend."

Magruder forced a smile. "Yeah, now go, or you'll be seeing me sooner than you'd like." Then he took his gun and painfully turned himself around to face the oncoming horde.

With one last glance, the others, like sad, reluctant shadows, slipped into the jungle and down the path toward the table.

Winston Magruder, a man who had been vastly disappointed with promises and people this lifetime, finally found friendship and faith at the end of his journey.

As he watched the night wraiths creep from the jungle's edge, Winston was amazed to find that he wasn't afraid. He felt at peace—he seemed quietly secure in a soft cocoon of knowledge that he was part of something more than the simple coming and going of a single soul, the winking of a lone star in a confused cosmos. He had sifted through the muck of man's myopic self-esteem, greed, and selfishness in this lifetime, and finally, at the end, he had found a bright gleaming gem of faith and friendship, and the promise of ever after in the circle that is life.

Magruder fired the pistol rhythmically, pacing his shots, holding them back as long as he could. He fired until the hammer clicked on empty cartridges. As the tide of glistening, moonlit bodies overwhelmed him and he passed from this world toward the next, his last earthbound thought was, *Godspeed, friends.*

Chapter Thirteen

Gusts of wind lashed the tops of the trees, whisking sheets of charcoal clouds across a lightning-scarred sky. The smell of approaching rain lay heavy in the air. They ran hard, as fast as was safe along the dark jungle trail that would take them to the pine tree plain. They listened to the steady reports of Magruder's pistols, and each had been wrenched by the devastating knowledge and the stone cold fear the silenced guns brought.

The wind at their backs carried the cries of their pursuers. Those angry voices promised no negotiations, no compromise. Only survival or death lay in the darkness ahead.

In minutes, they had worked their way through the narrow strip of jungle to the pine tree plain. It was a straight run across the plain to another small stretch of jungle. Once through that, they would reach the clearing in front of the twin hills. Even with the moonlight as fleeting as it was, the course was clear. At question was their ability to stay ahead of thirty rage-filled fanatics wielding machetes and rifles. By the time they entered the plain, the pack was less than two hundred yards behind them. Travis realized at the rate their pursuers were gaining, his people wouldn't even make it out of the next stretch of jungle.

The plain was dotted with stands of trees. The course to the trail on the far side led them by a dense stand near the middle of the plain. Breath was coming in ragged gasps for all of them now, especially Michelle. They had to slow down and allow their oxygen-depleted bodies to recoup. Travis decided to delay the mob behind them. It was their only chance.

As they neared the trees Travis had selected, he called to Billy and Michelle. "You keep going. Don't stop 'til you're back in the jungle on the far side." He patted the carbine he carried. "I'm going to hold them here for a while."

"No!" cried Michelle as she stopped and turned toward him. "You can't stay! No, Travis, don't do this. Please!"

He grabbed her by the arms and spoke quickly, intensely. "Michelle, trust me! I'm not staying here. I'm going to shoot them as they cross the open plain behind us. I'm going to force them to stop and take cover, to give you a chance to reach the jungle and catch your breath. Once I've pinned them down and you're safely to the edge of the plain, I'm on my way to you. Understand, I have no desire to die in this stand of trees. I'll be right behind you. Now go!"

Billy took her arm. Reluctantly, she turned and together they ran.

Travis settled in behind a tree at the edge of the stand, sighted down his carbine, and waited for the runners to clear the woods. He only had a handful of bullets left, so he aimed carefully as the first of them entered the flat ground of the plain. He fired four times. Three men fell and a fourth stumbled back into the dark foliage. He could hear them yelling, cursing him from the safety of the jungle, working themselves up. A few minutes later, half a dozen more charged out, shouting and screaming. These men, having learned from the first casualties, scrambled across the hundred yards between them and Travis in a broken pattern, making it difficult to hit them. Those with guns fired sporadically at him as they ran. He used over a dozen rounds getting five of them. The sixth had almost made the distance. He was less than fifty feet away when Travis sighted him and pulled the trigger. Nothing happened. Reflexively, he pulled again. Still nothing—the magazine was empty.

The big Haitian had truly expected to be shot like his companions. When he saw Travis pull the trigger and nothing happened, he bellowed triumphantly and charged—his machete held high. Travis came out from behind the tree and turned the gun around in his hands, like a club. He stood up straight and waited for the charging man, not moving, inviting him. The fellow came on like a knife-wielding locomotive, swinging the machete at Travis's head. Just as the man swung, Travis dropped down and to the side. Swinging the gun like a baseball bat, he slammed his antagonist in the knees so hard that both the man's legs snapped cleanly at the joints. The Haitian yowled in anger and pain as he pitched forward, throwing his arms out to break his fall. The machete flew from his grasp and slapped the ground a few feet from him. Ignoring the pain, the Haitian immediately rose and began crawling toward his knife, dragging his broken legs. Travis jumped to his feet and clubbed the man into the dirt once more. Standing over him, chest heaving, Travis looked up to see the rest of the pack streaming out of the dark trees like silent, vengeful shadows. He dropped the empty gun and ran.

As he neared the jungle on the far side, he waved Billy and Michelle on. Having watched from the mouth of the trail, they turned and ran again. Reduced now to Billy's shotgun and the three or four shells he had left, they knew their only chance of survival lay in speed. They had to stay ahead.

Ten more minutes into their flight left them with the realization that their chances of survival were narrowing.

They were all exhausted, nearing collapse. In the wind-protected silence of the jungle, they drew loud desperate gasps of air into their burning lungs. They no longer ran—they had been reduced to a controlled stumble. Michelle hadn't said a word, but each step had become agony. Brave as she was, the pain, fear, and exhaustion were taking their toll. Travis could see that she was fading. He glanced at her, watching her struggle courageously. Her dark hair was sweat-matted and tangled. Her pants and the shirt were lacerated, her face scratched and bleeding.

He was again struck by the width and depth of his love. He was suddenly consumed with the importance of her survival. Somehow, he had to see her through this, no matter what it took. He reached for her, gently taking her arm, and together they staggered on.

Four men armed with rifles had broken from the pack as they reached the pine tree plain. The men had taken a narrow, seldom used shortcut that ran diagonally through the jungle and intersected the path that Travis and his companions were on, just before it reached the clearing by the twin hills. Two of the men had pulled ahead of the other pair and they burst onto the main trail, not thirty yards in front of Billy, who was slightly ahead of Travis and Michelle. Billy was blessed with the hard lean body and the strong lungs of a runner, and he had fared better than his companions. He also had superb reflexes. The two big men stumbled out into the center of the trail and looked around. By the time they saw Billy running at them and they began to raise their guns, Billy was already pulling the trigger of his shotgun, firing from the hip as he moved forward. The two men danced backward, lurching like violent puppets, as Billy emptied his gun at them. When the last shell ejected and the firing pin clicked on empty, the other two, who had arrived in time to witness Billy use the last of his ammunition, stepped out onto the trail. Travis and Michelle had come up from behind and were standing next to their friend. They could hear the shouts and cries from those behind them, as the two men in front of them smiled and raised their guns.

Exhausted physically and emotionally, drained of breath and spirit, the three of them, who had struggled so hard, held so tenaciously to life, finally succumbed to odds and fate. Billy sighed, resigned but angry, and looked the men in the eye as they prepared to kill him. Travis, sad beyond belief that the end was here and now, reached over and drew Michelle to him, turning his back to the men as he protected her body with his own. It was a futile gesture, but it was all he had left. There were no more tricks, no more reprieves; this was the end.

"I love you," he whispered. "I always will." But before Michelle could answer, the guns roared.

Travis flinched, anticipating the brutal impact of the bullets, but when the shooting stopped a second later, he was still standing. Glancing over to Billy, he saw that his friend was smiling. Releasing Michelle and swinging around, he saw the two guards lying dead in the trail, beside the other two that Billy had killed. Cody stepped from the jungle, holding his Thompson machine gun in his good arm. With one arm in a sling and a bandage wrapped around his head, all he needed was a piccolo player and a drummer. Travis had never seen a prettier sight.

Cody came forward and stopped in front of his friend. "Heard the shooting."

Travis smiled. "Yeah, thanks buddy."

Cody looked around. "Magruder?"

Travis shook his head. "He bought us the time we

needed to make it this far."

Cody nodded solemnly.

The cries behind them grew louder, and Cody motioned with his head. "Get going. I'll delay them for a moment or two, then I'll be right behind you." The others trotted off. The man with the long blond hair and the Custer mustache settled in behind a tree and waited. No more than a minute later he opened up on the first of the group as they rounded the corner in the trail, about sixty yards back. Cody kept their pursuers pinned down for a couple of minutes, letting the others reach the clearing at the base of the twin hills. Then he raced after them. Travis and the others were halfway up the slope to the pass when Cody reached them.

There was a low, intense wail to the wind as it whipped at their clothes and pulled at their hair. The full fury of the storm was only minutes away.

Many of the *houngans* and their followers had given up the chase, working their way back toward the site of the ceremony. They were sorcerers, not soldiers, and the price had become too high. The pursuers who had reached the edge of the jungle below consisted mostly of Nyakang's guards and a few hardcore acolytes. They were not to be denied their quarry. They all knew Nyakang did not accept failure well.

Bullets began to kick up the ground around Travis and his people as they climbed the hill. Cody turned and sprayed the jungle with his Thompson, giving his friends covering fire until they reached the pass, then dashed after them. As the revenge-bent horde started out of the foliage and up the slope, Cody turned and forced them back with another burst from his gun, then scampered the last few feet to the protection that the crest of the hill offered before it leveled into the pass.

He looked over his shoulder, down the hill to the plane that waited below on the strip, then turned to the others who knelt next to him. "Get out of here, all of you! Travis, Billy, get the engines started."

The moon broke free of the wind-surged clouds again and cast an ashen glow across the hills. In the pale light, Travis could see the look on Cody's face, and it told him what his friend intended to do.

"Get down to the plane! Now!" Cody shouted over the building wind. "Get it started and get out of here!" Again he looked at his friends, who hadn't moved. "We can't all go," he said in quiet exasperation. "By the time we taxi down, turn around and roll out, they'll be up and over this hill and all over the plane. They'll stand in front of us and shoot the props off. Then we're all dead."

Travis knelt there for a moment and stared at his friend, the strangest of looks on his face. He took a deep breath and glanced up at the somber windswept sky, then down at the jungle below. There were tears in his eyes— and anger—when he sat down heavily with his back against the granite wall and looked around at his companions. "Son-of-a-bitch! Somehow I just knew it was going to come to this. I guess I knew all along." For the first time that Cody could remember, he saw fear in his friend's eyes.

But along with the trepidation there was a resignation and acceptance. Travis tried to smile, but there was a touch of sadness in the corners of his mouth. "No, damnit. You're not going to stay—I am. It's the way it has to be." He had reached the chasm of his fears and stepped across it—he had come face to face with the demon that had tormented him and accepted the consequence. Travis had come to realize that the price in this cosmic process of spiritual evolution is experience.

There was no way around it, and no way over it. If someone had to buy the tickets for a safe journey home, this time, it was going to be him, alone. "Give me your gun, Cody. Take Michelle and get her out of here. Everybody! Get down to the plane now!"

Michelle's features changed from alarm to panic as realization dawned on her. "No, no!" she yelled. Then rising, she cried out, "No, Travis! You can't! Please, dear God ... Travis, don't do this! Please don't do this to me. I can't lose you again!" She came to him, throwing herself into his arms, clinging to him, tears flooding her eyes and running down her cheeks.

He drew her to him again and kissed her tears. Pulling her close he whispered, "I love you more this time than the last, Michelle, and I will love you even more the next. I'll find you again, I promise."

As he drew away, he reached into his pocket, pulling out the coin of the brotherhood. She knelt there, her trembling hands clenched at her sides, trying to be brave, trying desperately to understand. "Please Travis, don't ... don't do this ..."

He took her hand, put the coin and the chain in it, and closed her fingers around it. "Hold it for me until next time, my love," he whispered as he kissed her gently, one last time.

"Travis, you don't have to do this!" Cody shouted over the wind, suddenly terrified for his friend.

"Yes, I do," Travis shouted back fiercely. "I understand now, and it's okay. I want you all to go—to live."

At that moment, the Haitians below moved silently out of the jungle en masse and a handful of bullets ricocheted off the granite walls, forcing them all down behind the ridge. Before Cody could respond, Travis reached over and snatched the Thompson from his partner. He swung around to the crest, forcing them back with a burst. Then he turned to Cody again, and extended his hand, "Good luck."

Cody tried to speak but there were no words that could satisfy the emotions raging in him. He knelt, holding his friend's hand, not wanting to let it go. Knowing that when he did, he was releasing it for the last time.

Travis pulled his hand free, and turned to Billy. "Take them home, buddy. I'm counting on you." He gazed at them all for just a moment longer then turned around and went back to work with his gun, keeping the enemy pinned down.

Cody laid the last magazine of ammo next to him. He reached down and touched his friend's shoulder once more as he rose. Michelle was becoming hysterical trying to reach Travis as Billy held her. Cody grabbed her by the wrist, threw her over his shoulder, and the three of them raced down the hillside to the plane. Billy hopped up into the open cargo door, helped Michelle up and got her to a seat near the cockpit. Cody turned for one last glance at Travis at the crest of the pass, then climbed aboard. He took a quick look at Henri, who lay propped up against the inside of the plane, while Billy raced through the start-up procedures. In seconds the starboard engine roared to life. Moments later the port engine fired and the plane vibrated with the drone of the big propellers.

Thanks to plasma and painkillers, Henri was doing all right. He looked like he'd lost a fight with a giant Veg-a-matic, but he was conscious and he was talking—which was a good sign for Henri. As the engines warmed, Cody went up to check on Michelle. It was then that he saw the two swords, lying side by side on the floor of the airplane.

He paused as he spotted them, and Michelle, who was watching, saw the look come over him as he knelt and touched the blades. They could hear Travis firing sporadically. It was heating up for him on the slope. Cody ran his hand across the bright steel of the sword on the floor in front of him. Then, almost involuntarily, turned toward the direction of the hill. Suddenly, with a sigh, he picked up Billy's shotgun and the last dozen shells in the box next to it. He looked at Michelle. She began to cry again.

Cody knelt by her. "He's almost out of ammo up there. He's the bravest man I've ever known, but I don't think he can hold them. Together, we can. He's got nothing left to prove to himself or anyone else. He's my friend. I just can't let him go this alone."

"Do you want me to tell you that it's okay to go die?" she shouted bitterly through her tears. "Is that what you want? Well, I can't. I've lost all I can stand to lose tonight."

Billy swung around in the pilot's seat and watched what was transpiring, but he had his hands full checking instruments and holding the brakes as he revved the big engines. Cody looked across to his friend and, as their eyes met, he smiled sadly and nodded. Billy touched his temple in a final salute. Cody returned the gesture. He paused for a final moment and ran his hand down Michelle's cheek, erasing a tear, then stood and turned toward the cargo doors. As he moved across the cabin, he once again saw the swords. Picking them up, Cody stuck the weapons in his belt. With a final salute to Henri, there on the floor, and a quick touch of his fingers to his lips for Michelle, he turned and jumped out of the cargo door.

The backwash from the props and the gusts from the storm tore at him as he watched the plane turn and taxi down the strip. Michelle stared at him through tear-blurred eyes from the cargo door. She held onto a strap with one hand, the other hung at her side. She couldn't bring herself to wave, to say goodbye again. She simply watched as Cody stood there for a moment in the wind-torn moonlight, then turned for the hills.

Travis lay at the crest of the pass, sighting down the barrel of his Thompson and firing steadily. He was into the last magazine. The remainder of the *bokor's* minions could hear the plane taxiing, and, howling madly, they began moving out of the jungle, preparing to rush the pass. As the Haitians below charged, the wallop of a shotgun suddenly shattered the night and Cody dropped down beside his friend in the dirt of the pass.

Below and behind them, the plane turned at the threshold of the strip. Billy threw the throttles full open and it lumbered forward. As Cody and Travis fired with deadly accuracy, forcing the enemy back, Travis spoke over his shoulder. "Why?"

Cody ejected another smoking shell. "You already know the answer to that—'cause you couldn't have left me here either."

Travis smiled to himself and fired another burst, knowing that his friend was right. He was saddened somewhat by the consequences of his buddy's choice, yet satisfied to know that the bonds of any friendship could run as deep as theirs. It wasn't really selfish of him, for he knew full well that the decision to return would have been the only possible choice for either of them. As strange as it might seem, and as much as it goes against man's nature to cling to life, there are times that we simply find something worth dying for. In a cosmos full of deception, larceny, and counterfeit emotion, they had each found someone to believe in, and they couldn't let that person die alone. For them, that was reason enough.

Bullets slapped the ground around them and ricocheted off the rock walls of the pass, as the horde below made one last concentrated effort. Travis and Cody fired as fast as they could, no longer conserving ammunition. The plane was running down the strip, taking off.

The big Beechcraft rocked and shuddered as the hurricane's winds tore at it, trying to push it off the small gravel strip. Billy fought the controls and jammed the right rudder down, doing his best to keep her on the runway. Billy had the throttles rammed to the firewall, desperate for enough speed to get him in the air and out of the grasp of the terrible surface winds. Finally, as she broke free of the earth, Billy threw the gear up, put her nose into the wind, and began to climb out. The plane bounced and lurched as the fierce gusts clawed and shook her, but she was a strong lady, and those powerful engines gradually forced her up and away from the deadly surface winds.

As the aircraft roared into the air behind them, the two men in the pass fired until their weapons were empty. The plane soared into the moonlit cloud cover and in seconds was lost to sight.

Suddenly, everything was still but the wind. The handful of acolytes and the few guards left below were aware of two things: The plane and its occupants were gone, there was no more vengeance to be had there. But the men on the hill—those they would have. For them, there was no escape. Silently, slowly, the creatures below began to come forward, out of the jungle. When there was no longer any resistance, no more gunfire from the pass, they became bolder, spreading out in a grim phalanx as they scaled the slope.

The last sounds of the plane's engine were just fading in the wind when Cody lay his shotgun down and pulled one of the swords from his belt with his good arm. He turned to Travis, lying next to him. "This is yours," he said as he handed him his cutlass.

Travis tossed the Thompson aside and grasped the hilt of the sword, smiling grimly. "You're damned right it is."

Cody drew his sword, and together they stood to face the enemy coming up the slope. As they waited in the pass, one of the guards below them brought his weapon up, but the *houngan* next to him pushed the barrel down with his hand, shaking his head at the man. The *houngan* drew his long knife. The guard smiled and pulled his machete from his belt. These men were to pay slowly, painfully; they were not to receive the gift of a bullet.

Exhausted, bloodied, and battered, the two men turned to each other one last time. The wind whipped at their clothing and the night moon cast furtive glances from behind the racing clouds, its cold brightness glinting off the steel in their hands. Travis said. "Until we meet again, my friend."

"Sure as the moon rises and the sun sets," whispered Cody.

With a final nod, they turned to the business at hand—dying as well as they could.

The first of the acolytes to reach them paid dearly for their eagerness, for it was as if 300 years fell away in an instant. Bright steel swished in flashing arcs as the pair cut and slashed their enemy in silent determination. In some unexplained alchemy of identity, space and time, the past and present suddenly blended—spirit and soul fused. At the first slash of a cutlass, a nova of remembrance exploded within them, sweeping them up and carrying

206

them back across eons of time and memory. They were no longer modern men tied to the mores and codes of the 20th century, they were buccaneers, brothers of the sword, as in their hearts they had always been.

In the final moments, they stood together, swords in hand, as they had three centuries ago, holding the pass. The end had come.

As the majority of their attackers were just reaching them, they heard the drone of the Beechcraft's engines again, over the storm. A quarter-mile away, the plane broke out of the heavy, rain filled clouds and roared down at them. Everything stopped for a second as both assailants and defenders watched the oncoming aircraft. One or two of the guards on the slope fired a few rounds as the aircraft zoomed overhead, not two hundred feet above them. At the moment it passed overhead, Travis saw a box kicked out of the cargo door. End over end, it tumbled lazily out of the sky, toward the pass and the slope in front of them. It was halfway down, rolling in slow motion free-fall, when Travis recognized what it was. With a cry, he slammed into Cody like a linebacker tackling a stationary quarterback, knocking him over the backside of the crest, covering him with his own body.

The box of C-4 explosive, crammed full with detonators, struck squarely in the center of the slope, amid the majority of the attackers. A monstrous orange fireball erupted with a deafening roar, instantly incinerating better than three-quarters of the people in the pass and on the slope. Those few who were near the base of the slope and survived the explosion suffered massive concussions. With bleeding ears and noses, shocked senseless and beaten, they stumbled back into the safety of the jungle.

Travis and Cody, lying on the other side of the pass,

were insulated from the majority of the blast, and each suffered only a mild concussion. As they stood shakily, they turned to see Billy doing the impossible—landing the Beech once more, in the midst of near hurricane winds. They held their breath and watched the plane being tossed like a child's paper glider, abruptly rising and falling thirty feet at a time as the savage wind slapped and grabbed it. Inside the cockpit, Billy struggled to hold her steady enough to get the wheels down on the runway one last time.

She hit the strip hard, bounced up, and a gust of wind caught the starboard wing. Travis cried out as the other wing tip grated the gravel runway and it looked like she was going over. Slamming ailerons down and standing on the opposite rudder, Billy somehow managed to bring her back down straight and level once more, and this time the plane stayed on the strip.

Travis and Cody were already bounding down the hill before Billy even hit the brakes. Moments later, as they were being pulled through the cargo door by a jubilant Michelle, Billy pushed the throttles forward. There was no time to turn around and taxi back, the hurricane was on them. Billy took a quick look at the runway he had left. He figured with this kind of wind coming at him, he still had enough strip to get out. Clothes drenched, sweat beading off him, Billy fought the controls and the wind while praying for one more impossible takeoff. They lurched forward, bouncing and skidding down the strip. The wings shuddered and flexed, looking as if at any second they would rip from the shaking fuselage and fly away on their own. The big engines whined as Billy forced every ounce of horsepower out of them. They were being buffeted so badly that everything in the plane was shaking. The wind shrieked through the open cargo door, grabbing and snapping at the canvas and the cargo nets that held the treasure down. As Billy desperately tried to gain enough speed for takeoff, two things soon became frighteningly apparent: First, the end of the strip was coming up way too fast. If they didn't become airborne in the next twenty seconds, they were going to become a permanent part of the low rise of mangroves at the north end of the runway. Secondly, and imminently more important, he was losing control of the aircraft. The plane was beginning to skid sideways toward the edge of the runway. No amount of rudder or aileron was any longer counteracting the fierce winds. It was as if a giant hand were nudging them off the airstrip into the mangroves. At this speed, with the tenuously held cargo, as soon as they hit the mangroves, everything was going to come apart like a shattered gumball machine. Billy struggled tenaciously against his diminishing control, applying all of his skill, every piece of knowledge he had, whispering harshly under his breath, "Come on, baby, come on!" Ten seconds lapsed ... fifteen ... he could hear Travis shouting in the back of his mind somewhere that the plane was sliding off the strip. Michelle screamed. There was no more runway.

In a reflex action he yanked the controls back into his solar plexus, waiting for the impact as the plane plowed into the marshlands and everything came apart at the seams.

The very second that Billy drew back on the controls, a huge gust struck the plane head on. The rush of wind lifted the plane up for a moment, just long enough for momentum and control surfaces to do their jobs. There was that almost imperceptible click of weightlessness as the wheels left the ground and the plane became airborne. Almost hesitantly, the plane began its labored ascent into the turbulent night. The cries of alarm became shouts of elation behind Billy as he raised the gear and battled his way up toward the clear western sky.

Up to this point, there had been no time for anyone to get to the seats of the plane. They had all stood in frozen fascination, holding straps and nets while they watched Billy perform aviation magic, pulling rabbits out of hats that they were certain were empty. As the plane continued to lumber upward, Travis got Michelle and Cody to their seats. Cody, his swollen arm in the makeshift sling, and head wound bleeding again, gratefully collapsed into the copilot's seat. Michelle took the seat behind him. Travis went back to check on Henri, and to close the cargo door if possible.

Kneeling by Henri, he looked down at the small man, bandaged like a poorly wrapped mummy, his trusty sax next to him, "How you doing, buddy?"

Henri looked up and somehow managed a bit of a buck-toothed smile. "Henri feel like he been run over by a stinkin' bus, mon." Then painfully, he reached over and touched Travis's knee. "But it okay 'cause Henri goin' to U.S. of A."

Travis smiled, fierce emotion welling up in him. "You're damned right you are, Henri. You're gonna be a U.S.A. citizen."

Henri grinned again, satisfied, then lay back against the side of the plane and closed his eyes.

Travis got up and moved to the cargo door. The brilliant moon hung like a pendant in the sky. High, dark clouds whipped across its scarred face. Below him, the Isle of Tortuga was slipping away, being swallowed by the full force of Hurricane Allen.

As Travis stared down at the receding island, caught for a moment in the kaleidoscope events of the past few days, he suddenly felt Joba's powerful presence again. The words came clearly to him in the rich baritone of his devoted friend. *"As it is your destiny to sail this course, it is my path to guide and protect you. Remember, I am here, as I have always been. Some things cannot be changed by time and space. But take heed, all your trials are not yet over. Until we meet again, my captain, as we most surely will."*

Travis smiled sadly and whispered into the wind, "God bless you, my friend, until we meet again."

Chapter Fourteen

With one last look at the island, Travis took a deep breath and slowly exhaled. It was over—they were going home.

He moved carefully across to the far side of the wind-swept opening, to the handle on the sliding door. He had just grasped the handle, when from the corner of his eye, he saw a movement at the back of the plane. He turned as one of the canvas tarps covering the treasure moved. Suddenly, it was tossed back, and out from underneath it emerged an enormous albino in a camouflaged uniform. Colonel Juele glared at Travis as he crouched, pulling his pistol from his holster.

As Juele had trekked through the jungle toward the plane, he planned a revenge that would provide him possession of the treasure as well. The Colonel reached the aircraft while the others were still dealing with Cody's crash. He crept aboard the plane and hid under the tarp. He would let them fly to their clandestine strip in the States. Meanwhile he would kill all but the pilot along the way, dumping their bodies in the ocean. When they landed, he would kill the pilot and hide the treasure. With the wealth of several lifetimes secured, he would seek political asylum. It was the perfect coup.

Travis turned for a rush, but Juele's gun was already out and aiming at his chest. "Don't," the big man growled. There wasn't quite enough headroom for the two men to stand totally erect, so they crouched, glaring at each other.

"Back," Juele growled again, "or I shoot you now. I don't care."

Cody and Michelle had swung around in their seats, watching the drama, unable to help. Juele kept his gun on Travis as he urged him toward the front of the plane. As the Colonel walked forward, he moved by Henri, paying little attention to the wounded Haitian. No sooner had he passed Henri, than the little man struggled to his knees and swung his trusty saxophone at the back of the Colonel's legs. There was a resounding crack as the sax struck the side of Juele's knees and he cried out in pain. He swung around, his face contorted with rage, and fired point blank into the Haitian. The impact of the bullet slammed Henri against the inside fuselage, and he slid to the floor, unmoving. Before Juele could bring the gun back around, Cody rammed the control yoke forward with his good hand, forcing the plane into a sudden dive. Juele lost his balance and was thrown backward, then forward, almost into Travis's arms. Travis grabbed the wrist that held the gun. The two men struggled, and the weapon exploded twice, punching holes in the ceiling of the plane. While Billy leveled the aircraft, Cody quickly snapped open the survival kit attached to his seat. He pulled out a flare gun and yelled to his partner. Travis, seeing the flare gun, understood immediately. He attempted to force the big man back toward the cargo door. The colonel, sensing the direction, began resisting and pushing forward. Suddenly Travis sidestepped him and spun him around, turning the man's back toward the cockpit. Cody aimed and fired. The flare struck Juele in the center of his spine. The man grunted as the projectile drove itself into his flesh. As it ignited into white-hot phosphorus, he screamed, clawing at his back. Flailing around, he released his grip on Travis, who took a step back and front-kicked him in the chest. Colonel Juele stumbled backward, out of the open cargo door, his eyes wide in terror, and made one last desperate grab for the side of the plane. His large fingers grasped the door and for a split second, he stood suspended, half in and half out of the opening. But inertia and wind were against him. As they ripped him loose, he screamed one last time and disappeared.

Billy held the aircraft straight and level and the other three scrambled to Henri's side. Fearing the worst, knowing as badly injured as Henri was, he couldn't survive the additional shock of a gunshot wound, they gathered around the brave young man. Travis lifted his head. Henri lay there, his eyes closed, clutching his precious sax to his chest.

As Travis cradled his head, Henri's eyes opened and he whispered. "Henri's chest hurt bad. I think Henri gonna die now."

There were tears in Michelle's eyes. "Oh dear God, no," she moaned as she took Henri's hand.

Cody started to move the saxophone, expecting to see a gaping wound, but there was no blood anywhere. Then he noticed the hole in the front of the sax. Michelle and Travis saw Cody smile and couldn't understand. Cody turned the sax to them. The bullet had entered the front of the horn. It was a hollow point and began to spread out on impact, rather than penetrate. That, and the thick metal of the twenty-five-year-old sax, saved Henri's life. The bullet went into the front of the horn and out the back. It continued into the body of the sax, but it never made it out the back side. The pain Henri was experiencing was from the impact of the instrument being slammed against his breastbone. It was painful, certainly, but not fatal.

Henri looked up, puzzled, as his friends began to laugh. Cody turned the sax to Henri, showing him the hole. "No, Henri, you're gonna live to chase those big-breasted American girls after all. But your sax is dead."

Travis patted Henri on the shoulder. "I think you're one excellently lucky guy."

Henri grinned and nodded. "Ya, mon, excellently lucky!"

Travis put out his hand, which Henri took hesitantly. As they shook, Travis said, "Henri, we are all in your debt. As Pierre once said, thanks just isn't enough in a situation like this. I think you just earned yourself a full membership in the Tortuga Treasure Club." He looked over at the others for agreement, and they all nodded. "I don't think you'll have to worry about working when we reach the States, partner, and we'll get you through the immigration people."

Henri beamed "This Henri's dream! Go to U.S. of A. and have lotsa bucks too!" Then for a moment he paused, and with a more serious look said, "Even better, Henri have good friends."

"Yeah, you do," answered Travis

Billy looked back over his shoulder from the controls, and shouted over the engines and the wind. "Hate to be a party pooper, but we've got more problems, serious ones. Cody, Travis, come here." As they reached him, he tapped the fuel gauge for the starboard engine. It was already down to one third and the engine was throwing out a stream of white smoke. "I think one of those guys who fired at us when we dropped the C-4 hit a fuel line. My guess is, the fuel's squirting out onto that hot engine and vaporizing. It's not gonna be long and we're gonna have a fire. Then we're finished."

Cody took one look at the smoking engine and turned back to Billy. "Shut it down, Billy, it's our only chance."

Billy looked at him. "You know what that means."

Cody sighed. "Yeah, I know. We gotta empty this friggin' plane of weight or we'll just fly right into the ocean on one engine."

"That's about it," replied Billy. "I hate to say it, but all the cargo has got to go. We empty her and we might, just might, make Key West on one engine. We can't go back to Haiti, or even the Caicos Islands because of the hurricane. The only other place close is Cuba, and that's out for sure."

"Holy bloody hell," Travis moaned. "We've got to dump the treasure?"

"That's it," Billy yelled from the controls, "and you better start now. We've got to get the cargo out before I shut the engine down, and it needs to be shut down now!"

Travis took one more look at the smoke pouring out the back of the engine, sighed, and nodded. "Okay, let's do it."

So, in the early morning hours of August 5, 1980, the last of the brotherhood pushed their hard-won treasure out of the cargo door, dropping it into the belly of mother ocean.

Father Timothy O'Brien looked out from the wheelhouse of his eighty-five-foot freighter and gazed at the star-filled sky. It was hard to believe that, just two hundred miles behind him, an avalanche of wind and rain lashed at the coast of Haiti, tearing at the dilapidated roofs and tired walls of his mission there. He prayed for the children in his care, for Father Phillip, and for the sisters who helped them.

He had agonized over this decision, but in the end he knew he had to save the ship. His insurance had lapsed; he had no money to pay for it anymore. He was four payments behind, and if the bank's people found it, they'd repossess it for sure. He had to get out of the harbor at Port de Paix and they desperately needed more supplies from the States, so he took off on another "run."

Six years ago he had been assigned a failing mission on the northwest coast. He and Father Philip did their best to renovate the mission, then opened the doors to the orphaned children of the area. Within a week they were inundated. There was never enough food, medicine, or beds, and every time he watched a child die from a simple staph infection or easily cured bronchial pneumonia, every time he gazed at those helpless, imploring eyes as they held out their skinny arms for the extra cup of milk that wasn't there, his conscience cried that there had to be more he could do.

Finally, two years ago, he bought the ship with the small inheritance he had received when his father died. Actually, he paid half down and financed the balance with a Miami bank. He contacted various local charities in South Florida, talked with hospital administrators, and begged for commitments from anyone who would listen. Then, with his ship full of food and medical supplies, he headed back to Haiti.

His father had been a Louisiana shrimper, and most of his childhood had been spent on the ocean. It was a perfect arrangement. He was able to free himself somewhat from the parameters of his position by making occasional runs, and provide the desperately needed supplies for his children. But in the last few months, money had become a real problem. He was still able to procure some supplies through various churches and organizations, but he needed cash to buy fuel and make his loan payments. It had come to the point where he had to use different ports to hide the ship when he brought it into the States. The bank didn't give a hoot about children in Haiti, it wanted its money or it wanted the collateral. Lately, it had been reduced to a shell game between him and the repossession people.

So once again, as he did so often, he prayed for a small miracle, knowing the power of faith.

The droning of a low-flying aircraft brought Father O'Brien from his musing. He watched, as out of the darkness on the horizon came a twin-engine plane, flying perhaps 500 feet above the water. As it passed over him, illuminated by the moon, he thought he saw something fall from the aircraft. A second after the plane roared over him, he felt a solid thump on the forward deck and his eyes were drawn to a golden explosion, just in front of the forward hatches. Scattered across the entire front deck were thousands of circular golden objects. He and his first mate, a young Haitian from the mission, just gaped open-mouthed. "Take the wheel, Peter!" he yelled. "I'm going down."

When he reached the deck, he couldn't believe his eyes. There, crushed and splintered, lay the scattered remains of an old chest, and spread across the deck was the contents of that chest. Father O'Brien knelt and picked up one of the coins, staring at it in the moonlight. Dear Lord! It looked real! He bit it, and it gave just slightly, with the soft firmness of gold.

He looked up at the sky and crossed himself. There were tears in his eyes as he spoke. "Thank you, Father. Thank you for the lives you saved tonight with just the touch of your hand."

Turning toward the distant drone of the aircraft, he smiled, "And thank you, brothers, whoever you are. God bless you, and keep you in his hands."

So it was, that nearly a thousand coins of the

Brotherhood's treasure made their way back to Haiti, to be used in the building of a new mission and school, as well as supplying medicines, food, hundreds of new beds, and milk for those outstretched hands. Life is a circle.

With a reluctance bordering on despondency, they had dragged the wealth of kings to the cargo door and pushed it out into the night. The treasure was of no value if they were all dead, buried in the ocean with a plane too heavy to fly on one engine. From the cockpit, Billy urged them on. He was forced to back the power off on the failing engine and they were losing altitude rapidly. It was he who saw the lights of the freighter on the ocean and, just for the hell of it, flew over them as Travis kicked out the last chest of coins.

With the treasure gone, Billy climbed slowly up to three thousand feet, then chopped the power on the starboard engine, stood on the left rudder, and feathered the prop. They lost a thousand feet in the process of stabilizing the disabled aircraft, but in a few minutes, he had her flying straight and level. He trimmed the plane out as best he could and kept a hard left rudder down. It was going to be a long four hours back to Key West.

Cody turned to Billy, who still sat hunched over the controls, patches of perspiration darkening his khaki shirt under the arms and around the neck. He smiled. "You know, those propellers out there are just big fans to keep the pilot cool. When they stop spinning, pilots start sweating."

"That's real funny," muttered Billy, not taking his eyes from the gauges. "You better hope that last one keeps spinning, or you're gonna see some serious sweating in this tin tube."

As the last of the brotherhood's treasure disappeared

into the dark sky, Travis turned to the others. "Well, so much for two lifetimes and three hundred years of waiting. Gone! Poof! Just like that!"

Michelle moved forward and took Travis's hand. "No, you're wrong; there have been more treasures discovered here than were stored in chests. I found you again." She turned and took Cody's hand as well. "I watched this man willingly offer his life for ours tonight, and in turn, I saw you do the same. I had no idea that the bonds of friendship and love could run as deep as what I have witnessed with all of you. Travis, the real wealth is what I hold in my hands now."

There and then, they realized that the greatest treasure they had found was their belief in each other, and the imperishable bond of love they shared. They, the children of time, had discovered faith in themselves and in spirit. They had been given a priceless gift, the certainty of everlasting life, time and again.

The next three hours were anxious, but uneventful. It was when they passed the last of the western-most Bahamian Islands and neared the Florida Coast that things took a turn for the worse. The sun had just crested the horizon, blushing the pale morning sky. They were half an hour out of Key West when Billy began to shake his head, looking at the gauges in front of him.

Travis, in the right front seat, couldn't help but notice. "What's up, Billy?"

"I've been running this engine almost wide open. I've had to, in order to keep us flying. What's up is the engine's over-heating and we're running out of fuel. It's gonna be close, real close."

For a moment, no one said a word. They had been through so much, survived the impossible, and they were so close to the coast ...

Travis broke the tense silence. "We'll make it," he said firmly. "We're gonna make it! Back it off as far as you can, just keep us in the air for another sixty miles, buddy. Remember flying isn't dangerous, crashing is what's dangerous."

Billy managed a small smile as he worked the throttles and watched the gauges. "I'll do what I can to keep us from the second option."

For the next tension-filled twenty minutes, they all sat hunched forward, watching the plummeting needle on the fuel gauge, praying silently for one last miracle. Billy called the Key West tower and told them he was nearly out of fuel, requesting to be cleared for an immediate long final approach.

Gradually, the sight of land emerged from the morning mists in the distance. "There it is, folks," whispered Cody. "Home."

"Come on baby!" coaxed Billy. "Just a little longer."

They were five miles out of Key West when the engine coughed the first time. Billy quickly gave it a little more throttle, while speaking over his shoulder: "Don't think we're gonna make it, folks. Bring Henri up behind us and pad him with whatever you can find. Then everybody buckle down."

The engine coughed again and the plane shuddered, losing a hundred feet of altitude as the big prop missed a beat. "Jesus," Billy moaned, working the throttles forward. "Come on, baby, just a couple more miles ..."

The needle of the gauge was past empty, and the engine was running rough, its cylinders stumbling, missing. But Key West was dead ahead. They could see the white strip of sand that was Smathers Beach, just in front of the airport.

They had less than a thousand feet of altitude left when the engine sputtered one last time and died. They were half a mile off shore. "This is it!" yelled Billy, feathering the prop and shutting her down as the plane dropped toward the ocean at a frightening speed. "Tuck your heads down and hold tight. We're going in."

A handful of early morning beachcombers stopped and stared at the low-flying aircraft, coming in at them with the inconsistent drone of a troubled engine. Suddenly, there was no sound at all, and the plane fell toward the sea.

Bob and Margaret Fletcher were having their usual early morning breakfast by the picture window of their ground floor condominium overlooking Smathers Beach. Even at ground level, they still had a lovely view of the beach, the ocean, and the sunrise. Bob, sixty-one years old, a retired manager of a meat packing plant in Chicago, had fallen in love with the Keys ten years ago on their first trip down. When he retired, three years back, they bought themselves a little condo and now shared the quiet, tropical leisure of the islands. Bob was passing Margaret the sugar when he looked out the big window and saw the plane coming at them, no more than a hundred feet off the water.

As the ocean raced up at them, Billy drew back the controls to bring the nose up a bit. He could see the beach two hundred yards ahead. They were dropping like a rock, but with a little luck, they might just make that strip of sand. As the aircraft lost the last fifty feet and the water rushed up at him, he pulled the nose up hard and flared the plane into a stall. He was still about a hundred yards out when the craft slapped the water the first time. Breaking free of the impact, it skipped up ten feet into the air and glided another fifty yards before smacking down solidly again. This time, when it touched, it was less than twenty yards offshore. The beachcombers had long since panicked and fled, leaving the beach clear.

The plane skipped over the final stretch of water, then skidded onto and across the small strip of beach. Its momentum was only slightly diminished as the fuselage plowed in between two streetlamp poles, on its way across the street toward the condominium on the other side. The wings struck the solidly planted poles and were ripped from the plane in a single, jarring, incandescent explosion, as the lamp posts came crashing down, bulbs bursting, blowing sparks and blue electrical fire across the road.

The sugar bowl never quite made it to Margaret's outstretched hand, as both of them stopped, frozen, arms extended, watching the crashing plane careen toward them. When it hit the water the first time, Bob stood, the sugar still in hand. When it hit the water the second time, he was backing toward the living room wall.

As the aircraft skidded over the beach, crashing through the lamp poles, and screeched, metal grinding on asphalt, across the road, Margaret lost it. She was a big woman, not given to rapid movement, but today was an exception. She screamed, turning the table over as she rose to her feet and lumbered at Bob like a lineman after a fumble. She flew into Bob's arms as he stood plastered against the back wall of the living room, his eyes the size of softballs. The wingless fuselage of the plane ground over the four-lane street, shooting sparks like the Fourth of July fireworks from its undercarriage. It plowed over the sidewalk and onto the manicured lawn of the condominium, furrowing a track across the perfect grass, as its momentum finally slowed. With one last jarring bounce, the nose of the plane decimated the concrete patio and buried itself in Bob and Margaret's plate-glass window, taking out a good piece of the surrounding wall, before finally halting.

When the shards of plaster stopped falling and the tinkling of glass ceased, Billy looked over the nose of the plane to find himself in Bob and Margaret's living room. The older couple stood huddled against the far wall in petrified silence, not ten feet from the front of the plane. Travis rose up from the front seat and quickly looked around at everyone. Miraculously, they had all survived. The only one he couldn't see was Henri, who was behind the seats, wrapped in canvas and cargo netting. He was undoing his safety belt to check, when he heard the little Haitian grumble, "Henri ain't never flyin' in no stinkin' plane ever again, mon!" Travis turned to Cody and Michelle and they smiled.

Billy swung in his seat to face his friends. "Well, they say any landing you walk away from ... Sorry about your plane, Cody."

Cody just grinned. "Billy, my boy. Considering the situation, that was one of the best damned landings I've ever seen. Forget the plane, we're still alive. I'll buy another."

"Well, not out of your share of the treasure," Billy replied sarcastically.

"Don't bet on it," said Cody, as he slipped his hand under his seat, unlatching a small secret compartment and coming up with a fat canvas bag.

"That's the bag the emeralds were in!" gasped Michelle.

"Correction, that's the bag the emeralds *are* in," replied Cody, smiling. "I tucked it away while I waited at the plane for you guys, just in case ... The way I figure it, there's probably close to three million in stones in here. My share will cover my losses nicely."

Travis just shook his head and grinned. "You did it again."

"Yeah, I guess I did," said Cody with his usual aplomb. "Now let's get out of here. I can hear sirens."

Travis opened the cockpit door and they all crawled out, onto the splintered remains of the wing, and into the living room. Travis and Michelle helped Henri.

Cody walked over to the Fletchers, still standing against the wall. "Sorry about dropping in on you unexpectedly like this. Here, I think this will cover your expenses nicely," he said, as he deposited a golf ball-sized emerald in the sugar bowl Bob still held.

Waving goodbye to the still frozen Fletchers, they pried open the front door of the apartment and walked out into the bright morning sunlight.

Chapter Fifteen

Travis Christian sat on the bar stool, holding the coin, watching it reflect the sunlight as he turned it with his fingers. He gazed out across the water and thought back over the last two months. It had been an unparalleled adventure, an experience that had changed his spiritual concepts and altered his personal beliefs, giving new dimension to his faith in himself, his fellow man, and his God. He was aware now, more than ever, of the width and depth of spirit, the undeniable immortality of the human soul, and the everlasting power of love.

He was certain, beyond any doubt, that some things are forever.

His attention was drawn to the walkway of the hotel when, out from under the parasol of flowering trees, came Michelle and Henri. They had been downtown to pick up some extra reeds for Henri's new sax. Tonight was Henri's debut with a local band at the Casa Marina Hotel Lounge. Things had gone surprisingly well at immigration—and for the others at customs. The group had all decided on a story of the search for, but not the discovery of, a treasure in Haiti. They did mention a modified version of the conflict with the Ton Ton Macoute and a certain Colonel Juele. They left out their encounter with Magruder. Having witnessed the "disappearance" of the chief of the Haitian Secret Police, there was no doubt that the Ton Ton Macoute would want Henri's head if he returned to Haiti. It made a solid case for political asylum. Henri was on his way to becoming an American citizen—a fairly wealthy citizen, actually.

Cody, with his myriad connections, was able to move the emeralds without a problem. When all was said and done, they netted a cool two and a half million dollars from the stones. True, they had lost the bulk of the treasure, but $500,000 each had a way of soothing the loss.

Michelle was flying home to Haiti on Monday to see her father. Most of Haiti's phone system had been knocked out by the hurricane, but two days after the storm, she managed to contact him through the French Embassy in Haiti—to assure him she was safe, and make certain he had survived. She had spent the last three weeks in Key West, with Travis. It was time to go home and relate the remarkable tale to her father, and to explain to him why he would need to find an overseer to take her place.

Billy was off to the South Pacific for three months, in his own Beechcraft C-45. It was the one place he'd always wanted to see. Now he had the time, and the money.

Travis and Cody were also leaving on Monday, but in a different direction. They were headed for Barbados— Michelle would meet them there inside of a week. They were going to research the history of a child who had been born in the spring of 1669, on the second largest sugar plantation in Barbados. The child's father had died before he was born and the boy—Travis was certain the child had been a boy—had most likely taken the name of his mother's family.

It was that name which prompted this investigation into the past. Travis' great-grandmother had told him that the first of the Christian family had been a swashbuckler from the isle of Barbados. She claimed he was as daring a rover as had ever sailed the Caribbean, leaving a trail of bloodied swords and broken hearts from the Windward

Islands to the Carolina's, where Travis's family eventually settled in America.

Up until recently, he had always thought it a fanciful story intended to tantalize a child's imagination. However, while looking through the diary that Anne Catherine had left, Michelle discovered Anne's full name in the back of the book. When Michelle handed Travis the diary and he read the name there, he was suddenly aware how complex the tapestry in the circle of life could be.

The lady who had borne the son of her buccaneer lover was named Anne Catherine Christian.

Could it be, he wondered, as he stared at his last name written in a book 300 years old, that the first in his lineage had actually been the son of Anne Catherine? *What was he like?* he thought to himself.

Travis thought of ol' Will Devon then, and smiled, for surely there must be a tale worth the telling there.

Life is a circle, and we are all children of time.

BACK ON THE ROAD TO KEY WEST *(The Golden Scepter)." Book II*

An ancient map and a lost pirate treasure, a larcenous Bahamian scoundrel with his gang of cutthroats, a wild and crazy journey into South America in search of a magical antediluvian device, and perilous/hilarious encounters with outlandish villains and zany friends will keep you locked to your seat and giggling maniacally. (Not to mention headhunters, smugglers, and beautiful women with poisonous pet spiders.)

You'll also welcome back Rufus, the wacky, mystical Jamaican Rastaman, and be captivated by another "complicated romance" as Kansas and Will struggle with finding and keeping "the girls of their dreams."

Kindle Book only $2.99

CLICK HERE TO PREVIEW OR PURCHASE FROM AMAZON.COM:

http://www.amazon.com/dp/B00FC9D94I

ALONG THE ROAD TO KEY WEST (The Truthmaker) Book III

Fast-paced humor-adventure with wacky pilots, quirky con men, bold women, mad villains, and a gadget to die for...

Florida Keys adventurers Kansas Stamps and Will Bell find their lives turned upside down when they discover a truth device hidden in the temple of an ancient civilization. Enthralled by the virtue (and entertainment value) of personally dispensing truth and justice with this unique tool, they take it all a step too far and discover that everyone wants what they have.

Seasoned with outrageous humor and sultry romances, *Along The Road To Key West* carries you through one wild adventure after another. This time, Kansas and Will are forced to wrest veracity and lies from con artists, divine hustlers, and political power brokers while trying to stay one step ahead of a persistent assembly of very bad guys with guns.

In the process, from Key West, into the Caribbean, and back to America's heartland, our inadvertent heroes gather a bizarre collage of friends and enemies – from a whacked-out, one-eyed pilot, and a mystical Rastaman, to a ruthless problem-solver for a prominent religious sect, a zany flimflamming sociopath, and a Cuban intelligence agent. In the end, it all comes down to a frantic gamble – to save far more than the truth. So pour yourself a margarita and settle back. You're in for a high intensity Caribbean carnival ride!

Kindle Book only $2.99

CLICK HERE TO PREVIEW OR PURCHASE FROM AMAZON.COM:
http://www.amazon.com/dp/B00G5B3HEY

SOMEWHERE ON THE ROAD TO KEY WEST (The Emerald Cave) Book IV

In the fourth book of "The Road To Key West" series, Kansas Stamps and Will Bell once again find themselves hip-deep in madcap adventure – from bizarre to hysterical. The captivating diary of an amateur archeologist sends our intrepid explorers on a journey into the heart of the Panamanian jungle, in search of *La cueva de Esmeralda* (The Emerald Cave), and a lost Spanish treasure. But local brigand, Tu Phat Shong, and his gang of cutthroats are searching for the same treasure. It's a cat and mouse game – up the perilous Fangaso River, through the jungle and the boisterous mining towns, and into "The Village of the Witches," where nothing is as it seems...

If that weren't enough, one of the Caribbean's nastiest drug lords has a score to settle with our reluctant heroes. (Something to do with an ancient golden medallion they "borrowed.") The word is out. There's a price on Kansas and Will's heads, and a conga line of hit men trailing them. As they careen across the Southern Hemisphere, our adventurers encounter some fascinating ladies as well, and experience an extraordinary romance. Be careful what you wish for...

Kindle Book only $3.99

CLICK HERE TO PREVIEW OR PURCHASE FROM AMAZON.COM:
http://www.amazon.com/dp/B00NOABMKA

ALSO..... BE SURE TO READ

THE NEW MADRID RUN
A #1 Nationwide Bestseller for Books in Motion Audio Books

The New Madrid Run, is a tale of desperate survival on an altered planet: In the aftermath of a global cataclysm caused by a shift in the earth's poles, a handful of survivors face the terrible elements of a changed world as they navigate a battered sailboat from the ruins of Florida into the hills of Arkansas via a huge rift in the continent (the New Madrid fault). They survive fierce storms and high seas pirates only to make landfall and discover the greatest challenge of all....

Kindle Book only $2.99

CLICK HERE TO PREVIEW OR PURCHASE FROM AMAZON.COM:
http://www.amazon.com/New-Madrid-Run-Michael-Reisig-ebook/dp/B004PLNKWU/ref=sr_1_1?s=digital-text&ie=UTF8&qid=1419118641&sr=1-1&keywords=the+new+madrid+run

FOR SI FI HIGH ADVENTURE:

THE HAWKS OF KAMALON
A #1 Nationwide Bestseller for Books in Motion Audio Books

Great Britain, Summer, 1944

Are you a fan of Jack Higgins or Robert Heinlen? Do you remember The Magnificent Seven? Did you like the first Star Wars? If the answer is yes, you're in for a galloping, interplanetary ride with "Hawks."

A small squadron of British and American aircraft departs at dawn on a long-range strike into Germany, but as they cross the English Channel, the squadron vanishes.

Captain Ross Murdock and the '51 Squadron are cast into a whirlwind adventure of intrigue, treachery, and romance as they are "culled" back and forth across the universe, outwitting and outrunning the Germans, while they attempt to foil the invasion of Azra by the neighboring continent of Krete – a thousand light years from Great Britain....

Kindle Book only $2.99

CLICK HERE TO PREVIEW OR PURCHASE FROM AMAZON.COM:

http://www.amazon.com/Hawks-Kamalon-Michael-Reisig-ebook/dp/B004QGYHUI/ref=sr_1_1?s=digital-text&ie=UTF8&qid=1419116826&sr=1-1&keywords=the+hawks+of+kamalon

A SPECIAL THANKS to my good friend, Cris Wanzer, at Manuscripts To Go, for doing an excellent job on the formatting and "final eyes" on this book, and for always being there when I needed her.

Michael Reisig

ABOUT THE AUTHOR

Michael Reisig has been writing professionally for nearly 20 years. He is a former newspaper editor and publisher, an award-winning columnist, and a best-selling novelist. His works have been optioned for motion pictures, sold to overseas publishers, and produced for ebooks and audio books.

Reisig has always had a yearning for the sea. He attended high school and college in the Tampa Bay area of Florida. After college, he relocated to the Florida Keys, established a commercial diving business, got his pilot's license, and traveled extensively throughout the southern hemisphere, diving, treasure hunting, adventuring, and writing about his travels. He admits that a great many of the situations and the characters in his novels are authentic, but nothing makes a great read like experience...

Go to amazon.com, or Michael's website at michael-reisig.com, to learn more about his works.

Made in the USA
Lexington, KY
26 February 2015